D0328034

LOGAN FELT LIKE AN INTRUDER

Christine's silence was beginning to get to him. He wasn't going to stand around in her kitchen feeling awkward if he wasn't wanted. "Look," he said in a low voice. "We can skip the coffee if you'd rather—"

"No!" Christine didn't want to be alone, not just yet. "Please don't leave," she said breathlessly. "A cup of coffee is the least I can do after the trouble I've put you to."

"You haven't." His tone was very quiet. "But I don't want to put *you* to any trouble."

Christine was aware of the silent question in his eyes, and the oddest thought went through her mind. It would be easy to trust this man, almost too easy. "It's no trouble at all," she said, and blessed him with her first genuine smile of the evening....

ABOUT THE AUTHOR

Oregon author Sandra James likens *Guardian Angel* to her first Superromance, *A Family Affair*. "They're both close to my heart," she says. Sandra has wanted to tell the story of Christine Michaels, the heroine of *Guardian Angel*, for a long time, and she finally felt ready. "I cried while I wrote it," Sandra admits. "I kept the Kleenex box handy, and readers may want to do the same thing!"

Books by Sandra James

HARLEQUIN SUPERROMANCE

205–A FAMILY AFFAIR
249–BELONGING
277–STRONGER BY FAR

Don't miss any of our special offers. Write to us at the following address for information on our newest releases.

Harlequin Reader Service
901 Fuhrmann Blvd., P.O. Box 1397, Buffalo, NY 14240
Canadian address: P.O. Box 603,
Fort Erie, Ont. L2A 5X3

Sandra James

GUARDIAN ANGEL

Harlequin Books

TORONTO • NEW YORK • LONDON
AMSTERDAM • PARIS • SYDNEY • HAMBURG
STOCKHOLM • ATHENS • TOKYO • MILAN

Published May 1988

First printing March 1988

ISBN 0-373-70306-6

Copyright © 1988 by Sandra Kleinschmit. All rights reserved.
Except for use in any review, the reproduction or utilization
of this work in whole or in part in any form by any electronic,
mechanical or other means, now known or hereafter invented,
including xerography, photocopying and recording,
or in any information storage or retrieval system, is forbidden without
the permission of the publisher, Harlequin Enterprises Limited,
225 Duncan Mill Road, Don Mills, Ontario, Canada M3B 3K9.

All the characters in this book have no existence outside the
imagination of the author and have no relation whatsoever to
anyone bearing the same name or names. They are not even
distantly inspired by any individual known or unknown to the
author, and all incidents are pure invention.

® are Trademarks registered in the United States Patent and
Trademark Office and in other countries.

Printed in U.S.A.

PROLOGUE

DEEP IN THE HEART of northern Idaho, a single dirt track wound its way through dense, seemingly impenetrable forest. Tall, majestic cedars and huge firs lined the way like a natural canopy. In the chill, shaded world below, an outdated van the color of mud labored steadily uphill. Then suddenly the twisting, pot-holed road came to an abrupt end.

The van rolled to a halt. A man jumped out. For a moment, he stood silent and watchful.

His domain was surrounded by a proud stand of jack pines. Beyond the perimeter of trees, a mountain stream dashed through wooded gullies, bubbling and gurgling in the silence of the late afternoon. A small, sturdy cabin stood in the center of the clearing, the home he had crafted and built with his own hands.

There was nowhere like it on God's earth. Surrounded by the wilderness, the smell of damp, pine-scented earth, this was land that was pure, unspoiled and unsullied. This was life, as life was meant to be lived. A man could ask for nothing more.

Except someone to share it.

The cabin door creaked as he opened it. His booted feet trod across the rough, wooden planks, past waist-high knotty-pine cabinets. He tossed a chunk of wood into the pot-bellied stove in the corner.

The man's concessions to modern-day technology were few. There was no telephone, no television, not even a radio. There was a battery-powered generator, but he rarely made use of it.

No one knew of his secret hideaway, and that was as he wished. He could imagine what they'd have said. That he was a hermit, a recluse. They didn't understand that he was merely a simple man who wanted but one thing—to live out his life with the woman of his dreams.

How lonely it was without her. She'd been gone only a week, but already it seemed a lifetime. But soon, very soon she would be his. And then his dreams would become a reality....

CHAPTER ONE

A FULL MOON HOVERED in the darkness, surrounded by an eerie halo of silver. Hazy gray clouds streaked across the sky, occasionally obscuring the moon's brilliance.

Far below, high on a hill at the end of a dead-end street, stood a house. It was large and homey-looking, flanked on three sides by a wide porch. Twin patches of light gleamed from a pair of narrow windows, dappling the shrouded landscape outside.

Inside, a lone figure stood, gazing reflectively into the night. Small in stature, the woman was simply dressed in dark slacks and a long-sleeved sweater. She appeared almost plain, her shoulder length hair the same monotonous brown of a washed-out photo. Had she moved but a single step, the light from the dining room chandelier would have turned the strands into a rich mass of honey, streaked with gold. There was an element of contrariness in her features. Her cheekbones were high and delicate, her mouth full and expressive. Her brows were surprisingly dark and winged, set above black-lashed hazel eyes.

Christine Michaels smiled slightly, still staring into the distance at the twinkling of bright, multi-colored lights that provided such a stark contrast to the cold and lonely night. Boise, Idaho, like the rest of the world, had welcomed the holiday season with open arms. Just one day after Thanksgiving, the streets downtown were already gaily decorated, the local storeowners prominently displaying the latest offerings.

Christmas. It was a time for mistletoe and magic, for joy and loving, for angels and miracles. It was also a time for fond and treasured memories. But where Chris was concerned, the remembrances evoked by the holiday season were among the most painful possible.

Oh, she had tried not to think of it. Yesterday, as the family gathered around the table for Thanksgiving dinner, she had been as cheerful and talkative as her four-year-old niece Wendy. And throughout the week she had been home, she had managed not to burst into tears every time she looked at Josh, the other addition to Char's family.

Yet in all the years that Chris had lived in this house, her mother had never failed to begin her Christmas preparations the day after Thanksgiving. This year was the exception.

The boxes that held the treasured holiday mementos were still tucked away in the attic, dusty and unused since last Christmas. Chris had no doubt that if she hadn't been home for Thanksgiving this year, everyone would have been oohing and aahing as each precious item was removed. The miniature manger and stable, nestled in a snowy bed of angel hair, would have assumed its rightful place on the seat near the bay window. Proud toy soldiers would have marched their way across the mantel top.

Chris knew it was consideration for her that lay behind her mother's reasoning, but somehow that only made things worse. It also made her realize that it was too soon to spend Christmas with her family.

Too soon? Her thoughts mocked her. It had been two years. Two long, lonely years since...

A gust of wind found its way through a tiny crack and stirred the lacy white curtains. Her hand finally fell away from the window, and she turned slightly.

Her eyes drifted to her father. He was sitting in the living room, peacefully dozing in his recliner, the evening news forgotten. A jumble of newspapers lay scattered at his feet. It was a familiar sight, one that kindled an odd twinge of nostalgia. For a moment, Chris wished it were possible to turn back the clock and relive the carefree years she'd spent beneath her parents' wing.

But the sight of her mother juggling her two grandchildren on her lap wasn't quite so comforting. Chris was helpless to prevent her eyes from veering in that direction. There should have been three, she couldn't help thinking. Wendy, Josh, and Scottie....

The sound of a high-pitched giggle reached her ears.

"*That's* Mommy?" a little voice shrieked. A stubby finger jabbed at the photograph album Elaine Jordan held in her lap.

"That's Mommy," the child's grandmother confirmed, her voice ripe with laughter and satisfaction.

Chris shook herself free of the pensive mood that had claimed her. She slid her hands into her pockets and glanced through the arched doorway that separated the dining room from the living room. Wendy was still giggling at the sight of her mother's second-grade school picture. In the photo, Char's dark hair was springing with tight banana curls. She was conspicuously missing her two front teeth, but nonetheless flashing an uninhibited grin at the camera. Six-month-old Josh leaned over curiously as well and showed his appreciation by dribbling onto the protective plastic covering.

As efficiently as her four-year-old hands would allow, Wendy promptly grabbed the bib tied around his neck. She lifted it to his face and began to scour his mouth with it. The baby let out a furious squeal that resulted in his grandmother playing referee to two pairs of small, opposing hands.

Once again, bedlam reigned supreme in the Jordan household.

The faint lines of strain on Christine's forehead were softened by her amusement. On hearing the ruckus, her father's eyes drifted open. He heaved a hearty sigh at being interrupted in the midst of his evening nap, but as Chris started across the room, she noticed his shoulders shook with a soundless chuckle.

She stopped next to his chair. "Starting early, aren't they?" Paul Jordan observed. He sent her a look from the corner of his eye. "Comes naturally, I suppose."

With her usual brisk proficiency, Elaine had already managed to placate the feuding siblings by turning their attention away from each other. Wendy was now sprawled at the foot of the chair, still inspecting the photo album, and Josh was busy investigating a small ball of bright red yarn his grandmother had dropped into his lap.

Chris glanced at her niece and nephew, then wrinkled her nose at her father. "We weren't that bad, were we?" she countered mildly. "After all, think of what life would have been like with three sons instead of three daughters."

"Infinitely quieter," he grumbled, but his daughter saw the twinkle in his eye.

"Hah! About as quiet as a basketball team," she retorted.

That was how Paul Jordan had always referred to his three daughters. His basketball team. It had always been a joke between Paul and the customers of his sporting goods store. Paul was a big, husky man, and none of his daughters ever managed to surpass the height of five-foot-four. And the only sport any of them had enjoyed was a wild sled ride down the hill behind their house, something that involved far more fun than skill. Torn coats, scraped noses and six skinned knees had attested to that fact more than once.

At home, the senior Jordans had adopted other nicknames for their offspring. Chris, the eldest, had been dubbed "the thinker," but she possessed the same motherly instincts as Elaine. "Doctor" Char had every child in the neighborhood running to her with their bumps and scrapes. The baby, "glamor girl" Diane, had often found herself in hot water for raiding her mother's closet and makeup vanity without permission, and then using both herself and her sisters as guinea pigs.

Somehow it came as no surprise to anyone when the eldest member of the "team" set her sights on psychology, and so it was Chris who eventually became the doctor in the family. Char wasn't untrue to herself, though, and was now a registered nurse, though her family was her number one priority. Jet-setting Diane was a cosmetic consultant for a major department store chain throughout the western states, and she loved every minute of it.

"You love having Wendy and Josh around and you know it," Chris said softly to her father. Wendy chose that moment to screech a hearty protest when Josh latched onto the end of a dark braid and pulled it toward his mouth. "Even though I think they're giving you a preview of what's ahead," she teased.

"I'm not about to argue with you on either count," Paul declared.

Chris laughed. "I didn't think you would."

Her father snorted. "Think you've got me all figured out, don't you, Doc?"

"Not me!" Chris feigned shock, then lowered her voice to a whisper as she nodded at her mother. "But I think I know a woman who does."

Paul's gaze traveled to his wife. An odd pang struck Chris as she watched the brief flare of emotion on her father's face. With thirty-five years of marriage behind them, the bond between her parents was stronger than ever. They'd had their ups and downs, good times and bad, but Chris knew that their devotion to each other had remained constant and unwavering. She wouldn't have had it any other way, yet for an instant, Chris was faintly envious. Her parents had the kind of marriage she'd always wanted for herself, the kind she'd been so certain she would have when she'd married Bill almost ten years earlier. But that was before the divorce.

And before Scottie.

Chris wasn't aware of the bleakness that had crept into her expression, but the man beside her was. Getting over Scottie had been quite a struggle; as a psychologist, Chris knew better than anyone what a slow, arduous climb it had been. For a long time she had believed that the faint hurt and the nagging feeling of emptiness would never disappear. But that had changed, and now she could go for weeks at a time without thinking sad thoughts of her son.

Yet always—*always* when she and her parents were together, Scottie was never far from their minds, and all of them were almost painfully aware of that. Paul, like his wife, knew what lay behind Christine's determination to maintain her careful facade of well-being, but he wasn't sure how to approach Christine, or if he should even try. It was as if they were all afraid to say what was really on their minds.

After a moment, her father reached out and caught her hand. "You don't know how much it means to your mother and me to have the three of you home again." He hesitated. "Especially you, Christine."

Oh, but she did. Even without the betraying rustiness in her father's voice, Chris would have known. Up until two years ago, she had managed to spend nearly every Thanksgiving, Christmas and Easter at home with her parents and sisters. Holidays had always been such special occasions for them. Even Diane, hectic as her schedule often was, always managed to head back to Boise at least twice a year.

But that had changed two years ago.

Chris's parents had made the long drive to Coeur d'Alene to visit her on several occasions, and there had been the usual monthly phone calls exchanged as well. It wasn't that she was afraid everyone would shower her with pity, or smother her with comfort. She knew better. But Chris simply hadn't been able to bring herself back to the home she had known for the first twenty-four years of her life, a home that represented all she held dear...and reminded her far too keenly of all she had lost.

Returning to Boise had been as hard as she had always known it would be. Chris felt she had coped as well as she could, but the strain of the past ten days had taxed her greatly.

But it would break her father's heart if he knew how difficult it was and so she felt her way carefully. "It's good to be back," she told him, squeezing his fingers slightly.

"Then maybe you'll change your mind about Christmas."

Chris bit her lip. She had known this was coming, ever since she'd informed her mother earlier that afternoon of her decision to spend the holiday alone again this year. The timing hadn't been the best. Not when she was leaving for Coeur d'Alene tomorrow morning. But she didn't want her parents to harbor any false hopes again.

She shook her head, evading his gaze. "It's not that simple," she said in a low voice. "And I've been here a week and a half already." She didn't offer any further excuse; any she might have come up with would have sounded feeble and weak.

"When you get to be my age, every minute counts." There was a brief pause. "I hate to see you leave, not knowing when you'll be back again."

The sounds of Wendy and Josh playing faded into the background. Chris stared at her father, and for a brief moment, there was just the two of them.

He was aging, she realized suddenly, then wondered if she hadn't blinded herself to it. His movements weren't quite as brisk as they'd been the last time she'd seen him; the ribbon of iron gray that streaked his temples was longer, wider. But she took comfort in the knowledge that for a man in his early sixties, he was in excellent health. Her mother saw to that.

Chris had always prided herself on being a strong woman, but that wasn't the case right now. She knew what would happen if she stayed any longer. But just as strong was the fear that she could end up hurting both her parents, and that was something she would never do intentionally.

"Pop, please don't misunderstand," she began. "I-I'm really glad I'm here, but to come back for Christmas..." She hesitated, then lifted her shoulders helplessly. "I just don't think I can," she said, her voice very low.

The resigned expression in her father's eyes cut into her far more deeply than his disapproval would have.

Paul was silent for a moment, but then he nodded. "I know, Chris. You're a woman who has places to go, things to do and patients to see." If only it were that simple, he thought silently. But he smiled at his quip, released her hand and rose from his recliner. Chris opened her mouth, an unfamiliar lump in her throat, but he clapped a hand to her shoulder before she could say anything. "Your mother's been raving all week about that spiced cider you brought along with you. How about a sample?"

Her father understood her as no one else ever had, and Chris knew his attempt to lighten the suddenly intense atmosphere was deliberate. A hot ache filled her throat, and she found herself unable to speak. She could only nod as she and her father began to move toward the kitchen. Chris remained silent as she lifted a jug of cider from the refrigerator and poured it into a saucepan. While the cider heated on the stove, filling her nostrils with the spicy aroma of cinnamon, she listened with half an ear as her father talked about the garden her mother had planned for the spring, the load of firewood they were having delivered on Monday.

Chris forced a smile when her father took a long, hearty pull from the cup she placed in front of him. "It's good, isn't it?"

"Even better than your mother said." He set the cup on the table and lifted his eyebrows quizzically. "Apples from your orchard?"

Chris nodded. "I even used an old apple press I found in the cellar." Her smile was valiant, if a little wobbly. "Looks like something out of a mail-order catalog from 1880. I think it even outdates the house."

Chris had bought an aging house, complete with a small acreage, just after her divorce from Bill a year earlier. It had been built at the turn of the century, and in Chris's mind, what it lacked in modern conveniences, it made up for in sheer, old-fashioned charm. There was even a roomy guest cottage, but Chris had been far too busy with the main house to turn her attention to it. Rejuvenating the house had served to take her mind off the divorce and ... other things, as well.

Eyes downcast, she poured herself a cup of cider. She turned away from the stove just in time to glimpse a grave expression on her father's face. It was a look that nearly pulled her up short, but she completed the few steps to the table in spite of it.

Aware that her father's thoughtful gaze hadn't left her, she finally glanced up at him.

"What time is Diane due back?" she asked. Diane had spent the afternoon and evening with several friends from her college days.

"Knowing Diane," her father said dryly, "we'll know when we see her, and that may well be tomorrow morning."

Chris pretended to be shocked. "Are you the same man who wouldn't let me out of the house until I'd told you what, where, who, when and why?"

"Only until your twenty-first birthday," he put in mildly. "After all, you had to set an example for your sisters."

"An example? Come on, Pop, Diane's the youngest. And it's practically a fact of life that the baby of the family always ends up being spoiled."

They both laughed, but the spark faded from her father's eyes much too quickly for Chris's peace of mind. The next moment, she knew why.

"How are you, Chris?" he asked very quietly. "How are you, really? I mean, with Christmas coming and all..."

In the second before Chris dropped her eyes, she saw the concern on his face. There was a tight little silence, and Chris found it impossible to speak.

If only she could turn back the clock to happier times, she thought wistfully. Back to the days when life had been simple and uncomplicated, when the worst thing on her mind was how to struggle through the next semester in geometry. Or to the time an eager, radiant mother had so proudly introduced her newb his father.

How was she? No longer bitter, no longer angry, no longer frightened.

But before Chris had a chance to say a word, a little whirlwind burst through the swinging door into the kitchen.

"Look, Aunt Chris! Gran said this is you when you were in kindergarten. And you've got just as many freckles as me!" Wendy sounded absolutely delighted as she ran toward the table waving a small wallet-sized picture before her.

In that special way only a child possessed, the little girl's entrance managed to lift the melancholy mood that had prevailed the second before.

"Practically born with 'em, she was," Paul provided cheerfully. "Just like you."

Chris eyed her father's ruddy complexion, the reddish-brown hair streaked with silver. "And we both know who to thank for that, don't we?" She lifted her eyebrows meaningfully.

Wendy had clambered into her aunt's lap, but the look she leveled at Chris's nose was one of puzzlement.

"What happened to all your freckles?" she asked doubtfully. "You don't have so many now."

Chris chuckled and hugged her niece. She glanced sideways at her father, then lowered her head. "There's this neat little trick I learned from Aunt Diane," she began in a conspiratorial whisper. "They disappear just like magic with a little bit of makeup."

The youngster's eyes gleamed. "Mommy has makeup. If I use it, will they go away?"

Chris bit her lip, struggling to keep from laughing. Wendy had inherited not only her aunt's freckles, but apparently her dislike for them as well.

"Char won't thank you for this," Paul put in wryly.

"But I'm the last person she'll point a finger at." Chris chuckled, thinking of unsuspecting Diane.

"I'm not sure how Char will take her four-year-old turning into a sixteen-year-old overnight, and someone may have a tale or two to tell." His eyes dropped to Wendy, who sat absorbing every word.

As if on cue, there was a pounding thump of footsteps on the back porch. The screen slammed and the door opened. A snatch of chill, fragrant air whipped into the kitchen, preceding Char and her husband Rick.

"Whew! Is it ever freezing out there!" Rick, a tall, slender man with hair and eyes as dark as his wife's, laid his hands on Wendy's cheeks. Wendy giggled, burrowing closer into Chris's arms.

Chris wrinkled her nose at her brother-in-law. "Pick on somebody your own size."

A decided gleam entered his eyes. "Great idea," he murmured. Spinning around, he reached for Char, who was on her way into the dining room. Chris caught a glimpse of the surprised pleasure on her sister's face as Rick slid his arms around her waist and pulled her toward him.

Chris looked away when his head ducked down. Her smile faded. Brief as the kiss was, she couldn't deny that it bothered her.

She and Bill had been like that once. In those days, Chris had felt on top of the world. She was strong. Successful. Sure of her husband's love and just as confident of herself. She was the woman who had it all. Career, home, husband and child.

It seemed a lifetime had passed since then.

She certainly didn't begrudge Char her happiness, though. Rick had just been made a junior partner in the accounting firm he was with, and she knew he worked very long, hard, demanding hours. He and Char didn't always get to spend much time together.

But deep inside Chris, there was a gnawing emptiness. She swallowed her sigh, one hand idly stroking Wendy's braids.

The door into the kitchen swung open and Elaine walked in, holding Josh on her hip. "So this is where everyone's run off to," she started to say. She stopped when her gaze lit on the two cups that sat on the table. "Aha! That's what smells so good. Why don't you heat some for all of us, dear?" She addressed herself to Char.

Moments later, the seven of them were gathered around the kitchen table, Wendy with a glass of chocolate milk in front of her instead of hot cider.

Josh, now settled on his father's lap, made a disgruntled sound, apparently not at all happy with the situation. He frowned at the soda cracker he'd been given, pushed it aside and reached for Rick's cup.

"You might have a hard time with this, young man." Rick tipped the mug up to Josh's mouth. The baby wasn't used to drinking from a cup, but he made a determined effort. When the warm liquid reached his lips, he pulled a horrible face.

"Uh-oh." Char glanced at Chris. "A traitor in the ranks. Josh doesn't like your cider." Everyone laughed, and Char propped her elbows on the table. "You know," she commented, "this reminds me of all the other Friday nights we have spent together just like this. Diane's even off with her friends again. If we dragged out the Monopoly game, it'd be just like old times."

Wendy chose that moment to tip her glass. The milk took a rapid and unerring path toward Rick and the baby. Josh burst into tears as the cold liquid drenched the front of his crawler.

Elaine had already thrust a towel at a startled Rick, and was busy mopping up the table before he even had time to react. Chris eyed her sister. "Maybe you'd like to rephrase that?" she teased.

"Please do," Paul said solemnly.

"It's *almost* like old times." Char laughed and reached for the baby. "Let's get you cleaned up and ready for bed, little man."

This time it was Rick who pleaded solemnly, "Please do."

Josh's unhappy whimpers could be heard from the living room while Char changed him into his sleeper. Elaine had just finished warming his bottle when Char returned to the kitchen. Josh's wail ceased the second he spotted the bottle. He gazed at it the way Wendy would have eyed cotton candy.

"That's what you wanted all along, isn't it?" his mother crooned. She would have taken the bottle from Elaine and gone back into the living room, but suddenly Chris stood next to her, a multitude of conflicting emotions sweeping through her.

She spoke before she lost her nerve. "Wait, Char," she said quickly. She glanced from the bottle to Josh, then finally to her sister's face. "Do you mind if I...?"

The baby was in her arms almost before she knew it. A hundred different sensations squeezed into her heart. Though she had teased and played with Josh during her stay, bounced him on her knee, she had never really *held* him, cuddled him close to her breast as a mother might do. She was painfully aware of the knowing looks exchanged between her mother and Char, and she felt a brief spasm of guilt. Then even that was gone as she nudged the swinging door aside.

No one followed her, and for that she was grateful. She carried Josh into the living room. The room was lit by a dim glow from the lamp in the far corner, and she sat down in the rocker near the fireplace. The bright blue bunny rabbit on the baby's sleeper winked up at her. Josh was staring at her intently, but his expression held no fear. Chris smiled shakily and brought the bottle up so he could see it. He gave an impatient grunt, his mouth already open.

He drifted off to sleep less than halfway through the bottle. Chris eased the nipple out of his mouth and set it aside. Josh blew out a bubbly sigh, his hand curled possessively against her breast.

Chris felt her heart splinter into a thousand tiny pieces. But along with the pain was a curious sense of pleasure. Josh looked contented and peaceful. She gazed at the dark crescents of his lashes, the tiny mouth that so resembled his mother's...and her own. The weight of his body, cradled lightly against hers, felt perfect, as perfect as she remembered. Sheer willpower alone prevented her from breaking down, and then instinct took over. Lulled by the gentle creak of the rocker, she let her mind and body relax.

A few minutes later, a small sound caught her attention. Chris turned her head to find Char standing in the dining room. When she saw that she'd been discovered, Char moved quietly across the room.

"You're leaving?" Chris asked softly.

"Rick's going out in a minute to start the car." Char held up a hand when Chris made to lift the sleeping infant. "He'll be back in when it's warm."

Chris's gaze followed Char as she sank to the floor in front of her, her legs tucked beneath her. "Josh wasn't as starved as you thought," Chris told her sister. She indicated that half-full bottle on the end table.

Char smiled slightly. "Just greedy."

The silence that followed was an awkward one. It was Char who finally broke it. "Mom says you're not coming home again for Christmas."

Chris stiffened, then nodded.

"You know how she stands on tradition." Char hesitated. "Last year just wasn't the same without you, Chris."

With her free hand, Chris gently traced the baby's chubby cheek. "I know," she said, her voice nearly inaudible. "But I can't, Char. I just—can't."

Her voice broke helplessly. Her eyes stung, and she blinked to fight back the tears. The shadows of the past had drifted back, and she was powerless to fight them. A babyish squeal, a gurgly laugh, a fist stuffed into an avid and eager mouth. Not much to someone else, perhaps, but it was enough to send Chris running. The act of a coward? Maybe. But at this time of year, Chris wasn't feeling very brave. Her arm unconsciously tightened around the sleeping infant she still held, as if she could somehow protect him.

When she was finally able to look at Char, she wasn't surprised to find her sister's soft brown eyes glistening with moisture. This wasn't any easier for Char than it was for her, Chris realized sadly.

In the kitchen, they heard Rick calling for Char, and both women rose to their feet. Chris couldn't help but feel a little relieved when Wendy ran in and Char began to bundle the two little ones into their coats. Josh never even roused.

As they neared the front door, Char somehow managed to pull her aside. "Chris?"

A tremulous smile was all Chris could manage. She didn't know when she would see her sister and her family again. "Don't tell me it's your turn to dish out a little sisterly advice," she tried to joke.

Char merely shook her head. "Will you do something for me?"

Chris wasn't sure she liked the sound of that, but she agreed.

"I want you to at least *think* about coming back for Christmas." Char took a step closer and kissed her sister's cheek. "Promise?"

The room grew suddenly quiet. A flurry of dread hit her, and Chris was agonizingly aware that all eyes were on her. She had to resist the urge to flee that very moment. She heard a dry, scratchy voice that sounded as if it belonged to a stranger. "I will," she promised.

And she knew, even as she spoke the words, that it was a promise she would never be able to keep.

CHAPTER TWO

"CHRISTMAS JUST WON'T BE the same without Christine."

Elaine looked up from the book she'd been reading, or trying to read. Paul had just voiced the very thought that had been running through her mind the entire evening.

The book closed with a dull thud. She dropped it on the nightstand next to the bed. "I know," she murmured.

From his place near the window, Paul sent her a sharp, questioning glance.

"Ever since she phoned to say she'd be here for Thanksgiving, I've had the feeling this was coming," she explained. "But I had hoped that once she was here, she would change her mind."

Paul turned, leveling a thoughtful gaze on his wife. "She's done so well this past year." He paused. The room was steeped in silence. "But tonight—" he shook his head, adding quietly "—I don't know, Elaine. I couldn't help but think she still hasn't gotten over Scottie after all."

Elaine's voice was just as quiet. "I think seeing Wendy and Josh brought everything back again. Coupled with the fact that Christmas is coming...."

"Sort of a double blow." Paul grimaced and sat on the bed next to his wife.

Elaine bit her lip, her expression deeply troubled. "I wish there was something we could do," she murmured. "I hate the thought of her being alone again during Christmas."

Paul's hand reached out to cover his wife's where it lay on the bedspread. "It's her choice, though." He sighed. "We could move things to Coeur d'Alene this year, but I don't think Christine would thank us."

"That's not the solution either." Her eyes met Paul's. "We both know Christmas is no longer a happy time for her, and we both know why. I wish she would let someone help her along, now that Christmas is so close. And I wish she didn't live so far away. I'd feel better if I knew someone were there to keep an eye on her."

At first Paul looked surprised, but then he smiled slightly. "She's thirty-four years old," he reminded his wife. "She's been on her own for a good many of those years. So what would you do? Send her a guardian angel instead?"

The expression on Elaine's face was both anxious and wistful. "If I could," she said slowly, "that's exactly what I'd do."

SATURDAY MORNING DAWNED in a pale, watery sunrise. The sky was a cold, threatening gray that shrouded the earth and mocked the sun's arrival. The silhouette of a tall concrete structure rose against the dismal skyline, one of Coeur d'Alene's latest additions to urban development.

Inside the building, a neatly folded newspaper in one hand, his morning cup of coffee in the other, a man left the kitchen and walked into the dining room of his condominium. Though it was Saturday, it was business as usual. He was dressed in a dark, severely cut suit that might have belonged to a Wall Street banker or a

Washington, D.C., politician, and he possessed the same polished exterior. This was a man who was the very picture of success and sophistication, something borne out by the elegant furnishings of his home. Everything was neat, fastidiously and correctly placed, from the towels in the bathroom to the salt and pepper shakers carefully concealed behind cupboard doors.

But Logan Garrison was neither a Wall Street banker nor a Washington, D.C., politician. And he had purposely made his home on the opposite seaboard.

His appearance was also deceptive in more ways than one. In spite of his six-foot height, his build was far from heavy. Trim and wiry, his shoulders tapered to hips that were as narrow as they'd been in his college days. His features were an intriguing symmetry of planes and angles. Set beneath eyebrows as dark and thick as his hair, his eyes were a pale, crystalline blue.

He dropped the newspaper onto the table. Several swift purposeful steps carried him to the window, where he opened the drapes. His face wore the absorbed, intent expression of a man who knew exactly what he wanted, but it was little more than a mask. The past few years had held nothing but a series of question marks.

Those extraordinary eyes scanned the horizon. The sky was the color of pewter. Steep, pine-covered slopes rose misty and green, surrounding the lake that was the town's namesake. The day promised to be as lonely and dismal as he sometimes felt, but when the weather was clear, the view was impressive. On such a day, the colors of the lake and sky were so vivid and deep they were almost blinding. It seemed he had only to stretch out a hand to be able to touch them.

He'd wanted a place with a view, but there were times he'd thought it was a mistake. Because then, the lush panorama only served to remind him of a nightmare he had yet to forget. So close, close enough to touch...but hopelessly out of reach.

Once he'd made the decision to abandon his career, Coeur d'Alene had seemed as good a place as any to settle. He really hadn't cared, as long as he was far, far away from Florida—or New York. He hoped to hell he never saw another palm tree again in his life. As for his parents, they'd tried to lure him back to the place he'd left for good nearly twenty years earlier. He had no desire to see them, and he didn't doubt that the feeling was mutual. Nor did he doubt that they had made the offer simply because it was the "proper" thing to do. But for them to even suggest it, particularly his father, was something that made him see red.

The phone rang at that moment, and Logan picked it up to find Ned Gibson on the other end.

"Hi, ya. Look at this morning's paper yet?" Ned asked.

Ned was a sergeant with the city's police department. The two men had met six months ago while Logan was in the process of obtaining a license to start his security business. Initially Logan had suspected Ned's efforts to strike up a friendship weren't entirely what they seemed. He'd thought that Ned was perhaps a little in awe of a man who'd spent nearly fifteen years with the F.B.I. But as a stranger in a strange town, he'd been pleased to discover that wasn't the case at all.

"Not yet." Logan pulled the cord around and took a seat at the dining room table. "What's up?"

"Had another robbery last night."

By now he'd flipped the newspaper open to the city section. The headline glared up at him: Robber Strikes Again.

Ned spoke again while Logan quickly scanned the article. "It was that stereo shop on Market Street.

Somebody jimmied the back door. Just about cleaned out the storeroom."

"So I see." His eyes still on the newspaper, Logan lifted his brows. "Still feel like bragging about the crime stats here?"

Ned's voice was a little sheepish. "There's certainly been a rash of robberies the past few weeks. One of the office buildings near the square has been hit twice. Folks aren't likely to be quite so trusting. I'm beginning to think maybe you're the one who's behind all this," he joked. "Trying to beef up business."

Logan smiled slightly. The city was the largest in northern Idaho, but it was the kind of place where people thought nothing of leaving their back door unlocked. It was also true that with person or persons unknown on a crime spree, many of the local businessmen were getting a little edgy. Logan's office had received double its usual number of calls this past week, and he had an appointment early this afternoon to see about setting up night patrols at the mall downtown.

"You might be interested in knowing we're due to put a security system in that office building near the square," he told Ned. "The owner of the one right across from it got smart. We just finished installing a system in that one yesterday." He reached for his coffee and took a sip before asking, "Any increase in home burglaries?"

"Not so far. But with Christmas only a month away, it's bound to happen. That reminds me, how was your holiday?"

Just like every other holiday, Logan reflected silently. He'd spent Thanksgiving alone, exactly the way he'd spent countless other holidays. It was really no different from any other day. He was surprised to find himself a little bitter. It wasn't like him to be mawkish or sentimental. At least, it hadn't been until Denise had died in Miami.

The thought was far from comforting. Logan had no desire to spend the rest of his days feeling sorry for himself with every holiday that rolled around.

"I holed up in front of the TV with a beer and a bowl full of pretzels to watch the Seahawks. Great game, Ned. Did you see the play that sent it into overtime?"

Ned groaned. "Are you kidding? Why the hell didn't you call me? Linda wouldn't let anyone lay a hand on the television, so I was stuck with a houseful of kids and in-laws."

Logan knew Ned well enough to realize he really wasn't complaining. With four kids, Ned was very much a family man.

"By the way, while I'm thinking of it, Linda said to mention that the invitation still stands. Since you didn't come Thursday, you're invited for Christmas dinner."

Logan was silent for a moment. He really did appreciate the offer, just as he had when he'd been invited for Thanksgiving. He'd have felt like an outsider, though, and he really had no wish to intrude on Ned's family.

"Thanks anyway," he said finally. "But I may have other plans by then."

He wouldn't, and he had the feeling Ned knew it, too. When he hung up the phone a few minutes later, he tried to tell himself it didn't really matter.

But something inside told him it did.

CHRIS TIGHTENED HER GRIP on the steering wheel. Her eyes were narrowed in concentration, although the traffic heading north was light. Her gaze flitted from the ribbon of highway stretched out before her to the ominous clouds overhead. It didn't take a meteorologist to realize that those clouds were full of moisture. And with the temperature flirting with the freezing mark . . .

A sigh escaped without her being aware of it. One gloved hand crept around to knead the knotted muscles in the back of her neck. She felt exhausted, yet tense.

The day hadn't started out well, and the threatening weather only made a bad day even worse. She tried not to think about this morning's tearful goodbye, but she couldn't help it. Chris hated goodbyes; they only served as an unwelcome reminder that she'd never even had a chance to say goodbye to Scottie.

Char and the kids hadn't dropped by to see her off, and for that Chris was grateful. But she didn't thank her sister for planting the seed in her mother's mind. Her mother hadn't insisted that she come home to Boise for Christmas, but what she had asked of Chris was just as impossible.

Her mind carried her back to the conversation that had taken place in her room that morning.

First her mother had asked when she would be home again.

"Soon," Chris had tried to reassure her. "Soon." But not at Christmas.

The thought must have shown in her face, because Elaine had squeezed her hands. "You know I've never asked much of you."

"No." Chris made the admission almost reluctantly.

"Much as you know we want you here with your family, I won't say another word about having you back at Christmas."

Chris said nothing.

"But before you go, there's something I want you to tell me."

She had no choice but to listen.

"I need to know you won't spend the day alone."

Christine's eyes clouded. She shook her head, but her mother had been adamant. Chris was left with the impression that if she hadn't agreed, she wouldn't have gotten any farther than the front door.

Yet another promise she couldn't keep. First Char, now her mother. She was, she decided ironically, well on the way to becoming a pathological liar.

Losing a child was never easy, and the first year was always the hardest. Yet she'd gotten through it, and she'd thought she'd been doing so well—in all but this one thing. She couldn't even think of Christmas without thinking of Scottie.

She had stayed away from home too long. From Boise, and her family. Chris was well aware of that, and yet her emotions had won the war against logic. If such a situation had arisen with one of her patients, Chris had no doubt about her advice. *Deal with it openly and honestly. You'll do far more harm than good if you keep everything bottled up inside you. There are times you need to go back, before you can go forward.*

It was hard. As difficult as she expected. But going home to Boise for the first time in more than two years had been a test of sorts, a final exam. It was a test Chris wasn't convinced she had passed.

She would be lying to herself if she didn't admit that part of the reason she had avoided her family was Char's two dark-haired innocents. Chris was stung by a pang of guilt, but she couldn't deny what was in her heart.

As for Christmas, she knew she couldn't spend it with the people who loved her the most. Why? she agonized silently. Was she afraid of what someone might say? Nothing that hadn't been said before. *We all know how you feel, Christine...* But they didn't. Not her mother, or her father. Not Char, and not Diane. How could they? she reflected with a rare bitter twist. None of them had ever lost a child.

She wanted nothing more than to retreat and lick her wounds in private. Cowardly, perhaps. But at least it was the truth.

The glare of headlights suddenly flashed into her line of vision. Chris focused her full attention on the road. She glanced at her watch. Five-fifteen. With any luck, she'd be home in an hour.

Darkness was complete and total by the time she reached the eastern extremity of the lake. It had rained earlier, and when she finally reached the city limits, the streets were still wet and slippery. She drove slowly, struggling to see the dividing line between the lanes.

She was home. Home.... She should have been glad—relieved, if nothing else, that she'd made the long trip safely. But all she could feel was a cold hollowness in the region of her heart.

The night seemed to grow darker, the clouds more threatening. Even as she cast a worried glance through the windshield, a fine gray drizzle began to fall from the sky.

Scottie had died on a night like this. A night *exactly* like this.

Numbly she stopped the car for a traffic signal. Her eyes squeezed shut as she struggled against a feeling of failure. She shouldn't have held Josh last night. Dammit, she shouldn't have! Then she wouldn't be suffering this awful yearning inside.

She couldn't go home like this, she realized. Her house was too big, too dark, too...empty. What she needed was work. A horn blared behind her, and she seized on the thought. She would stop by her office, sort through the mail that had piled up in her absence.

Maybe take a few case files home with her. Therapy for the therapist, she decided sourly. It seemed ironic that she could help others when she couldn't seem to help herself, but Chris was also aware that in the past two years, her work had been her only salvation.

Her expression was grim but determined when she pulled into the parking lot a few minutes later. Trailing tendrils of ivy crept up one side of the two-story, stately brick building that housed Chris's office. Two other buildings exactly like it flanked the large, flagstoned courtyard that was known as the square. It was complete with benches, daintily tended flower beds and a small gurgling fountain in the center. In spring, summer and fall, it wasn't unusual for the workers in nearby shops and offices to head for the square on their lunch break.

Various businesses occupied the buildings. One was a regional headquarters for an insurance group. The other had been taken over by the school district's administration. Several other doctors and psychologists besides Chris occupied the second floor of her building, while downstairs there was a pharmacy, a florist and a medical supply house.

It was still drizzling as she stepped from the car. She didn't bother to pull up her hood, but ran quickly toward the door. Chris had worked too many solitary evenings alone here to be frightened by either the silence or the darkness. Yet as she switched on the light and started up the stairs, she had the vague sensation that something was different.

But things looked exactly the same. She let herself through the door marked "Christine Michaels, Ph.D., Counseling Psychologist." Jean's desk was just as cluttered as it had been last Friday, but Chris wouldn't have traded Jean for the most efficient receptionist in the world. She had a knack for putting patients at ease beyond anything Chris had ever seen.

While flipping through her mail, Chris thought of the meager contents of her refrigerator. She was still a little on edge from the drive, and not really hungry. But when she was through here, she would need to stop by a grocery store for a few staples. Hurrying a little, she collected several patient folders. She tucked them beneath her coat to shield them against the rain, then left her office and headed downstairs.

She had no sooner stepped outside than an ear-splitting wail shattered the air. A siren, some distant part of her mind acknowledged. But the sound was so loud and overpowering it seemed to surround her, hold her captive.

She saw lights coming at her from a distance. They belonged to some kind of emergency vehicle. It raced straight at her, closer and closer; then another and another, their overhead lights glowing ominously in the darkness.

Chris's heart began to pound. It was just like the night Scottie died. First the ambulance, then the police. Her breath came jerkily; her muscles tensed. She couldn't take it. It was like reliving a nightmare. Something inside her snapped. Her only thought was to get away.

She wasn't more than ten feet from her car when she heard the screech of brakes. Doors slammed. The glaring circle of a white-hot spotlight blinded her. Chris threw up a hand against it and stumbled to a halt. Then a voice like a foghorn penetrated her consciousness.

"Police! Hold it right there!"

CHAPTER THREE

THE PANIC INSIDE Chris climbed higher. She realized dimly that some sort of alarm must have sounded since the piercing wail wasn't coming from any of the police vehicles. Strange, she thought vaguely. The building hadn't had an alarm system when she'd left last week.

Her arm was seized in a grip that wasn't exactly painful, but it was far from gentle. A man loomed before her.

"What were you doing in that building, lady? And where do you think you're going?" The harsh voice belonged to a burly sergeant who was quickly joined by two other policemen.

Chris opened her mouth in a vain attempt to explain, but to her horror, the sound refused to pass the tightness in her throat. She was shaking, she thought disbelievingly. Literally shaking. All she could do was stare back at him dumbly.

A movement in her peripheral vision caught her attention. Chris saw that a man dressed in a suit had stepped up behind the uniformed officers. He was dark, some distant part of her brain registered. Dark hair, bronzed skin, but there was a flash of brightness in his face. Still struggling to find her voice, her eyes met his, the only pair in the entire swarm of faces surrounding her that wasn't entirely hostile.

Those eyes seemed totally at odds in such a dark, hard-featured man; the irises were so pale they were almost transparent. China blue, some faraway segment of her mind telegraphed. For a split second, they seemed to hold her pinned, caught by some nameless, fleeting emotion.

But the shrill whine continued to slice through the night, piercing and relentless. It echoed in her ears, over and over and over until she wanted to scream.

Chris swallowed sickly. She had to fight to keep from covering her ears with her hands, but she knew she didn't dare make a move. "Please," she finally managed faintly. "The siren..."

The man in the suit moved away. The silence, when it finally came, was almost deafening.

"All right, lady. Start talking." The burly sergeant swept her with a disdainful glance and repeated his demand. "What were you doing inside that building? And what are you hiding under your coat?"

Chris resisted the impulse to close her eyes. If only someone would switch off those dreaded lights. But they continued to whirl and flash a nightmarish red pattern all around her.

She looked away for a fraction of a second, forcing herself to speak. "I—I work here. I didn't know about the alarm, you see..." Her weak voice sounded anything but convincing, she realized.

The sergeant's gaze continued to drill into her. "If you work here, why didn't you know?"

A logical question, and one she hoped she could answer to his satisfaction. Moving very slowly, she displayed the patient file folders she'd tucked under her coat. "My name is Christine Michaels, *Dr.* Christine Michaels. My office is in this building. I've been on vacation the past ten days, and there was no alarm here when I left, I swear. My office is on the second floor, and I stopped by on my way home." She bit her lip.

They were all staring at her so suspiciously. This was just what she needed, she despaired silently. All she needed was to be dragged off to jail; a fitting ending for a far-from-perfect day.

She dropped her purse on the ground before her. Her legs felt like jelly. How she remained standing was a mystery. Yet somehow she managed to inject a note of soft-spoken authority into her voice. "If you'll just open my wallet, you'll find my driver's license." She nodded at her purse. "There's also a certification card from the State Board. If you need to check further," Chris added, "you could always call the building superintendent. Norm Henderson is his name."

One of the officers bent down to retrieve her purse. At the same time, the suited man edged over to the sergeant and whispered something in his ear. Who was he? And why was he here? Chris couldn't help but wonder about his air of quiet authority.

The purse was pressed back into her hands, still unopened. At a nod from the sergeant, the group began to disperse. Chris had the distinct sensation it wasn't because of her declaration; whatever the man in the suit had whispered to the sergeant appeared to carry far more weight. It irritated her a little, since she had the feeling he wasn't a cop.

The sergeant turned to her. "You can go now." His voice was still a little gruff, but there was a hint of both apology and respect in the way he tipped his hat. "Sorry about coming down on you so hard, but we do need to check these things out."

Chris's nod was jerky. It was an understandable mistake, so she wasn't really angry. Nevertheless, her insides were still churning.

"In the meantime," he continued, "if I were you, I'd wait until Monday before going back to your office."

The sergeant turned away, but when she realized he intended to leave, she took an involuntary step toward him. "Wait!" she cried breathlessly.

He half turned, a polite but detached expression in his eyes. Chris suddenly felt rather foolish. The other man still hadn't moved, she noticed. "I still don't understand what happened. Why didn't the alarm go off when I went inside?" She floundered uncertainly. "And I've never even heard any of the other tenants in the building mention that an alarm was being put in."

The sergeant lifted his eyebrows and inclined his head toward the dark stranger. "That's the man you ought to be talking to. Knows a lot more about it than I do." With that, he tipped his hat once more and disappeared into the darkness.

Chris was left alone with the stranger. She could feel his gaze boring into her. She took a deep breath and squared her shoulders. She was shoring up her defenses, she realized subconsciously, but she didn't quite know why.

Perhaps it was because of those china-blue eyes, a point of beauty in such ruggedly configured features. China blue? There was nothing fine or delicate about this man, and she decided it wouldn't be wise to make an enemy of him. There was something very keen, a little too penetrating in his glance. Chris had the strangest sensation that he looked not only at her, but through her. She shivered, but whether it was from the cold or the fine gray drizzle that persisted in falling, Chris wasn't certain.

"Welcome back, Dr. Michaels."

Her eyes flashed upward. Finding no hint of mockery in the soft-spoken voice, she half expected to see it on his face. Instead, she caught a glimpse of wry humor, reflected in the slight tilt of his mouth as he added, "Not quite the homecoming you expected, was it?"

She shook her head. "No," she murmured, narrowing her eyes against the glare of the streetlight. "No, it certainly wasn't, Mr.—"

"Logan Garrison." He held out his hand.

Her gaze dropped. Chris stared at his hand for a second, feeling curiously reluctant to touch him. Her reaction puzzled and confused her, but common courtesy preempted an analysis. In any case, Chris wasn't sure she'd have wanted to make one.

"You're not with the police?" Chris inquired as she extended her hand.

The handshake was brief but firm, not the least bit too familiar. Logan Garrison, she decided, probably wasn't half as dangerous as he looked.

He shook his head. "I own the company that installed the security system. You've been away...how long?"

Chris slipped a hand into her pocket. The drizzle had ceased falling, but the air was very chill and damp. "About ten days."

"There's been quite a number of burglaries in town since then. Someone broke into that building—" he pointed over her shoulder toward the school district offices "—twice now."

She frowned. "Anything taken?"

"Enough." Logan lifted his brows. "Computer equipment, mostly. At any rate, Norm Henderson didn't want to be next on the list. We just finished installing the system yesterday."

"Are you sure it's operating the way it should?" She certainly didn't want to tell him his business, but on the other hand... "I was outside when it went off."

"When you went in, you triggered a silent alarm that's relayed to a central monitoring station at the office. There's a five-minute delay before the audible sounds. Hopefully the police will have arrived by then. If not, the idea is that the audible will frighten off the intruder."

Five minutes. She didn't think she'd been inside any longer than that. "Guess it works like a charm," she muttered.

"We usually just call the police when an alarm sounds and let them handle it. I happened to be at the office when this one went off, and it's the first time I've used equipment from this particular manufacturer. I thought I'd better check to make sure it wasn't an equipment failure."

"It obviously wasn't," she said flatly.

He merely smiled, seemingly amused by her faint disgruntlement.

Chris tried to smile back, but she was still a little too shaken up to manage anything more than a slight twisting of her lips.

And she sensed he was looking right through her again. She shifted uneasily, unaware that she did so. "Well." She cleared her throat, hoping she sounded far more confident than she felt. "It was nice meeting you, Mr. Garrison, but you're probably as anxious as I am to leave—"

"You said you were on your way home."

His voice checked her abrupt movement as she turned toward her car. Chris glanced back over her shoulder. There was a note in his voice that made her hesitate. "Yes."

"Do you mind if I follow you?"

Chris chewed her lower lip uncertainly, then fought an almost hysterical impulse to laugh. Had it been so long since she'd fielded a pass from a man that she couldn't even recognize one?

She turned back then, her eyes wide. "Why?"

Her directness didn't appear to put him off. "Because I'd like to make sure you get home safely."

There it was, that edge of authority she had suspected all along. *Was* he making a pass? Perhaps she was mistaken, the way the police had mistaken her presence here tonight. Chris stared at him a second longer, a little puzzled by the low intensity in his voice. She didn't understand why it seemed to matter to him, or why she would have felt guilty if she had refused. But she knew she would have, just as she was suddenly very certain that whatever type of man Logan Garrison was, dangerous or otherwise, he was not a man on the prowl.

"Please," he added very quietly.

"It's a long way." She hesitated briefly. "I live about five miles out of town." She had relented before she even realized it. But if Chris had been hoping her words might change his mind, she was in for a disappointment. He simply smiled once more and opened the car door for her.

DR. CHRISTINE MICHAELS was nervous, Logan decided, watching as she exited her Audi sedan. Her gaze immediately flitted to where he had pulled up behind her on the gravel drive. Nervous and just a little apprehensive, he amended silently.

He was both puzzled and curious by what had happened back at the square. He couldn't forget the expression on her face. There was more to her reaction than simply being surprised or startled by the police on a cold, rainy night. Her frozen features, the anxious distress in her eyes... Logan was well acquainted with the look of sheer, blind panic. He'd seen it far too many times not to recognize it.

He had also been seized by another sensation, one that he almost hated to acknowledge. He wished he could have been indifferent to Christine Michaels's plight, but he couldn't. Dear God, he couldn't.

She reminded him of Denise. Lord, but it hurt to admit it. As if that weren't enough, she reminded him of Denise the last time he had ever seen her. She had been so close then, close enough to touch....

But this woman's eyes weren't the deep blue of a wintry sea. Still, there had been something in the way she had looked at him, something pleading. Just like Denise, he realized silently.

A dull, familiar ache unfolded in his chest. He suppressed the urge to slam the door of his BMW, inwardly cursing this woman who had roused sleeping demons with merely a look.

Logan met her midway between the two cars. "You live alone?"

Chris hesitated, watching as he made a slow, sweeping survey in all directions. The spotlight above the garage centered the two of them in a hazy pool of light. To her right, her house was a rambling jumble of points and angles. Beyond the perimeter of light, the world was dark.

A prickly unease trickled down her spine. Again, she had the sensation that this man was all seeing, all knowing. When his eyes finally returned to her, she nodded slowly.

"Maybe I should come in with you then."

Presumptuous? Or just cautious? It occurred to Chris that she hadn't acted very wisely in telling a perfect stranger that she lived alone, especially when the nearest house was over a mile away. As if he could read her mind, he glanced toward the road, giving Chris the opportunity to study him. His profile was stark and unyielding, the contours of his mouth rather grim. Despite his air of calm detachment, she fleetingly entertained the notion that his generosity wasn't entirely on her behalf.

"You've been gone ten days." There was just a hint of reproach in his gentle reminder. "And with so many burglaries lately..."

There was no need for him to go on. Only then did Chris realize he had turned back to her, and she'd been staring. Stop being so silly, she chided herself. He'd hardly been ogling her—not that there was much to ogle at the moment. She probably looked as tired, damp and disheveled as she felt.

"You're right," she finally agreed. With an inward chuckle, she pushed a limp strand of hair from her eyes and started toward the back porch.

He was directly behind her as she ascended the narrow wooden steps. Opening the door, she switched on the light and stood aside, waiting for him to precede her. Chris was surprised to see one corner of his mouth tilt upward when he brushed past her. For the first time that day, she felt some of her tension ease.

"You're sure you're not a cop?" She posed the question after he poked his head into her living room.

His gaze found hers briefly, then slid beyond into the dining room. "I used to be," he admitted. "Sort of."

"Sort of?" Chris raised her eyebrows.

"I spent quite a few years as an FBI agent." The admission seemed to come reluctantly.

"No wonder you're so suspicious." She wrinkled her nose and sent him a curious glance as they began to retrace their steps down the hallway. "I'd have thought that Coeur d'Alene would be a little tame for an ex-FBI agent.''

That was exactly the point, Logan agreed rather grimly. But he didn't say so to Christine Michaels. She'd finally lost that woefully stricken look that tugged so painfully on his heart.

Chris stopped near the kitchen doorway, suddenly wishing she'd taken the time to brush her hair while he'd looked through the house. Her gaze met his briefly. In the small silence that followed, she guessed that Logan Garrison was a very private, solitary man. Yet in spite of that, he seemed almost lonely.

''Would you like to stay for a few minutes?'' The invitation was issued before Chris could recall it, and then she decided she didn't want to. Perhaps *she* was the one who was in need of a little company. When he said nothing, she added rather uncertainly, ''I could make some coffee if you like.''

She wished he would stop staring at her. His gaze was direct and unwavering, a little too piercing for her to be entirely comfortable with.

''Coffee would be fine,'' he said with a smile that transformed his whole face. It made him appear less harsh, more approachable somehow. At the same moment, his eyes softened to a subtle blue. ''You sure you're okay now?'' he asked very softly.

The question caught her off guard. For an instant, Chris could only stare back at him. He knew, she thought numbly. He knew of the sudden, irrational panic that had flooded through her at the sight and sound of the police sirens. She could see it in his eyes, hear it in his voice. She sucked in a harsh breath, silently wishing the earth would swallow her whole.

This man seemed so utterly in control. And she had practically fallen apart in front of him, and in front of the police as well. Chris felt embarrassed and foolish, yet oddly touched by his concern.

Quickly she glanced away. "I'm fine," she murmured. She didn't sound as convincing as she'd hoped, however. The week spent with her parents, fighting back the bitter memories, had taken its toll. And tonight, with the sirens screeching in the darkness, had added but one more bruise to an already battered heart.

Several seconds went by. The silence was anything but comfortable. "I should probably explain," she muttered finally.

"You don't have to," Logan said softly. "Unless you want to, of course."

She didn't, and that was the whole problem. It was difficult to talk about Scottie at the best of times; she couldn't even think of doing so with a complete stranger.

But was he a stranger? a tiny voice inside prodded. From the moment he'd set eyes on her, he had known of the turmoil in her mind and heart. And perhaps because of that, he had ceased to be a stranger. His presence here in her home was somehow reassuring.

Chris's silence was beginning to make Logan feel like an intruder. If she wanted to be alone, all she had to do was say so. His eyes fell to her fingers, clasped together before her. The pads of her thumbs swiped against each other, over and over. It was a nervous gesture, and again he wondered about her. Such a scared little girl...

The thought brought him up short. This was no young girl he was facing, in spite of the fact she was so small and gentle. Back at the square, she'd given him a glimpse of the cool, competent woman he suspected she really was. And no matter how she tried to hide it, he also had the feeling that Christine Michaels was a woman who'd had her share of ups and downs.

But he wasn't going to stay where he wasn't wanted. "Look," he said in a low voice. "We can skip the coffee if you'd rather—"

"No!" She didn't want to be alone, not just yet. Thoughts of Scottie were still so close. "Please don't leave," she said breathlessly. "I . . . a cup of hot coffee on a night like this is the least I can do after the trouble I've put you to."

"You haven't." His tone was very quiet. "But I don't want to put *you* to any trouble." He paused, his gaze never wavering from hers. "Especially if you're not up to it."

Chris was aware of the silent question in his eyes, and the oddest thought went through her mind. It would be easy to trust this man, almost too easy. Again, Chris didn't quite understand her feelings, but she was a woman used to following her instincts. Working in a field where there were hardly any clear-cut answers, they were often all she had to rely upon.

"I'm fine," she said again, and this time she knew it was the truth. As if to emphasize the words, she blessed him with the first genuine smile of the evening.

Logan caught his breath. Lord, she was pretty. The smile sparked tiny gold lights in her eyes, showing him a hint of impishness he found wholly unexpected. So why did he have the feeling she didn't smile like that nearly enough?

He followed when she led the way into the kitchen, a large rectangular room with white painted cupboards on one wall. The entire outside wall was composed of a brick-to-ceiling fireplace. The wide window above the pine-plank table was covered with gauzy red gingham curtains, tied back with starched white ribbons.

"Are you cold?" Stupid question, Chris chided herself. The house had been closed up for over a week, and the temperature outside was very chilly. She still had her coat on, and a hasty glance over her shoulder revealed that Logan had slipped his hands into his pockets. His shoulders were hunched up ever so slightly.

But at her question, he shook his head. "I'm fine." He must have caught her look, though, because the corners of his mouth edged up in a sheepish half smile. "Fine," he repeated. "It seems to be the standard reply tonight, doesn't it?"

It certainly did. Chris smiled weakly and hurried into the living room to turn up the thermostat.

When she reappeared in the doorway, Logan thought of asking if she needed any help. But in spite of what had happened earlier, he suspected Christine Michaels was far from being a helpless female. So he sat down at the table and asked the question that had been running through his mind the last few minutes.

"What kind of medicine do you practice?"

"Oh, I'm not an M.D. I'm a psychologist." She chuckled at the look of surprise that flitted over his features, then moved toward the cupboard. "You know, as in Ph.D. I handle a general caseload, a little bit of everything actually."

What, then, was he supposed to call her? *Dr.* Michaels? That sounded so formal. They hadn't met on a professional basis, nor had it been a friendly social occasion. But he had the feeling she could use a friend. For that matter, so could he.

As if she were aware of his dilemma, she glanced at him over her shoulder. "Everyone calls me Chris, except for my patients. *And* my dad," she added, pulling two cups from the cupboard. "When he calls me Christine, I know he means business."

The warm fondness in her voice was unmistakable. Logan thought of his own father. He was glad Chris wasn't facing him. Psychologist or not, he knew it wouldn't have taken a great deal of insight to recognize the coldness that had entered his face.

"Your father lives in Coeur d'Alene?" He spoke out of courtesy more than anything else. He hadn't forgotten the polite rules of civility after all, and he couldn't help thinking his mother would have been elated.

Chris shook her head. "My parents live in Boise," she announced without turning around. "I've got another sister there, too, and the youngest lives in Seattle."

"Boise," he repeated. "Is that where you've been?"

"I was there for Thanksgiving." Chris moved to the cupboard on the other side of the sink. Logan absently watched as she rummaged through the contents of the bottom shelf, but his mind was elsewhere.

So Dr. Christine Michaels had two sisters. Logan would have bet she came from a close-knit family. At the thought, an odd pang went through him.

Chris finally turned around. "You're not going to believe this, but I can't seem to find the coffee." Suddenly she stopped. Then, marching across the room, she snatched a piece of paper from beneath the Coca-Cola magnet on the refrigerator. There it was, right at the top of her grocery list: coffee.

"Wouldn't you know it," she muttered. "I can't find the coffee because there *is* no coffee. I meant to stop in town tonight, but . . ." She sighed and looked across at Logan. "I don't suppose you like tea?"

Her expression was so forlorn that Logan felt a rare laugh rising in his chest. "Tea would be fi—"

Her eyes widened.

"Great," he finished, then was unable to hold back a deep chuckle.

As it turned out, Chris ended up adding tea to her list as well. She was full of apologies as Logan got to his feet.

"Tell you what." Logan halted just before they reached the door that led onto her back porch. "I'll supply the coffee if you'll have breakfast with me tomorrow."

Chris laughed. "You must be a glutton for punishment. I am not what's commonly known as a 'morning person,' especially on weekends."

"It doesn't have to be early." His quick reply surprised him a little. "If you want, we could stop by your office afterward and I'll show you how the security system works. Minus the lights and sound effects," he added when a faint look of distress crept into her eyes.

Chris felt herself relax. "Next you'll be throwing in a side trip for my groceries, too."

"What better way to spend a Sunday?" His smile faded when she seemed to consider. "Unless you have other plans, of course."

Time seemed to drag, though he knew only a few seconds had passed. He didn't want her to refuse, he realized. He really didn't. . . .

"No," she murmured at last. "No other plans." She smiled up at him with that same breathtaking smile she'd given him earlier. "In fact, I think I'd like it," she added softly.

"How's ten o'clock sound?"

"Sounds fi—" This time she was the one who couldn't hold back a laugh. "Sounds just about right."

"Great." He opened the screen and headed down the porch steps.

Chris peered into the darkness. "See you tomorrow," she called after him.

He acknowledged with a small nod just before he got into his car. Chris closed the door and locked it. She was still smiling, but she wasn't quite sure why.

When she was halfway up the stairs, the reason suddenly struck her. Breakfast with Logan Garrison... She was actually looking forward to it. Quite a lot, if she were honest with herself.

The day hadn't turned out so badly after all.

CHAPTER FOUR

As WAS HIS HABIT, Logan arose early the next morning. Sunday was no different from any other day of the week.

His thoughts drifted to Christine Michaels as he dressed. He found himself admitting that he had mixed feelings about his upcoming breakfast with her. A part of him wondered what on earth had possessed him to issue such an invitation in the first place. A desire for company? Or perhaps it was a simple, basic need for human warmth and contact.

Another part of him scoffed at the notion. He possessed a solitary nature. For years he had depended on no one. What was the sense in forming ties that would only be broken? It only made it so much harder to walk away. He'd learned that at a very young age.

He had come here to be left alone. No more assignments. No more pressure. The work that had once been so satisfying had become a constant and painful reminder of something he wished to hell he could forget. So why had he sought out someone, when he really had no need of anyone but himself?

It was an ingrained habit, he supposed. Courtesy of his upbringing. Christine Michaels had seemed so alone. And if nothing else, his mother had seen to it that he never forgot his manners.

But he was being cynical, something Denise had always hated. She had once vowed to cure him of that.

Given the chance, Logan had no doubt she would have succeeded. Even when he was at his most disagreeable, she had always managed to wheedle a smile from him.

"There!" she would say. "Now doesn't that feel better?" And then she would laugh, in that spirited, boisterous way she had.

With a muttered curse, Logan dumped the remainder of his coffee in the sink. Walking back into the living room, he idly speculated that the weather was responsible for his dark mood this morning. The day had dawned just as bleak and dreary as yesterday. Even the lake was rolling in waves, proclaiming its mood in white-capped agitation.

He grabbed his jacket from the closet, but as he did, his gaze trickled around the living and dining room. The strangest sensation suddenly crept over him. He had the feeling he was viewing the room for the first time, through the eyes of a stranger.

He'd put the entire condominium into the hands of a decorator, a flighty woman whose name he couldn't remember. The living room was the picture of success and sophistication with its floor-to-ceiling bookcase lining one entire wall, filled with dozens of thick, leather-bound volumes. Here and there were touches of smooth, polished brass and clear, sparkling glass. The camel-back sofa and chair were white, along with the drapes and carpet. Ivory, the decorator had called it.

Once more his gaze scanned the room. White on white. Color without color. A home...that was not a home.

For the first time, it struck him that the place didn't look lived in. It was sterile, lacking any traces of warmth. So cool... No, not cool. Cold. Cold, austere and intimidating.

A surge of anger ran through him. Cold. Intimidating. Was that how the blasted decorator had seen him?

A muffled curse escaped his lips. He wasn't heartless. There had been many times when he'd wished that he were, but he wasn't. Dammit, he wasn't!

He suddenly realized he hated this room and vowed then and there to make some changes. Better yet, he would move. Clear across town.

Yet the oddest thought struck Logan as he slammed the front door, shutting out the sight of his living room.

His parents would have loved it.

CHRIS WAS JUST COMING DOWN the stairs when a knock sounded at the back door. She hurried down the steps, wondering a little at her haste.

It was true that things sometimes looked different in the cold light of day. Chris was a little ashamed of her display of weakness last night, and because of that weakness, the prospect of facing Logan Garrison left her feeling both uncomfortable and embarrassed. In spite of her momentary lapse last night, she wasn't the kind of woman who needed a crutch, and it was somehow important that he know it, too.

But none of that seemed to matter when she opened the door. Her first thought was that his hair wasn't nearly as dark as she'd thought. Neatly feathered and angled back, it was the color of rich, dark chocolate. Her second was that she was glad to see him, and the reason why wasn't really important.

His dress was casual—jeans and a plaid flannel shirt, covered by a brown suede jacket trimmed in sheepskin. Chris was glad she'd opted for slacks and a sweater.

"Hi," she greeted as she opened the door wide. "Come on in."

Logan gazed back at Chris and felt his vague depression evaporate like early-morning dew on a sun-kissed field.

"Hi." His voice was deep and low, very pleasing to the ear. "How are you this morning?"

Those keen, penetrating eyes examined her, not with critical concern, but with a genuine interest that kindled an oddly heart-warming feeling deep inside her.

"Oh, I'm fi—" She broke off when his dark, heavy eyebrows winged upward in warning. Chris laughed. Logan's answering smile was slow in coming, but when it did, it was definitely worth waiting for.

"You know," she said as she slipped into her coat, "I really do owe you an apology over what happened last night. If I had come home first instead of stopping off at my office, I'd have known about the alarm Norm had put in." She gave a self-deprecating sigh. "My secretary left a message on my answering machine and warned me not to come in until Monday."

Logan shrugged. "It's not the first time something like that has happened. Infrared systems are sensitive to changes in heat radiation, while utrasonic sensors detect changes in air currents. We've had alarms triggered by air conditioners kicking in, by pets wandering around in the middle of the night.... Just last week, we had a residential alarm go off at seven in the morning. Someone hadn't locked or closed the front door all the way, and the wind blew it open." He smiled. "That was one embarrassed homeowner."

Tell me about it, Chris groaned silently. "I think I'd rather buy a Doberman," she muttered aloud.

Not surprising, Logan thought to himself. Again he wondered briefly at her reaction last night, but he said nothing. He paused near the hood of his burgundy BMW. "Where should we go first?" he asked. "To breakfast? Or your office to check out the alarm?'' He opened the passenger door for her.

Chris slid inside. The air was cold and faintly damp, the result of an early-morning rain shower.

"Might as well get the worst over with right at the start,'' she told him stoutly. "Unless you think it will take too long.''

Logan shook his head; she didn't miss the flicker of approval in his eyes. "It shouldn't take more than a few minutes,'' he assured her. "Unless you get into technicalities, security systems aren't half as bad as they look—or maybe I should say not half as bad as they sound,'' he amended dryly.

"You don't know me.'' Chris chuckled, trying not to look too doubtful. "Jean, my secretary, badgered me for ages to get a computer system installed to cut down on paperwork and bookkeeping. She finally talked me into it about a year ago, and I decided I might as well learn how to use it, too. I sat down one night after work and tried to type a letter. I've been under strict orders ever since not to lay even so much as a finger on it, or I'll find myself without a much-needed helping hand.''

As it turned out, Logan was right. He showed her how to enter the digital code in the control panel behind the door in the front entry. Chris vaguely recalled thinking last night that something was different, but in her haste she hadn't even noticed it.

By the time he was finished, Chris was feeling much more at ease about entering and exiting the building when the system was armed.

"There. You see?'' he asked when she'd programmed the code for the last time. "It's not so bad now, is it? And you should feel safer if you're here alone at night.''

Chris dug her hands into her pockets. "I still think I'd rather buy a Doberman," she said, not entirely in jest.

"Are you trying to tell me you're just an old-fashioned girl at heart, Dr. Michaels?" Logan's tone was teasing. It surprised him. Why, he hadn't teased anyone since...Denise. Sobering as that realization was, Logan still couldn't deny that it felt good—it felt damn good—to be standing here with Christine Michaels.

"I am, at that," Chris claimed lightly. "And this old-fashioned girl could use an old-fashioned breakfast."

"I did promise you that, didn't I?" He took her arm and would have led her back to where his car was parked in the lot, but Chris quickly pointed out that they were only a block away from Beth's, the best restaurant in the city.

It was Logan's turn to play the skeptic when they stepped inside the restaurant. It was tucked into a corner of an aging brick building that also housed a hardware store and a mail-order office. Logan had passed the restaurant many times without even realizing it was there. One glimpse of the matchbox-sized counter, jukebox and half a dozen vinyl booths lining the wall, and Logan felt as if he'd stepped back in time.

Chris happened to catch sight of his expression. "You haven't discovered this place yet, I see."

He shook his head.

Her eyes sparkled. "I know it's small, and it doesn't look like much. Beth doesn't serve anything fancy, but you've honestly never tasted food like this before."

The polite reply on his lips never made it to fruition. The door to the kitchen swung open and availed Logan of any number of mouthwatering aromas. He made no demur when Chris headed toward the booth nearest the kitchen. He really hadn't been hungry before, but now...

They pored over the menu they were handed moments later by a pleasant, heavy-set woman Chris introduced as Beth. "They have the best apple pancakes here." Chris sighed. "Just stuffed with spiced, juicy apples and smothered with whipped cream."

Logan glanced up at her. "You," he surmised with a lift of his brows, "must have a sweet tooth."

"I do," she said with unrepentant honesty. "I can never decide between the apple pancakes and the cherry crepes."

"Smothered with whipped cream, too?"

She grinned. "Powdered sugar."

Logan shook his head and went back to the menu, eventually deciding on blueberry waffles.

While they were waiting for their breakfast to arrive, Chris couldn't help but notice what a terribly attractive man Logan was. His was a face of striking symmetry—high cheekbones, straight, narrow nose, strongly angled chin. His features possessed a dark elegance as well as a hint of ruggedness.

Chris felt an odd little shiver trace up her spine. His eyes, such an unusual silver blue, were sometimes piercingly intent. She had noticed it several times since they'd met. There were some who might think he was a hard man. Maybe even ruthless. Yet when Christine looked at him, all she could remember was how compassionate he had been to her last night.

"You haven't lived here long, have you?" It was Chris who broke the comfortable silence that had cropped up.

Logan accepted the coffee Beth delivered before glancing up at her. "Six months probably isn't long to a native like you."

"I don't know if I qualify as a native." Chris chuckled. "Although I have lived here for nearly ten years, so maybe I am." Chris studied him, a hint of laughter in her eyes. "How about you? Where do you hail from? Chicago?"

Logan shook his head, thinking how much he liked it when she smiled.

"I didn't think so." She tipped her head to the side as if to consider. "You don't have a Midwestern twang."

His mouth twitched at the corners. "Thank you," he returned gravely.

"Where then? San Francisco?"

His gaze met hers over the rim of his coffee cup. "I did live there for a while," he admitted.

"Phoenix?" When he opened his mouth, Chris frowned good-naturedly. "Don't tell me. You lived there, too."

Logan nodded. "You can add Pittsburgh and Denver to the list, too."

"You've certainly moved around a lot. All FBI assignments?" she guessed.

He inclined his head slightly. "Best way to keep an agent out of trouble."

Out of trouble? Or out of danger? Chris wondered wryly if the psychologist in her wasn't coming into play. She'd learned that what a person *didn't* say sometimes divulged a great deal more than what he chose to reveal.

"Actually," he added after a moment, "my last assignment was in Miami."

"That's a long way from here."

A ghost of a smile touched his lips. "I was about to be transferred to Spokane. In fact, I'd just made the trip out to see about housing when I made up my mind to resign."

"But you decided to stay anyway?"

He nodded. "I like it here," he said softly. "It's different from anywhere else I've ever lived. The pace and lifestyle of the people here is less frantic—more easygoing."

Chris chuckled. "And that's why you decided to open an alarm company? You were hoping things would liven up a bit?"

His expression was a little sheepish. "My very first case involved an interstate jewelry theft where the thief managed to bypass an elaborate security system," he told her. "I've always been rather intrigued with different systems since then. Spokane is so much bigger than Coeur d'Alene that I thought my chances of getting my company off the ground were better here than there."

"Less competition?"

Again he nodded.

"Plus the fact that you couldn't resist our small-town atmosphere?" She found herself teasing him.

He smiled slightly. "I'll admit I've had enough of big city life." Coeur d'Alene was hardly a bustling metropolis, though its location near the lake attracted swarms of vacationers during the summer months.

Chris picked up her coffee. "Maybe I shouldn't be bragging, though, with all the robberies that have been going on. I saw the article in yesterday's newspaper about the latest one." Her eyes met his. "It probably doesn't seem like all that many to you, but five thefts in less than two weeks is quite a few for Coeur d'Alene." She paused. "I doubt if I'm the only one who forgets to lock the door when I leave in the morning."

Logan eyed her over the rim of his cup. "You really should lock up," he said, his tone gently admonishing. "Especially since your place is so remote."

Remote. While it was true that her nearest neighbor lived over a mile away, Chris had always thought of her home as rural and secluded. But remote? Now, as she turned the word over in her mind, it kindled an involuntary shiver.

Beth bustled over then with two steaming plates. Chris wasted no time in sampling her crepes, savoring the rich, sweet taste of warm cherries. When she saw Logan watching her indulgently, she gave a sheepish but unrepentant grin.

They passed the next few minutes in silence, then she took advantage of the lull to backtrack slightly. "Your company," she commented. "You work mostly with security systems? Installing alarms, that kind of thing?"

"I have two installers who do the actual on-site work," he clarified. "But that's primarily what it entails—selling and leasing alarm systems. When I started up just over six months ago, I spent most of my time trying to drum up business. I have about a dozen people working for me now, and I'm just starting to branch out a little. In fact, I just firmed up a contract this weekend to provide night patrols at the shopping mall downtown."

"Sounds like all these robberies lately are good for business," she commented.

"True," he agreed slowly, then frowned. "But these days, I don't think anyone can be too careful."

After Beth came over to refill their coffee, Chris glanced across the table at him. "How long did you say you were with the FBI?" she asked curiously.

It was on the tip of his tongue to say that he hadn't, but something in her eyes stopped him.

He was silent for so long that Chris didn't think he intended to answer. Then he said finally, "Fifteen years."

She felt her jaw drop. "Why, you couldn't have had too much more time before you could retire."

The words emerged before she thought better of it. If she had been looking, she would have noticed Logan's fingers tense to a white-knuckled grip around his cup.

As it was, she glanced up in time to see his expression freeze.

"I'm sorry." She hesitated. "I didn't mean to pry. You must have had a reason for leaving."

His voice was clipped. "I did. I decided it was time to get off the merry-go-round."

Judging from the guarded tension in his face, Chris suspected there was more to his resignation from the FBI than the reason he'd just stated. He made it sound as if the decision had been almost a whim, but she wasn't convinced.

A brittle silence followed. She tried not to let his reaction bother her, but she couldn't suppress a pinprick of hurt. She was used to patients letting off steam. Sometimes it helped just to have a sounding board.

But something told her that Logan Garrison was not a man to be openly hostile. He was the kind of man to hold on to his pain, to keep it tightly bottled up inside him. The kind to suffer in silence, just like her.

The comparison startled her. It was also disturbing, for it reminded her that no matter how cool and controlled a person appeared, that wasn't always the case.

How well she knew. There were times after Scottie had died that she felt she would explode; times she wanted to cry or scream or rage. But she couldn't. Dear God, she couldn't.

It seemed the past, where both of them were concerned, wasn't the best place to visit.

Somehow she managed to keep her voice calm. She even managed to curve her lips in a parody of a smile.

"Something tells me this would be a good time to change the subject."

Logan took a deep breath, cursing himself soundly as he did. The last thing he wanted was to hurt her. She had such gentle eyes. Such hauntingly gentle eyes, flecked with amber and ringed with gold. But more and more he was beginning to think she was a woman at odds with herself.

He wasn't the only one with darkness in his heart, of that he was certain. He'd seen the shadows in her eyes. But although Christine Michaels possessed a presence that was calm and serene, there was a time or two this morning when he'd caught a glimpse of impishness that surprised him, given her quiet demeanor. He liked it, though. He also liked her frankness, something he'd had precious little experience with.

But he didn't particularly like himself at that moment. "I'm sorry," he said very quietly. "I guess I'm just not used to talking about myself."

"I noticed," Chris stated dryly. "You still haven't told me where you're from. You'll have me thinking you were raised by wolves."

Wolves? Logan was unwillingly amused. She didn't know how apt a description that was.

When Chris glanced up at him once more, she saw that his smile didn't quite reach his eyes.

"I grew up in New York. Long Island."

And that, Chris decided wryly, was that. But she noticed he didn't call New York his home.

"Can I ask you something?" It was Logan who posed the question this time.

Chris was relieved to note he appeared to have relaxed. "Sure."

"How is it a pretty lady like you has managed to stay single all this time?"

Slender, winged eyebrows arched further. "Are you taking potshots at me because I happen to be over thirty, Mr. Garrison?"

"Not very likely. I happen to be nearer forty than thirty myself."

His expression had softened considerably. Chris was very glad, without quite knowing why, or even *wanting* to know why.

"I haven't," she said softly, holding his gaze evenly.

"You're divorced?"

She nodded. "It's been final just over a year now." She paused, her fork poised on the edge of her plate. There was a faint cloud in her eyes as she murmured, "It seems funny to think of myself as being single again."

Meaning that she still felt married? Certainly it came as no surprise that she had been married. Logan couldn't help but wonder if her divorce was responsible for the well of pain he sensed in her.

Chris provided the answer, or at least part of it, when she added, "I was married for almost nine years."

Nine years. So it wasn't as if she and her husband had married and then found out later that they weren't right for each other. Nine years was plenty of time to build a strong relationship. Provided two people loved each other, of course.

Logan's mind drifted to his parents. Had they ever loved each other? It was a question that had plagued him since he was a boy and he had begun to realize that some marriages were built upon such values as mutual love, understanding and respect.

"I'm sorry," he said after a moment.

Chris shook her head, her voice very quiet. "Don't be. I'm not bitter." *Not about the divorce, anyway.*

"Bill and I both realized it was the best thing for both of us."

"No kids, I take it."

Logan wasn't prepared for the undeniable look of pain that flitted across her face at his offhand remark. Once again he branded himself an unthinking fool. He knew the answer, even before the words passed her lips.

"One," she said finally. "A little boy. His name was Scottie." The infinitesimal pause seemed to last forever. "He's gone now," she added softly, so softly Logan had to strain to hear.

He studied her as she pretended an absorbed interest in her food. It had been a long time since he had met a woman who was utterly without guile, or a man, for that matter. Her fine-boned features were so expressive, it wasn't hard for him to interpret her, to chart and gauge every nuance of emotion as if it were plotted on a map. It was a skill that had served him well over the years.

Perhaps a little too well, he couldn't help thinking. Chris's teeth were digging into her lower lip, as though she was trying very hard to keep it from trembling. With her hair spilling like dark gold honey over her sweater, a tiny smattering of freckles dotting her nose and cheekbones, she looked rather young and innocent. And so damned hurt and vulnerable he felt some nameless emotion spear his chest.

Before he'd even realized it, his hand came out to cover hers where it rested on the tabletop. "This time I *am* sorry, Christine. And please don't tell me not to be."

"I wasn't." She gave a tiny shake of her head. "I was just thinking that . . ."

"What?" He sensed how difficult this was for her.

"That this is the first time I've said Scottie's name aloud in—" her smile was tremulous at best "—why, it's been so long I can't even remember."

He watched her solemnly, his breakfast forgotten. "I didn't mean to pry, Chris. Or to remind you of something that's obviously still very painful for you."

His skin was warm, the touch of his hand reassuring. Chris marveled at how comfortable and secure she felt with this man. It seemed impossible that she had known him less than a day.

"Are you trying to tell me this might be a good time to change the subject—again?"

Logan laughed, the craziest thought running through his mind. Chris couldn't remember the last time she had said her son's name aloud. And he couldn't remember the last time he'd laughed so much in one day. His laughter sounded rusty and alien to his ears, but it felt good. It felt damn good.

In the next half hour, he was relieved to note the sadness had vanished from Christine's eyes. Her voice was pleasing, low and occasionally husky as they chatted over a second cup of coffee.

His own enjoyment came as something of a surprise, a very pleasant surprise. Logan was well aware that a year ago, he wouldn't have noticed, or cared, if the world had come crashing in around his head. But who was he trying to fool? A week ago he wouldn't have cared either. But right now . . .

By the time Logan stepped up to the cashier, check in hand, he was in a rather complacent frame of mind. The food? he speculated. Or the company? He silently chided himself. As if he really had to ask. . . .

"WHERE TO NEXT?" Logan asked when they were seated once more in his car. "The nearest grocery store?"

Chris looked at him blankly.

"You're out of coffee," he reminded her, holding back a chuckle.

A rare blush stole into Chris's cheeks. "I know," she said quickly. "But that doesn't mean I expect you to—"

"I want to, Chris." His gaze met hers. "And it's no trouble. Really."

"All right." She relented with a low laugh. "But only if you promise to stay for that cup of coffee I promised you last night."

The car engine purred smoothly to life. Logan sent her a quick glance before he pulled onto the street. "You're probably just looking for someone to carry in all the heavy bags," he teased. "Some strategy for a psychologist. I can see right through you, you know."

He and Christine had similar tastes in food, he noted a short time later, as he watched her pile items into a cart. Lean meat and fish, fresh fruits and vegetables. Last but not least, a stop at the in-store bakery for a dozen chocolate chip cookies. Undoubtedly to indulge her sweet tooth, he decided.

His amusement stayed with him while they made the drive back to her place. A sack in each arm, Logan followed her into the kitchen.

Chris stowed the half-gallon jug of milk in the refrigerator and turned to him. "Let me take your coat," she offered.

Logan deposited the sacks on the counter. They stood facing each other while he stripped off his jacket. Chris found herself unwittingly comparing him to Bill.

Bill was of average height but muscular, with a tendency toward brawniness. Logan was taller. The top of her head just barely reached his shoulder. His build wasn't at all heavy; instead he possessed a lithe trimness. Standing so close to him, Chris was aware of Logan in a way that was both pleasing and just a little disturbing. She looked up at him, fighting a sudden sensation of breathlessness. "You can go into the living room, if you like. I'll bring the coffee in when it's ready."

One corner of his mouth turned up. "Are you trying to get rid of me again?"

His tone implied great seriousness. Chris, who had resumed the task of unpacking her groceries, glanced back at him, apologies spilling from her lips. "Why, of course not. I just thought you might be more comfortable..." She broke off when she discovered his amusement.

Logan thought she looked enchanting as she turned to him rather hesitantly, one hand clutching a head of lettuce, the other a shiny green cucumber. Almost as enchanting was the spray of freckles sprinkled across her nose and cheeks.

He left her alone and went into the living room, not because he wanted to, but because he sensed Chris needed a moment to herself. He had the feeling that she wasn't used to a man's presence in her home.

He took in his surroundings, willing his mind from the woman in the kitchen. The neutral color of the walls and furniture gave the high-ceilinged room a light airy look. But it was the finishing touches that drew his attention—the charcoal sketches of mice and rabbits and owls hanging on the walls, the granny-squared afghan draped across the old rocker in the corner, the ancient steamer trunk that served as an end table. They lent the room a warm and welcoming atmosphere. And above the fireplace, occupying a place of honor, was a gilt-framed portrait.

It was Christine's family. He knew it, even before he moved across to study it.

The photograph had been taken outdoors, beneath a huge elm tree, an emerald field of grass stretching in all directions. There were five of them in all: Chris stood between another honey-blond and a dark-haired woman. Behind the three were a silver-haired man and a sweet-faced woman. Chris was smiling directly into the camera, a radiance in her face that he had yet to glimpse. She looked no different than she did now. Only the fact that her happiness seemed to shine from within her warned him that the portrait had probably been taken some time ago.

His gaze dropped to the cherrywood mantel below. Spread out on the rich wood surface were various knickknacks and treasures, small, delicate vases, tiny ceramic figurines. Apart from the collection was a wooden carving, perhaps six inches high, of a mother holding a sleeping child. Drawn by a force he didn't quite understand, he picked up the carving. Why it held such fascination for him, he couldn't fathom.

But all of a sudden Logan felt hollow, so devastatingly empty it seemed he would crumble to dust with the slightest touch. This was a home, a *real* home, he realized numbly. The kind of place where love and laughter filled every nook and cranny. It was nothing at all like the mausoleum he'd grown up in, where every feeling was preempted by cold, stoic propriety.

How long he stood there, Logan could never have said. It was only when Chris entered the room that he roused himself from his trance. "This is your family?" he asked.

"Yes. My parents and my sisters Char and Diane." She smiled. "Dad's always called us his basketball team."

Rich pride echoed in her voice. At the realization, Logan felt an unfamiliar feeling slice through him. Envy?

Aware of a pinprick of guilt, he remained motionless, wanting to face her, but unable to.

Her eyes had dropped to the carving he still held in his hands. "You like it?"

Logan nodded. His fingers ran over the smooth wood once again, the movement almost caressing.

Several steps away, Chris watched him. There was something almost personal in the way his fingers gently stroked the carving. "It's my favorite, too," she said, her expression very soft. "For obvious reasons, though. My grandfather carved that for my grandmother after my father was born."

He found himself admiring the workmanship. It was exquisite. "He must have been a carpenter," he murmured.

Her lips curved in a smile. "Woodworking was just a hobby, a winter hobby since he was a farmer. He gave away a lot of what he did, mostly toys. That carving came from an old oak tree on the farm that had to be cut down."

Logan carefully replaced the carving. He saw that she held two cups of coffee, and he relieved her of one. "They're still alive?"

Chris shook her head. "Both of them died when I was just a kid. It was kind of a ritual to eat Sunday breakfast with them. I remember being held close, and the smell of cinnamon rolls...my dad still loves cinnamon rolls on Sunday." Her smile turned wistful. "I can't say I remember what my grandparents looked like, but what I have are the best kind of childhood memories, I guess.''

The best kind of childhood memories... Logan's heart twisted. He felt the emptiness spread clear to his soul. He had to force himself to speak. "This isn't the old homestead, is it?''

"Oh, no. When my grandparents retired, they sold the farm and moved into Boise.'' She nodded toward the sofa, indicating that they should sit. "I'm not sure I'd even want to guess when this house was built,'' she continued when he'd taken a seat at the other end. "There's a fireplace in nearly every room, but there was no central heating system, other than that antiquated wood stove in the dining room. And I just didn't have the heart to take it out. But the first thing I had done when I bought this place last year was replace the heating and plumbing. As well as doors, windows and floors...''

In spite of her weary sigh, her face was animated, her cheeks flushed with excitement. It was obvious she took great pride in her home. And she had managed to undertake refurbishing the old house without detracting from its old-fashioned charm.

"Isn't there another house near the road?'' he asked. "I saw an overgrown flower garden.''

"Flower garden? My goodness, you don't have to be so polite. The yard there is so overgrown with weeds, I'm surprised you even noticed it.''

Lord, but she sounded sweet when she laughed the way she was doing now.

"It was probably intended as a guest cottage,'' she told him. "Or maybe a mother-in-law type of arrangement. I think it's about twenty years old, so the inside isn't really in bad shape, once you wade through all the dust and cobwebs." She laughed. "It's small, but really pretty nice."

Logan was surprised at how relaxed he was. Chris had a knack for making him feel very welcome and at ease. He realized he felt much more at home here in this house than he did in his own home.

It was with genuine reluctance that he rose a short time later.

"You're leaving already? I'd love to have you stay for dinner."

Did he only imagine the disappointment in Christine's voice? He hoped not. Nonetheless, he gently refused. "After being gone for a week, you probably have a lot you'd like to get done before you go back to work."

Chris thought of the stack of files she'd brought home from her office last night. "That's just the reminder I needed," she said dryly, handing him his coat.

Together they walked to the back door. He wondered what she'd have done if he reached out and grazed her lips with his. He didn't, because he sensed that Christine Michaels needed a friend as much as he did.

Instead he opened the screen and stepped onto the porch. "Looks like it's raining again," he commented.

Chris frowned as she peered outside. The sky was the color of lead, dark and dismal. A hazy gray shroud seemed to cling to the earth. Nonetheless, there was a distinct nip to the air.

"You'll have to be careful then," she called after him, watching as he descended the narrow wooden steps. "The roads always ice up sooner out here than they do in town."

On the verge of entering his car, Logan paused. Her warning had an unexpected effect. He felt himself acknowledge with a mechanical wave, get in the car and start the motor. But as he drove away, he was helpless to prevent the sudden bleakness that seeped into his heart. He stared straight ahead, his eyes fixed on the narrow ribbon of road. But in his mind, he saw a face, the face of a young woman, whose midnight eyes were dark with anxiety, her beautiful features lined with a terrible fear.

You'd better be careful... Chris's word's echoed in his mind once more. He muttered a violent curse, wishing he could empty his mind as well as his heart. When, he asked himself savagely, was the last time anyone had exhibited such concern over his well-being?

Only Denise had cared. Only Denise.

THE MAN AWOKE WITH A START. For a moment he stared into the stark blackness of the night, his mind filled with images of softness and light.

He had dreamed of her again.

His footsteps made no sound as he slid from the bed and moved across the rough plank floor to a small wooden desk. He struck a match to the wick of an oil lamp. He stepped back to watch as pale golden light filled the room.

His lips curled as he picked up a small framed photograph. A petite, chestnut-haired woman smiled back at him, her eyes shining with love.

Calloused fingertips roved over each of her delicate features. Eyes, nose, mouth.

"You're mine," he whispered to the picture. "You've always been mine."

And again his dream came back to him, as real, as elusive as ever. It only reminded him that his dreams were so unsatisfying, and his arms were so lonely. He ached to hold more than empty air; he yearned to hold her, and touch her and make her his.

But he contented himself with the knowledge that it was time now. He'd worshipped her from afar for too long already. It was time they were together again, just the two of them, and he'd already taken steps to that end.

And then she would be his for all eternity....

CHAPTER FIVE

EARLY MONDAY MORNING, Chris opened the frosted door to her office. She looked cool and professional in a tailored maroon suit, her shoulder-length hair pulled into a sleek twist at the back of her head.

"Welcome back! How were things at home?" Her voice bright and cheery, Jean Anderson followed Chris past the lacy-leafed ferns in the reception area to an inner office decorated in soothing grays and pale blues. She placed a hot, fragrant cup of coffee next to the Rolodex file on the desktop. Eyebrows lifted, brown eyes alert and sparkling, Jean rested slim hands on her hips to await the verdict.

Home. Oddly enough, the word reminded Chris of Logan Garrison. Her trip to Boise last week was almost an afterthought. "Couldn't be better," she replied, wearing a tiny smile. "It was good seeing my parents again."

Shrugging out of her coat, Chris surveyed the woman who was her secretary, receptionist and office bookkeeper. She had hired Jean a year and a half earlier when her other secretary had decided to retire. If Chris had had to pick one word to describe Jean, heaven-sent would have been her resounding choice. Though crisp and efficient, neat and fastidious in work habits as well as appearance, Jean was very much a motherly type of woman, the kind that one instinctively liked.

"I hope you're all rested up." Jean chuckled as Chris hung her coat in the oak wardrobe in the corner. "Now you're going to have to make up for being gone so long." With a flourish, she moved to flip open the leather appointment book that sat in the center of the desk.

"That bad, huh?" Behind her, Chris eyed the calendar.

"Let me put it this way." The other woman laughed. "If you're lucky, you may have time for lunch—a very short lunch."

"How did things go here?" Chris asked. Jean had taken most of the week off, too, though she had come in to the office several mornings. "No emergencies?" Chris took her place behind the desk and stowed her purse in the bottom drawer.

When she looked up, Jean's expression was hesitant.

"Don't tell me," Chris said quickly. "Tom Chamberlain again?"

Chris had been seeing the high-powered executive for the past six weeks. An intelligent, competent man, Tom had been devastated when his wife of ten years had filed for divorce. Totally unsuspecting that his wife wasn't satisfied with their marriage, he had tried easing his depression with the use of alcohol, but Chris was thankful he'd had enough sense to seek help before things got any worse. Still, she was worried over his lack of progress.

"He really scared me," Jean admitted. "He called at noon Wednesday, just when I was ready to leave. When I explained that you weren't here, he started talking wild...threatening suicide..."

"Damn!" Chris swore softly. "He was drinking again, wasn't he?"

"I got Dr. Williams to take the call," Jean added. "He managed to get him calmed down."

Chris nodded. "I'll give them both a call later and see if Tom can come in sometime this week."

On her way back to her own desk, Jean halted near the doorway. "I almost forgot . . . while you were gone, Norm decided to put in an alarm system. I'll have to show you how it works sometime today. There's been a rash of robberies in town lately—apparently the building across the way has been burglarized—" She broke off on seeing Christine's dubious expression. "Didn't you get my message?"

"Oh, I got it," Chris put in dryly. "Hours too late, but in time to find out that the system works just fine and dandy." At Jean's blank look, Chris went on to tell her how she had unwittingly triggered the alarm Saturday night.

"So you met Mr. Garrison." Jean eyed her curiously. "What did you think of him?"

Chris leaned back in her chair. "I think a better question would be what do *you* think of him." Slender brows lifted. "You're just dying to give me your opinion of him, right?"

Jean grinned sheepishly. "I am," she admitted. "I thought he was mysterious. Intriguing. But definitely low key," she amended hastily. "I couldn't help but think he's the kind of man who likes to blend into the woodwork, the kind who isn't always what he seems. Crazy as it sounds, the minute I saw him, every spy movie I've ever seen popped into my head. Maybe I've been watching too many *Mission: Impossible* reruns."

It was this insight that made her such a valuable asset. There were times when Chris thought Jean would have made a perfect psychologist.

But at Jean's last comment, Chris's lips curved. "What would you say if I told you he used to work for the government?"

Jean's eyes widened. "I knew it," she breathed. "Oh, I just knew it. For the CIA, right?"

Chris chuckled. "Nothing quite so mysterious," she told the other woman. "He spent fifteen years with the FBI."

The news only slightly lessened her secretary's smug look. At precisely that moment, the phone rang. Jean stepped across to Chris's desk and answered with a crisp greeting.

A second later, she punched the Hold button. "Speak of the devil. It's Logan Garrison—for you." Eyes sparkling, she handed the phone to Chris, then breezed across the room humming the theme song from *Mission: Impossible*.

Chris pulled the receiver to her ear. "Hello, there." The pleasure in her voice wasn't the least bit feigned. "You got home okay last night?"

Across town, Logan's heart gave a betraying thump. "Sure did," he replied smoothly, but only after the briefest of pauses. If Chris noticed, she gave no indication.

"I'll bet you're calling to take me to breakfast again." Her voice was teasing.

Logan laughed softly. "How about dinner instead? About seven?"

There was a small silence. "I'm not sure I can make it," she began.

Disappointment shot through him.

"I'm giving a lecture at the library tonight."

"That's too bad." He hated the cold formality of his tone, but he couldn't help himself. Did she think he was trying to make a pass? That he had mistaken last night for something it wasn't?

"I could make it for lunch though." Her voice sounded hopeful. "I'm afraid it would have to be a quick meal," she added apologetically. "My appointments this morning run till noon and I have another scheduled at twelve-thirty."

The tension seeped out of his muscles. "I could meet you at Beth's," he suggested. "How's that sound?"

"That would be perfect. Only make sure I order a salad, okay? I'm not sure my waistline can handle cherry crepes twice in one week."

Logan visualized her slender figure. She was small, but trim and shapely nonetheless.

Chris was smiling when she hung up the phone a few minutes later. Lunch with Logan, she thought, pulling out the folder for her first patient. It was a nice way to start the week, she decided.

THAT MEAL WAS JUST the first of many that Chris and Logan enjoyed together over the next few weeks. Sometimes it was only a sandwich shared at her desk; another time Chris invited him for dinner in the evening.

One Friday night Logan kept her on the phone so long the eleven-o'clock news was over by the time she hung up. They spent another Sunday together exploring Spokane.

After nine years of marriage, Chris had begun to take her moments of solitude for granted. It wasn't until the last year that she had discovered there was a vast difference between solitude and loneliness.

Nor had Chris realized just how desperately she needed a friend until Logan Garrison entered her life.

Not a soul mate, or someone who sought to probe every corner of her mind. Not a lover, but a friend.

And Logan was the perfect friend, one who accepted, who neither asked nor demanded more than she could give; a friend to talk with in the evening, someone to laugh with over the tidbits of the day, someone to share a companionable silence.

But they were two people who hadn't laughed nearly enough of late. Both knew it. Yet neither made an issue of it. Perhaps, Chris speculated occasionally, that was part of what had drawn them together in the first place.

The Friday that marked the end of the second week in December found Chris sitting in her office, her elbows propped on her desktop. Raising her eyes, she glanced toward the outside office. Jean had been flitting around all week putting up decorations. She'd had Carl, the janitor, help her place a stately looking Noble fir in the corner of the reception area. Lacy, glittering garlands draped the branches, and colorful ornaments bobbed from the tips. Bright red pots of holly filled the corners of the room. Jean also insisted on putting a miniature Christmas tree on the corner of Christine's desk and spreading an assortment of ceramic choir boys on the credenza below the window.

Chris didn't have the heart to refuse.

As it had last Christmas, as it had several weeks earlier at her parents' home, the holiday season had begun to take its toll. Chris was beginning to feel that the walls were closing in on her, as if she were being sucked dry.

Would it always be like this? The question gnawed at her. Would the season of cheerful tidings and good will forever remind her of Scottie?

With a sigh, she rose and replaced the patient folder in the filing cabinet. Hands in her pockets, she wandered over to stare out the window.

The weather had been bitterly cold all week. Heavy clouds the color of gunmetal blanketed the sky in all directions. A lonely leaf skittered across the street, swept by a forceful wind. Had the dismal weather sparked her pensive mood?

She really should leave, she decided on a long sigh. She was supposed to meet Logan in half an hour for dinner and a movie.

Just then the door to her office opened. Chris's head jerked up at the sound. Jean had left an hour earlier, at five o'clock, clucking disapprovingly that Chris wasn't leaving with her. With the rash of robberies of late, Chris had been just a little apprehensive herself. But she relaxed when she saw that it was only Carl.

He stopped short when he saw her standing near the window. "Dr. Michaels. I didn't know you were still here."

A tall, slender man in his mid-thirties, Carl Chapman had been the night janitor there for several years. Polite and quiet, Carl was a little on the shy side in Christine's view. She occasionally ran into him when she was working late. He was always dressed in drab, unobtrusive browns, and Chris recalled how Jean said he reminded her of a chameleon, able to blend in with his surroundings. He seemed a little embarrassed, and Chris sought to put him at ease.

"I wish I could say I was working late," she said with a faint smile. "But actually I've been playing hooky for the last few minutes." She glanced out the window at the ever-darkening sky. "Wishing for a change in the weather," she added.

A smile creased Carl's thin face. "It's not even officially winter, Dr. Michaels. Sounds like you can't wait for spring to arrive."

"Could be," she admitted. "I've always loved spring. It's a time for renewal. Not that I mind the snow, but I miss all the greenery. Especially the daisies." Her lips tilted faintly, but she knew it would take more than sunshine, warm days and blue sky to cheer her up. "Maybe I should move to Florida. It's one of the few places I'd find flowers in the middle of winter."

She and Carl talked for several more minutes. Chris was just reaching for her coat when the phone rang. She hesitated, tempted to let her answering service get it, but something made her pick it up.

The caller identified herself as the ward nurse at the hospital. "We have a patient of yours here..."

Moments later, Chris replaced the receiver in its cradle. She wasted no time in hurrying into her coat and grabbing her satchel. It appeared she wasn't the only one for whom Christmas was not a time of happiness.

Tom Chamberlain had just made good his suicide threat.

CHRIS'S TEMPLES WERE THROBBING by the time she emerged from Tom's room at the hospital. She stopped briefly at the nurses' station, then headed for the elevator. On the main floor, she started to walk right by the waiting area off the main lobby when suddenly something caught her eye. Broad shoulders, a pair of impossibly long legs, the tilt of a dark head that had grown rather familiar...

Logan couldn't have chosen a better time to pull his attention from the magazine he was idly paging through. He watched Chris come to an abrupt halt, saw a look of surprised pleasure flit across her features.

Then a slow smile inched across her lips, and Logan told himself what he had known almost from the start.

He had no idea what quirk of fate had brought him and Christine Michaels together, nor did he care. For longer than he could remember, he felt he'd been pushed off the merry-go-round of life. But he and Chris were good for each other. He knew it as surely as night followed day.

He rose just as she stepped up to him. "Aren't you the man," she asked softly, "I talked to less than an hour ago? You're off the hook, remember?" Chris had made a hasty call to let him know she had an emergency and wouldn't be able to make dinner.

His eyebrows lifted. "Sure you're not trying to beg off because it's your turn to buy?"

Her smile faded. She was glad she didn't feel the need to pretend with Logan. "I wish," she murmured, then hesitated. "I've got what's probably the worst headache of my life. I really don't think I'd be very good company tonight."

His eyes searched her face. Chris wasn't the type to complain, but she did look tired and tense.

"We don't have to go out," he told her. "If you'd rather, we could go to my place instead. You haven't eaten yet, have you?"

Chris shook her head. Her headache was at least partially caused from hunger. She hadn't been sleeping well this week—this morning she'd been awake before dawn—and the draining episode with Tom had sapped what little energy she had left. If she went straight home, she'd probably skip dinner entirely.

"All right." She relented with a sigh. "But don't say you weren't warned."

The hinge creaked a noisy protest as Logan opened the exit door for her. A nippy wind greeted them as they stepped outside. To the east, a few twinkling stars glittered a greeting. Chris inhaled a stinging mouthful of air. "Whew!" she muttered. "It's going to snow tonight."

In the process of pulling on a pair of leather gloves, Logan glanced at her. "Believe it or not, the weatherman says the skies will clear tonight. It's still supposed to be cold, but there's no precipitation in the forecast."

"Hah!" They trudged toward the parking lot, Chris making no secret of her disagreement with the local forecaster. "It smells like snow," she pronounced emphatically.

"It *smells* like snow?" It was Logan's turn to sound skeptical. "I've heard people say it smells like rain, but that's a new one on me."

Chris chuckled. Already she was beginning to feel better. Somehow being with Logan always managed to have that effect. "My mother always said that Dad and I were crazy, too."

"Your father has a nose for snow, as well?" he asked dryly.

Tucked inside the furry hood of her coat, Chris's head bobbed. "He certainly does."

"And are you and your father ever mistaken?" Logan was hard put not to laugh, and he had to chuckle when she hesitated.

Chris frowned good-naturedly as they stopped next to his car. "My grandmother always said if it rained when the sun was out, it would rain again tomorrow, and that's something I've never seen fail."

Logan accepted that theory a little more readily than he did Christine's "nose for snow."

"Now I see why you're a psychologist." He opened the passenger door for her. "The scientific community of the world isn't subjective enough for you, right?"

Chris rolled down the window and stuck her head out. "Three inches by morning," she called as he rounded the front fender, "or my name isn't Christine Michaels."

Logan merely shook his head. It wasn't until they were in his car, shielded from the cold, the heater blowing blessedly warm air, that he asked, "How's your patient?"

Chris sobered abruptly. Tom had been discovered unconscious by his brother. If he had been found an hour later, the pills and booze he'd consumed would have done the job only too well.

She stared out the window a few seconds before she spoke. "He'll be okay physically. Mentally..." She left the sentence dangle. She wished she could be as optimistic. But perhaps this episode would make Tom realize how serious a problem his drinking was. If his mind hadn't been clouded by alcohol...

She understood Tom, perhaps far better than anyone realized. She understood his despondency, his fears, his despair at facing a life without the ones he loved most in the world.

Logan maneuvered the car around a corner. "I have a friend, Ned Gibson," he said quietly. "He's a lieutenant on the police force. He mentioned just last week that the holidays are probably the busiest time of the year for the police—a lot of family beefs and that kind of thing." He risked a quick glance at her. "Guess that applies to you, too."

Chris expelled a long sigh of agreement. "It's funny, isn't it, that there are such extremes in the family unit. Some people can't get together without jealousy and pettiness coming between them. And there are others who are torn apart because they have no choice but to be alone." Against her will, she suddenly remembered the promise she'd made to her mother—that she wouldn't spend Christmas alone. But somehow she would get through it—alone or otherwise—if it was the last thing she did.

They passed the next few minutes in silence. It wasn't a particularly warm, comfortable silence, but neither was it an uncomfortable one either. It occurred to Chris that when she was with Logan, she didn't feel the need to be anything but herself. Patients sometimes tried to make her into someone she wasn't, a paragon who was all-seeing, all-knowing. Trust was implicit in a doctor-patient relationship. Still, her patients sometimes had difficulty in realizing she wasn't a miracle worker, either.

But with Logan, she didn't have to pretend to be wise and omniscient. She was only human; she didn't have all the answers. Logan accepted her at face value, and for that, Chris was grateful.

It didn't take long to reach Logan's condominium. He lived in one of the most elite areas of the city, though secretly she preferred her own aging house and acreage. She'd been to his place once before. Logan had forgotten his camera the day they went to Spokane, so they'd stopped to pick it up. It hadn't taken long, and she'd waited in the entryway. Now, as she glanced around his apartment for the first time, she wasn't surprised to find that it was tastefully—and expensively—decorated. Everything was neat and spotless, shining and in its proper place. He had always struck her as a bit of a perfectionist.

But her eyebrows shot up when he stripped off his coat and strolled into the kitchen, rolling up his sleeves as he did so. "You're going to cook?" she asked. "I thought we'd just send out for something."

Logan's lips curved at her mild astonishment. "Why not? I make what's probably the best twenty-minute spaghetti sauce you've ever tasted."

"Modest, aren't you?" she commented, tongue-in-cheek.

"Just honest. Besides, you'll see," he promised lightly.

He came around the bar a second later. She saw that he held a small bottle in his hand. "What's that?"

"Aspirin. For your headache." He handed her a glass of water.

Two small tablets were dropped into her palm. Had she mentioned her headache? Apparently she had, but for the life of her, she didn't remember it. She couldn't help thinking that nothing escaped him.

"Amazing," she declared teasingly. "Now I see why you were an FBI agent. Unfailingly honest *and* a mind like a steel trap. They could hardly turn you down, could they?"

He laughed, but for a second, there was an odd expression in his eyes. It was so fleeting, she couldn't possibly have guessed at its origins. But she was suddenly reminded that every once in a while she glimpsed pain in Logan's eyes, a pain she suspected ran as deep as her own.

She and Logan seemed to have developed a silent understanding. Except for that first day at Beth's, Logan hadn't mentioned either Bill or Scottie.

But much as she had come to like Logan, Chris was the first to admit he wasn't an easy man to get to know. She had the curious feeling that Logan was hiding something. No, that wasn't quite right. It was more like he was holding something inside.

But it didn't stop her from wondering about him. He was a man of impeccable manners. Smooth, polished and well-bred. What kind of home did he come from? And what secret lay behind the mystery in his eyes?

He had never claimed to be totally alone in the world. And as she had kidded him several weeks ago, he hadn't been raised by wolves. Since then, he had talked places, people, events. Yet not once—and Chris realized there had been many opportunities, considering how much she talked about her own family—had he mentioned anyone close to him. Surely there was someone...somewhere.

Logan refused any help in the kitchen, so Chris wandered around his living room. She felt a little silly over her curious reluctance to sit in one of the plush, velvety chairs, but she couldn't help it. She finally halted before a floor-to-ceiling bookcase. His collection was impressive.

"I wouldn't let anyone from the city library in here," she called through the wide, open doorway. "They'd be hounding you for donations from now until doomsday."

He looked startled for a fraction of a second, then shrugged. "I doubt they'd be interested. They're mostly law texts."

Chris chuckled. "Don't tell me you've got a law degree hiding up your sleeve, too." She was only joking, and it surprised her when Logan's expression turned sheepish.

Dazed comprehension set in. "You do, don't you?" she asked slowly.

Logan nodded. Chris had the vaguest sensation that he was avoiding her gaze as he quickly whisked away the snowy white tablecloth that covered the dining room table. He neatly folded it into squares and tucked it away in the sideboard. The perfectionist again.

"But—why don't you practice? I mean, especially after you left the FBI? With a little boning up, surely you could pass the State Bar..." Chris blurted the questions before she could recall them.

Logan centered two linen place mats on the glass-and-oak tabletop; stoneware plates, napkins, cutlery and spindly stemmed wineglasses followed. His reply was a long time in coming.

"I've never practiced law, Chris, because it would have pleased my father. Nor will I ever practice law because it would give him too much satisfaction."

His light tone belied his expression. Chris had one glimpse of his face, and that was enough. His eyes were pure frost, his features more taut and rigid than she had ever seen. Logan was always so calm, so controlled. But Chris suddenly had no doubt that when he chose, Logan could be an intimidating individual.

She stared at his retreating back, a little confused. What had he been trying to say? That he was the rebellious sort? The black sheep of the family? She had a hard time picturing him in such a role, either now or twenty years ago.

At least she knew he hadn't been raised by wolves. Her silent chuckle was slightly tenuous. Somewhere he had a father, but the subject was clearly a touchy one.

The incident appeared to have been forgotten when he reentered the dining room, a basket of bread in one hand, a salad bowl in the other. Chris was only too willing to turn the conversation elsewhere.

She was also willing to concede that he hadn't exaggerated his culinary abilities.

"I have decided," she pronounced, pushing back from the table half an hour later, "that you must be heaven-sent. No matter how hard I try, I always overcook the spaghetti, and who likes waterlogged spaghetti?''

Logan's gaze rested on her face. He wanted to apologize; he *needed* to apologize. He knew full well how abrupt he'd been with her earlier, yet the words refused to come.

"How's the headache?" he asked. He rose and would have taken her plate, but Chris beat him to it.

"What headache?" Her tone was airy. She vanished into the kitchen. Logan followed more slowly.

Later, when the dishes had been stowed in the dishwasher, they wandered back into the living room. Logan picked up the schedule for the night's television program. He noted idly, "There's not much on except the prime-time soaps. And an old Gary Cooper movie."

"A Gary Cooper movie! Which one?"

"*The Hanging Tree.*" He glanced up at her avid tone. "You're a Gary Cooper fan, huh?"

"Am I! Back in the days when men were men and women were women..." She ended the quote with a long, wistful sigh.

"Are you a *Gunsmoke* buff, too?"

She wrinkled her nose. "I like Gary Cooper better. My dad and I spent more afternoons than I can remember watching his movies on the Sunday matinee."

"You seem to have inherited quite a lot from your father."

"The only thing I've ever complained about are my freckles." She made a face and gestured at her cheeks. Her freckles were scarcely visible beneath the light layer of makeup she wore today.

The next moment Logan found himself on the receiving end of a not-so-subtle query. "Are you as good with popcorn as you are with spaghetti?"

"Better," he chuckled, and switched on the television. Chris curled up on the sofa, and Logan disappeared into the kitchen to make the popcorn.

Midway through the movie, Chris fell asleep. Logan reached above her head and turned off the light. For the rest of the movie, his eyes never strayed once to the television screen. He found it strangely companionable and altogether relaxing to simply sit there in the dark, watching Chris sleep. Moonlight spread its silver veil over her face, the tender curve of her jaw, the pouting thrust of her lip. She looked like a child, one hand tucked beneath her cheek.

Much later, he thought of waking her, then immediately dismissed the idea. Instead, he eased off her shoes, slipped a pillow beneath her head and draped a blanket over her. Lastly, he removed the pins from her hair, one by one, very carefully so as not to wake her. The task completed, he found himself reluctant to leave her. He picked up a few trailing strands of honey-gold hair. It curled around his fingers as if it had a mind of its own. He marveled at its texture; it felt like warm silk.

There was a rich, deep contentment inside him, a feeling he scarcely recognized. Yet he was also aware of a yawning emptiness, and he had never been more conscious of it than he was at that moment.

He sat back on his heels. "I'm sorry, Chris," he whispered, wishing he'd said the words earlier. "Some things don't come easily to me. But liking you is very easy." The blunted tip of one finger gently traced the arcing wing of one delicate eyebrow. "And you know what? I love your freckles."

Unconsciously, before he even considered what he was doing, he bent and touched his mouth to hers, the merest butterfly caress.

Did she smile? Or was it merely the fanciful yearning of a lonely man? Logan wasn't sure. But he did know that something drew his eye to the window just before he climbed into bed, and what he saw kindled a warm feeling unlike anything he'd ever known before.

It was snowing.

CHAPTER SIX

CHRIS WOKE SLOWLY the next morning. She stirred drowsily, feeling very secure, very warm. But when she started to roll over, she experienced a curious disorientation, as if she had slept on the wrong side of the bed....

Her lids snapped open. With stunning clarity she realized exactly where she was. She was in Logan's apartment, sprawled on Logan's couch, a cozy velour blanket tucked around her shoulders. She bolted upright ... and gazed into eyes that were as clear and blue as the sky on a warm, summer day.

Logan was standing at the end of the sofa, wearing a white cable-knit sweater, his arms crossed over his chest. He was freshly shaved and a pleasant, woodsy scent surrounded him. It hit her with all the impact of a freight train what an intensely masculine man Logan was.

But in spite of the ruggedly handsome picture he made this morning, Chris realized something else as well. He seemed more relaxed, more at ease than she'd ever seen him. His eyes were as keen and watchful as ever, but that sharp, knifelike edge he possessed—one of the first things she had noticed about him—had softened. Why it pleased her so much, Chris couldn't have said.

He nodded toward the wide picture window, where bold, bright sunlight filtered through. "Three inches," he said, an enigmatic smile on his lips. "That's a conservative estimate, by the way."

Chris fairly flew to the window. The world below wore an untarnished blanket of glittering white snow.

"I knew it," she breathed. "I knew it would snow. Can you believe that just yesterday I was yearning for spring—and flowers? But there's nothing like waking up and seeing the world outside covered with snow."

Excitement glowed on her face as she placed her fingertips on the glass and gazed out at the winter wonderland below. The gesture was so innocent, so unthinkingly childlike that Logan found himself walking a precarious balance between joy and pain. How long, he wondered silently, since he had experienced such wonder at one of nature's simplest of miracles?

But he couldn't deny what was in his heart. Watching her sleep last night, and again these past few minutes, had stirred emotions that had lain dormant in him for a long, long time—emotions he had thought were buried and would never rise again. He felt protective of her. He also felt as if he were the one who had awakened from a long, long sleep, only to discover life all over again.

"How was the movie?" Her eyes were the color of topaz when she finally turned to him.

His own rested on her rosy, sleep-flushed cheeks. "You tell me," he teased.

She grinned sheepishly. "Sorry about falling asleep on you," she apologized. She felt no embarrassment about having spent the night with him. They had known each other such a short time, yet she trusted Logan as much as she would her own family.

Chris ran her fingers through her sleep-tousled hair, trying to restore some order. It was then that she spied the neat pile of pins on the end table. Despite the thought of a moment ago, her heart gave an odd little flutter. Had Logan..? *Silly question, Doc,* she chided herself. Of course he had, since she hadn't.

But the strangest notion suddenly flew into her head. She had opened her eyes this morning to find him watching her, and her mind delved further back. She registered the fleeting sensation of warm lips brushing hers, the touch so featherlight she could have imagined it.... But that was ridiculous. There was nothing sexual in her friendship with Logan; they simply didn't have that kind of relationship.

Logan watched her hair slide through her fingers, remembering the texture and softness of it on his own skin. "I thought about waking you. I have a perfectly good guest room you could have used."

"Are you kidding?" Chris laughed aloud. "Getting to sleep may not always be easy, but once I do, I sleep like a log."

"I noticed." His smile widened. She'd barely roused when he'd kissed her.

She wrinkled her nose at him. "Besides," she went on, "your couch is very comfortable."

"You're welcome to it anytime. Which reminds me, I don't suppose you'd like a shower? I can't produce a change of clothes, but I think there's a new toothbrush in the medicine cabinet. I can have breakfast on the table by the time you're finished."

"Spaghetti again?"

He shook his head. "Bacon and eggs."

"Then you've got yourself a deal."

Logan's eyebrows shot up. "I thought you liked my spaghetti," he said mildly.

"Oh, I did—I mean I do." She chuckled. "But not for breakfast."

Logan pointed her in the direction of the bathroom. Chris glanced around curiously as she shed her clothes. The brown and ivory tiled room was easily three times the size of her own modest bathroom, large enough to accommodate an oversized tub equipped with a Jacuzzi and a glass-enclosed shower as well.

She gazed longingly at the tub but decided on a shower instead. She turned on the spray, then went in search of the toothbrush Logan had said she would find in the medicine cabinet. Somehow she wasn't surprised to find a new tube of toothpaste and shampoo as well. She half-expected to emerge from her shower to find that Logan had indeed produced a much needed change of clothing.

No such luck, however. But the shower, and the smell of bacon frying as she headed toward the kitchen, more than made up for it.

Logan laughingly banished her from the kitchen, but Chris paid him no mind. The table hadn't been set, so she took the task upon herself. It was while she was transferring a small carafe of orange juice into the dining room that she happened to glance out the window.

"Is that your dog?" she called. In the parking lot below, she had just spotted a furry animal curled near the front wheel of Logan's car.

Logan appeared in the doorway, carrying a plate heaped full of bacon and two perfectly cooked eggs. "Dog?" he echoed. "I don't have one, Chris. No pets allowed. The manager made that very clear when I bought this place."

Chris gestured at the window. "Pets or no pets, this one seems to have taken a fancy to your car. He's sleeping under it. I hope he wasn't there all night," she added with a frown. "As cold as it was, I'm surprised he's not half-frozen."

Logan came to stand beside her.

"You know," she began slowly, "maybe he's not sleeping at all." She bit her lip. "I'd better go check on him."

Logan caught her arm before she'd taken more than a step. "I'll go," he said quickly. "Your hair's still wet."

He had grabbed his coat and was gone before Chris could say another word. Breakfast forgotten, she watched as Logan approached his car, crouching down on his heels and stretching out a hand. Her heart lurched when the dog never even stirred, but her eyes widened when he stripped off his coat and wrapped it around the dog, lifting it high in his arms.

She threw the front door open wide when she heard his firm steps coming down the hall. "Is he hurt?" she asked anxiously. Chris caught only a glimpse of a small black nose and two paws buried within the folds of his coat.

Logan carried the dog into the kitchen. Chris was right behind him as he knelt down.

"First of all," he told her, "it looks like 'he' is a 'she.'" His voice carried a hint of amusement, but there was a faint frown etched between his dark brows. "Second of all—" he began to carefully unwrap the coat, making a bed of the warm folds as he did so "—it looks like she's about to burst at the seams."

It took a moment for Chris to glean his meaning. "You mean she's pregnant?"

He chuckled dryly. "As far as I can tell."

Chris blinked. "But you said no pets allowed...."

He looked up at her, his lips curving faintly. "I couldn't leave her out there in the cold, now could I?"

Their eyes met over his shoulder for a fraction of a second, and a special kind of understanding passed between them. Then Logan once more focused his attention on the dog. "Chris," he murmured, and she didn't mind his absent tone in the least, "do you think you could get me a couple of towels from the linen closet in the hall? She still looks cold."

Frozen was more like it, Chris decided when she returned to the kitchen. The dog was shivering violently as Logan gently began to dry her. Chris guessed that the dog wasn't a purebred; she looked like a cross between a terrier and a cocker spaniel. Her coat was a rich golden brown, but the fur was matted and badly tangled in places.

Logan had begun feeding the dog bits of bacon, the bacon that had been on his plate moments before. The dog wolfed them down hungrily. "Lord," he muttered, "she's starving."

"She is thin," Chris admitted, running a hand down the dog's back and sides. In spite of the small mound of belly, she could feel the dog's ribs just above her burden. "Does she have a tag? Maybe she belongs to someone nearby."

His fingers delved gently in the fur on her neck. He shook his head. "Not even a collar." His lips tightened as he added, "Maybe the owner decided to dump her when he found out she was pregnant."

Chris silently agreed. With her huge, pleading eyes—eyes that were now fixed trustingly on Logan's face—she hardly looked like a scraggly mutt, but she was certainly in need of a bath and a thorough brushing. She really was cute and lovable.

"Poor little mother," she murmured, kneeling down beside Logan. "Did someone desert you?" The dog nudged her nose beneath Chris's hand, and Chris began to stroke her head gently.

But suddenly the furry animal gave a short, sharp yelp—a sound of pain.

"Little mother?" Logan echoed. He looked at Chris. "It's not about to happen now, is it?"

He sounded so worried, so much like an expectant father, that Chris couldn't hold back a smile. Beneath her hand, the dog had started to tremble again, but her belly was rigid and taut.

"I think," she said dryly, "that we're about to find out. So unless you want a litter of pups born on your coat, maybe we should find a blanket." When he merely shrugged, she went in search of one and returned with an old car blanket a few minutes later.

"We had a dog when I was a kid, but not a female," Chris said as Logan made the animal comfortable on the blanket. "This is a first for me, I'm afraid. I've never seen puppies born."

A painful yap from the animal on the floor claimed their attention once more. The dog seemed to have entrusted herself totally to Logan's care, calming visibly at his slightest touch. He murmured soothingly to the dog, over and over with the ebb and flow of each contraction. He was, she marveled yet again, such an easy man to trust, in spite of his sharp-featured reserve.

But exactly who had charmed whom was strictly a matter of opinion, Chris thought wryly. Logan's eyes were dark with concern, but the harsh planes of his face were far softer than usual.

Chris was aware of a warm flow of pleasure in her veins as she watched Logan stroke the soon-to-be mother. But the feeling soon gave way to another emotion, kindled by the almost hypnotic motion of his hands on the dog's fur.

She thought of him sliding his fingers through her hair last night, searching for pins. It had been totally innocuous, she knew. But he had such strong, wonderfully masculine hands; long and lean-fingered, not at all fleshy. He'd pushed the sleeves of his sweater up to his elbows, and Chris noted the muscular definition of his forearms, coated with a layer of dense, silky-looking hair. Against her will, her eyes came to rest at the base of his throat, where a cluster of dark, bristly hairs spilled over the neckline of his sweater. Her gaze lingered there, and for one heartstopping second, she wondered if the rest of his chest and stomach were covered with the same intriguingly dark hair.

Her eyes squeezed shut. Warm heat suffused her entire body, and she had the sneaking suspicion that a telltale trail of red had crept into her cheeks—she, who had unabashedly counseled and discussed sexual mores, problems and practices with more men and women than she could remember!

Yet she was exceedingly grateful that Logan had confined his attention elsewhere. On one level, she was struck by his gentleness. On another, she couldn't ignore the wholly male aura Logan possessed. But it seemed almost wrong to think of him in such an earthy, sensual way.

"Open your eyes, Chris, or you'll miss out on the big event and *never* see any puppies born."

Chris opened her eyes to see the first tiny puppy make its way into the world, followed in quick succession by four more squirming little creatures. One by one, the mother nosed them gently against the warmth of her belly. Her tail thumped once, and then again and again, as she gazed up into the two human faces above her. It was as if she were saying, "See? I really did it!"

Chris looked on with a tiny smile. "Seems like you've got yourself a dog—or rather six of them."

As if she sensed she were the subject under discussion, the dog inched her nose forward, then licked

Chris's hand. Chris suddenly found herself under the scrutiny of those liquid brown eyes.

Logan glanced over at Chris, his eyes alight. "No," he disagreed lightly. "Looks like *we've* got ourselves a dog—" his lips twisted into a lopsided grin "—which makes us grandparents."

Chris laughed. Then, as if she found the sound highly pleasing to the ear, she laughed again, and this time Logan joined her.

He stroked the new mother under her chin. "So what do you think, little mother? If no one claims you, would you like to be adopted? We could call you Little Orphan Annie. Annie for short."

Annie licked his hand, apparently signaling her approval. Then, after making sure that her pups were still nestled against her, she lay back wearily.

Logan got to his feet and extended a hand to Chris. She took it unthinkingly, warmed both by the look in his eye and the heat of his skin against hers. He offered her a cup of coffee and she accepted.

"Are you really going to keep her?"

"I'd love to," he admitted readily. "I've never had a dog before. Or any kind of pet, for that matter."

The words were uttered in such a matter-of-fact tone that they almost failed to register. When they did, Chris had a hard time preventing her jaw from sagging. Never had a pet? Why, that was as much a part of childhood as nursery rhymes and cartoons.

"Then maybe it's high time you did," she said softly.

Logan was leaning back against the counter, cradling a cup of coffee in his hands. "Easier said than done, I'm afraid. No pets allowed, remember? Besides—" his thoughtful gaze rested on the new family in the corner "—I don't think a condominium is a very good place to keep a dog, let alone five puppies. My four-by-six deck hardly qualifies as a yard. A dog, even one as small as Annie here, needs some space, somewhere with a little room to run. You've got a great place," he added, almost absently.

"Thank you very much," Chris retorted pertly from her seat at the table. "Are you volunteering me?"

He laughed. "No, of course not. But for two cents, I'd keep her and say to hell with—"

When he broke off, Chris's brows arched, conveying a silent question.

Logan set his cup on the counter and straightened abruptly. "Wait a minute," he said slowly. "What you just said . . . about your place."

"*You* said it, not me," she teased.

He waved a hand. "Tell me if I'm being presumptuous," he began. "I'll understand if you think I am." He hesitated once more.

"What?" If he was trying to make her die of curiosity, he was succeeding beyond the shadow of a doubt. *"What?"*

"I was just thinking . . . about your cottage."

"My guest cottage?"

Logan wasn't quite sure what to make of her expression. Chris was a warm, caring person, but like himself, she valued her privacy. Logan respected that, and the last thing he wanted was to make her feel that he was intruding on her in any way.

He nodded, watching her closely. "You said it's in good condition, right?"

Chris paused uncertainly, not quite sure what he was after. "It's structurally sound, yes. The roof doesn't leak or anything like that. A thorough cleaning, a coat of paint on the inside, and it would probably be as good as new."

His eyes began to glow.

Chris broke into a smile. "Let me get this straight. You want to move Annie and her pups into my guest cottage?"

"Yes. No." He laughed, the sound oddly tentative. Two long strides carried him to the table, where he pulled a chair out and turned it around. He sat facing her, legs straddling the seat, arms braced on the upholstered back. "How would you feel about renting your cottage? To me," he clarified unnecessarily. "I could sublet this place. I'm sure I'd have no problem and...oh, hell, Chris. What do you say? Would you be interested in taking on a tenant?"

She'd had an inkling of what was on his mind, but Chris couldn't help wondering what had brought this about. Logan was not an impulsive man; he was too careful, too concise. She stared at him. "You want to move—" she snapped her fingers "—just like that?"

He hesitated for the longest time. When he spoke, there was a self-deprecating element to his voice. "You think your cottage isn't right for me, don't you? Or rather—*I'm* not right for the cottage."

The words cut her to the quick. For just an instant, before the harsh edge bit into his tone, he had looked like a hurt little boy. Now he only looked angry.

And Chris couldn't stand the thought of either one.

She reached out and laid her hand on his arm without thinking. Beneath her fingers, the muscles were rigid and tense, but she kept her hand where it was.

"That's not it at all," she denied softly. "You make it sound as if I think I'm too good for you. And that's not true, Logan. You know it's not."

As if I'm too good for you ... The words sliced into him. Though he despised himself for his bitter cynicism, he suspected Chris would have been running in the opposite direction if she knew just how right she really was. But he had no doubt about her sincerity. There was no guile in her, no jealousy or scheming or selfishness, nothing of the emotions he'd been surrounded by all of his life.

His anger drained away. It wasn't Chris he was upset with; his anger was directed more at himself than anything. But it was important to him that she understand.

"I'm sorry, Chris."

Chris knew the words weren't easy for him.

"It's true I haven't seriously considered moving," he admitted after a moment. "But it has crossed my mind—especially in the past few weeks."

His hand came up to cover hers. It was as if he were silently imploring her. But she also sensed that he was undergoing some kind of struggle deep within himself. Suddenly he rose and pulled her along with him, not stopping until they were standing in the middle of the living room. "Look around you," he said curtly. "Look, and tell me what you feel."

Her gaze swept the room, touching on the bookcases, the elegantly styled draperies, the sleek, modern furniture. The room was like a showcase, everything picture-perfect.

"You have a lovely home, Logan. Everything is— beautiful," she said after a moment, then frowned. "But surely you know that."

But he was already shaking his head. "Don't tell me what you see. Tell me what you *feel*." Her eyes widened; his sharpened. "There's a difference, Chris. I know it, and so do you."

He sounded so strange, almost resigned. A twinge of discomfort passed through her. There were homes that felt lived-in and welcoming. This wasn't one of them, but could she tell Logan that?

"Come on, Chris." His voice held a challenge now. "You don't have to be polite."

"All right, all right!" She relented with a sigh. "This isn't what I'd choose for myself. It's too sophisticated for me. Too polished."

She was still being polite, or perhaps tactful was a better word. But Logan said nothing.

He thrust his hands in his pockets and walked slowly around the room, finally stopping in front of the marble fireplace. His head was held high, the chiseled configurations of his face thrown into stark relief, as gossamer sunlight streamed through the windows. His expression, his eyes, betrayed little emotion as the silence mounted. And somehow it served as a warning; there was much that Logan held deep inside...perhaps too much.

When he eventually spoke, his voice was as empty and hollow as she had known it would be.

"I don't know," he said finally. "Maybe I'm getting old, Chris. Did you know I'll be forty in two years?"

Chris shook her head. She wanted desperately to go to him, but something held her back.

"Or maybe...maybe I'm just beginning to find out what I really want for myself—" he gazed slowly around the room "—and this just isn't it."

He sounded so tired, so utterly exhausted. The sigh he gave seemed to have been pulled from some deep, empty void inside him. It tugged on her heartstrings.

Logan said nothing for several seconds, leaving Chris with the notion that this man, who was always so cool, so very much in control of himself and his life, was lost...and floundering.

She was almost certain of it a moment later. The eyes that finally came to rest on her were bleak and cloudy, even a little confused.

"Do you want to know what I feel when I walk into this room?" he asked very softly. "I feel almost as if I don't belong here. I feel like a stranger, as if this is a stage for a play I have no part in. And yet this apartment—this entire blasted condominium—is just like every other place I've lived in. It's not my home; it's where I eat and I sleep, no more, no less."

He stared at her, and it was almost as if he were begging her to understand something even he didn't. "People change," Chris said hesitantly. "Their tastes change. We go out and we buy new cars, new clothes, new furniture."

He was silent for so long she was beginning to think he hadn't heard her. "Perhaps," he said at last, "but there's more to it than that, Chris." He gazed at her intently. "Would you be angry if I said there are times I envy you?"

Chris frowned. "I can't think why," she responded honestly.

"No," Logan said slowly. "No, I don't suppose you would. But one of the first things I noticed about you was how close you are to your family. And I know, as surely as I'm standing here with you right now, that if you ever needed them, or they needed you, you'd be there for each other. I doubt it would matter if they lived right across the street, or halfway across the country, you wouldn't be alone for long."

Her eyes met his squarely. "That's something I'm very grateful for, Logan."

For a moment he said nothing. There was a fierce pride in the rigid way he held his shoulders, but there was an air of vulnerability about him right now that caught her off guard.

"You should be," he finally said quietly. "But tell me something else, Chris." His gaze strayed to the insipid watercolor hanging over his fireplace. It never wavered from the painting as he spoke. "You're the kind of woman who carries pictures in her wallet, and I'd be willing to bet everything I own that you've got a wallet-sized snapshot of the family portrait above your fireplace. And probably your sister's children, too."

A pang of guilt knifed into her. Wendy, yes. But not Josh. *Not Josh.* Oh, God, she hadn't even realized . . . "Yes," she said weakly. "But nearly everyone—"

"Not everyone," he cut in harshly. "My father doesn't. He carries too many business cards—one for every occasion, I've always thought. Nor does my mother. Her wallet is stuffed with credit cards and invitations to upcoming events on her social calendar. As for me, I'm afraid I'm just as guilty. Of course, it would have helped if they had thought to make sure their only son had a family photo." His laughter held no mirth. "Oh, I suppose I could have clipped one from the society page. There've been plenty of those where my mother is concerned, and I can't count the times dear old Dad's hit the front page."

Once started, he couldn't seem to stop. Logan hated himself for the mockery in his voice. He hated himself even more when he turned and saw the look of hurt confusion on Chris's face.

"Dammit, Chris, I never meant to. . ." He hadn't intended to hurl barbs at her, and that's probably what it must have sounded like to her. But once started, he hadn't been able to stop. He was at her side in an instant, both hands gripping hers. "I'm sorry," he muttered feverishly. "The last thing I want is to lay this on your shoulders. You see why I hate to talk about my parents? I try not to even think of them."

She managed a brave, wobbly smile. "That's what I'm here for," she attempted to joke. The smile faded.

She tilted her head to gaze at him searchingly. She was more certain than ever that Logan came from a wealthy, elite background. "Who are you really, Logan? The son of some famous politician or something?"

"Famous? No, not famous," he said, almost to himself. "Notorious would be a better word—" a bitter smile played on his lips "—at least in my eyes. And my father isn't a politician."

This last was almost an afterthought. Chris hesitated but an instant. "Who, then, Logan? Please," she urged gently. "Tell me."

His grip on her hands tightened so fiercely she almost cried out. He stared back at her, but she knew he was seeing someone else entirely. His grip loosened abruptly. His expression was so taut and closed that Chris feared he had withdrawn into himself once more, but then he sighed and walked the few steps to the sofa.

Chris stood silently as he kneaded the muscles of his neck. After a moment, he turned his head slightly and glanced up at her.

"Have you ever heard of Robert Garrison?"

She shook her head.

"Good." His eyes crinkled faintly at the corners. "I try not to advertise the fact that I'm his son."

"Really?" She deliberately widened her eyes. "I'd never have noticed if you hadn't told me."

He chuckled. It was a dry, raspy sound, but Chris was relieved to note that some of the tension had left his features.

"If you lived back East," he told her, "you'd probably know the name."

"Practically a household word, hmmm?"

He shrugged. "Depending on the circle you travel in."

"I always knew you were a snob," she teased. "Maybe you should tell me what circle *you* traveled in." While she was trying to lighten his mood, she wasn't about to let him off the hook either.

Logan leaned back. He stared at the ceiling, lean fingers laced across his stomach. "I went to all the right schools, knew all the right girls, met all the right people, if that's what you mean."

"I knew it all along," she said lightly. "So where did it all go wrong?"

"It wasn't so much a matter of going wrong—" his lips curled in a twisted parody of a smile "—as a matter of things never going right."

A small silence settled between them. More than anything, Chris wished she could erase the somber, faraway expression from Logan's face.

"At the risk of sounding rather trite, or maybe like a nosy old busybody, I really do believe that confession is good for the soul."

"Say that often, do you, Doc?" He leaned his head back wearily.

"I usually don't have to."

He continued to gaze at her through half-lowered lids. "No," he said at last. "I don't suppose you do." He appeared to hesitate. "I've never been very comfortable talking about myself, Chris."

"Most people aren't." Her eyes encouraged him, but she wouldn't press him any further. She and Logan were no longer strangers; she felt they had *never* been strangers. It hurt to think that he trusted her so little that he would share nothing of himself. But just when she began to think they had reached that point, he began to speak.

"My father's an attorney," he said very calmly, and Chris had the strangest sensation that it was the calm before the storm. "A defense attorney. Big time. Big bucks. Very big bucks." He took a deep, indrawn breath. "He's good, too, or maybe I should say he's damn good at getting the job done, no matter what it takes. Robert Garrison, defense attorney *extraordinaire*, practically a legend in his own time."

His mouth thinned; his eyes were like chips of blue ice. What memories had drawn his face into such cold, harsh lines? He might pretend that whatever he was about to disclose didn't hurt, but his expression told the story only too well.

"My mother, just like her mother, and *her* mother before that, is the perfect social butterfly. It's obvious what my father saw in her. She was the lady with all the right connections. Marrying into one of the oldest and wealthiest families in the State of New York was probably the smartest thing my father ever did."

Chris leveled a searching look upon him. "You don't believe they were ever in love?"

Logan sat forward, propping his forearms on his knees, his hands laced together. "They don't know love as you know it, Chris. They never have, they never will. To them, love is measured in dollars and cents, in prestige and power." His voice was clipped and abrupt. "Even if they were in love once, and believe me that's a big if, my father's ambition and my mother's vanity killed it."

There was a faint frown etched between Chris's brows. "You sound very certain of that," she said slowly. She sensed a multitude of emotions churning away inside him, anger and resentment among them.

His lips tightened. "I am, though I'll admit even I wonder how the hell I'm qualified to make a statement like that."

Her frown deepened. "I'm not sure what you mean." She paused. "You lived with your parents, didn't you?"

"Summers and weekends, when I wasn't in boarding school." His bitter laugh raked over her nerves as he continued, "Oh, yes, I lived with them, but I never really *knew* them, and what I did know I never liked. I grew up watching my father defend slum landlords, underworld crime figures, corporate bigwigs involved in dirty deals. All people willing to pay top dollar for the lawyer who seldom lost a case. I saw my mother on her way out, my father on his way in, at the time when all poor little rich kids are packed off to bed."

All of a sudden, Chris had a very clear picture of the way Logan had grown up: a staunch, rigid upbringing that sent a fierce tide of anger surging through her veins. But in its wake, she felt almost sick.

My God, she thought silently, and closed her eyes. Only an hour ago, she'd felt it was a shame that Logan had grown up without a pet. He'd said his parents didn't know love as she knew it. Did he? Or had he grown up as lonely and desolate as she feared?

She didn't have to ask.

When her eyes opened, Logan was staring into space, his features carved into a remote mask. "They're still married, aren't they?" she asked.

He nodded. "For the life of me I'll never understand why they haven't gone their separate ways long ago. They share the same last name, but that's all."

His tone was one of utter weariness. It was as if all the anger and resentment that she had sensed in him moments ago had drained away, leaving only a bleak acceptance.

She laid her hand on his forearm without even realizing that she had moved. "I'm sorry," she whispered, a poignantly hollow sensation in her chest. "Oh, Logan, when I think of how you must have felt every time I've mentioned my folks, or Char and Diane..."

His face softened when he turned to find Chris's eyes suspiciously bright. If ever there was a time to tell her about Denise, it was now. And he wanted to tell her—he wanted to so badly. But at this moment, to speak of Denise would be like pouring salt on an open wound.

Very gently he covered Christine's hand with his. Their eyes melded, and the emotion he saw reflected in the hazy gold depths stole his breath.

"Don't be sorry, Chris," he murmured. "Nothing can change what happened." There was a brief pause. "I haven't wanted to look back, but perhaps I should have. I never really cared how I lived. All I knew was that I never wanted to be like my parents. I never wanted to need them, because they never really needed me. I never wanted to live like them, but I'm just beginning to realize... maybe I'm not so different from them after all."

Chris opened her mouth, but before she had a chance to say a word, Logan sighed. The smile that lifted his mouth was both sad and a little wistful. "How did we get started on this conversation anyway?" he asked, sounding as if he were talking to no one in particular.

His tone didn't fool Chris in the least. She smiled and found it supplied the release they both needed. "I believe," she said lightly, "it started when you mentioned you were thinking of moving. Which reminds me... you may change your mind once you've given the cottage the once-over, so maybe we should go have a look before I hand over the key. I do need to stop at the hospital to see my patient first, though."

The flare in his eyes was brighter than the most brilliant of suns, but it faded all too soon. "Chris," he said quickly, "you really don't have to do this. I wasn't trying to push you into anything, and maybe it's not such a hot idea after all.''

"I know that," she told him. "But you know what? The idea of having a new neighbor is beginning to sound rather appealing." An impish smile, the smile that so charmed Logan, lit up her face as she glanced toward the kitchen. "Or I guess you could say I have a soft spot for a guy who fed his breakfast to a starving little pooch...."

A man who had never had a pet, a man whose childhood had been as empty as hers had been full. It was time for this man to have a home, a *real* home. Perhaps for the first time in his life...

CHAPTER SEVEN

THE NEXT WEEK was a hectic one for Chris. Her patient schedule kept her hopping during the day. Between her work, her noonday shopping for furniture with Logan and evenings spent scrubbing and painting the cottage, she fell into bed exhausted every night. But it was one of the most rewarding weeks she'd had in a long, long time.

There were some tense moments during her sessions with Tom Chamberlain in his hospital room, but by the time he was discharged Wednesday afternoon, Chris began to feel they had finally started to make some real progress. It had been a rather hard way to learn one of life's lessons, but when Tom realized how close he had flirted with death, it had shocked him into seeing that he had a future as well as a past, and there was no point in dwelling in the past.

And then there were the flowers, the perfect way to end the week. Jean had carried them in just before lunch on Friday, opening the door with a flourish.

Chris's eyes had widened at the sight of the lovely arrangement. It wasn't made up of cherry red and white carnations, mixed with shiny green foliage like so many of the Christmas bouquets on display. Instead, it was like a burst of sunshine, buttercup-yellow daisies softened with lacy, delicate sprays of baby's breath.

Jean perched on the corner of Chris's desk, her eyes gleaming with undisguised interest. "Do I get to find out who they're from?"

Chris frowned at her good-naturedly and pulled the card from the small white envelope. It read: "For a very special lady." There was no signature.

"Apparently not," she said wryly and handed Jean the card. But Chris knew they were from Logan. Who else would send her flowers? Maybe it was his way of saying thank you for the cottage.

Jean hopped off the desk. "Why don't we call the florist?" she asked brightly. "Then you'd know who sent them."

Chris chuckled. "You make it sound as if I have legions of men falling at my feet."

Jean wore a sly look. "I can only think of one," she said triumphantly. "Unless there's someone else you're keeping secret?"

"Someone *else* I'm keeping secret?" Chris laughed and pointed toward the open door. "You *have* been watching too many spy movies lately. Or are you planning to jump ship on me and go to work for a private detective?"

Jean eventually went back to work, but when she left, she was humming the theme from *Mission: Impossible*, a rather familiar tune around Chris's office these days.

Throughout the day, Chris smiled every time her eyes came to rest on the floral arrangement. Even Carl commented on it when he came in that night. "What's the occasion, Dr. Michaels? Anything special?" He glanced at her inquiringly.

Chris eased back in her chair. "I'm not sure there is an occasion," she said softly, thinking of Logan. Then she smiled. "Which only makes it that much nicer." She reached out a hand to gently stroke one of the petals. "I just love daisies," she murmured absently.

Carl merely smiled, rounding the corner of her desk to collect the trash can.

She'd just finished dictating her last case file when Carl had arrived. Her work for the day finally wrapped up, she rose and retrieved her coat from the closet in the corner. Carl had gone into the outer office.

The last fading embers of sunlight had long since faded, and the sky was dark and moonless. For a moment, the sudden quiet was almost ominous. Several times tonight, after the other offices on her floor had presumably been closed for the night, she'd heard the echo of footsteps, the faraway sound of a door closing. Though she told herself it was only a straggler like herself, catching up on a full workday, the sound sent a prickle of unease up her spine. There had been two more robberies that week, one only a few blocks away. If she hadn't known that Carl would be around, she wasn't sure she'd have stayed after hours.

Carl was in the waiting area, dusting the furniture. Pulling on her coat, she gave him a tentative smile when he straightened. "I hate to ask you this," she began rather apologetically, "but do you think you could walk me out to my car? All these robberies lately have everyone spooked a little—including me."

For an instant Carl looked surprised, but then a smile lit his thin face. "As a matter of fact, I was just about to lock things up here and head out to my next job. So it's no problem—no problem at all."

He seemed so pleased that Chris couldn't help but think Carl was perhaps rather starved for company. Which really wasn't surprising, considering the solitary nature of his job.

She walked along beside him as he stowed his cleaning cart and supplies in the closet downstairs. Chris still wasn't entirely comfortable with activating and deactivating the alarm system, so she made no demur when he stepped up to the panel.

Outside she glanced at him curiously. "You have jobs at other office buildings, too?"

Carl pointed to another building on the square. "I'm usually through with your building by seven o'clock. That one comes next." He smiled at her. "I've been the janitor at several offices near the hospital for the past ten years. I also take care of half a dozen other businesses, but a couple of those are only once a week."

"Even so, you must put in a long day. Or maybe I should say a long night."

"It's usually well after midnight before I'm through," he admitted. She thought he seemed a little embarrassed.

By now they had reached her car. Chris frowned as she stopped near the front fender. "Aren't you afraid being out that time of night? Especially with all these burglaries lately?"

In typically male fashion, he scoffed. "It doesn't bother me," he said with a shrug.

"Nevertheless, you should be careful." Impulsively she squeezed his shoulder before slipping her key into the lock and opening the door. "Thanks for walking me out, Carl," she said warmly. "Have a safe night."

Chris dropped several hints about the flowers when she talked with Logan later that night. But to her surprise, he didn't confess to being the perpetrator behind the flowers. Card or no card, signature or no signature, she knew Logan had sent them.

At any rate, she certainly had discovered this week that once he made up his mind, Logan was not a man to let anything stand in his way. He had placed an ad in the newspaper's Lost and Found column in case someone had indeed lost Annie. Chris sincerely hoped no one claimed her, but considering the fact that she was a package deal complete with five tiny puppies, she doubted that anyone would respond. But Annie or no, Logan was determined to move into her cottage.

She had been surprised when Logan asked her to help him furnish the cottage. He'd decided to sublet his condominium exactly the way it was, complete with furnishings, and planned on transferring only his personal belongings. As he'd predicted, he had no trouble finding an occupant, Steve Johnson, another psychologist in Chris's building. It would suit Steve and his wife rather well, since they did quite a lot of entertaining. It was a miniature showplace, as Steve's wife delightedly commented, and Chris silently agreed.

Picking out furniture with a man seemed a rather intimate undertaking, and Chris had been a little uncomfortable about it at first. But being with Logan was becoming as natural as eating and sleeping, and her initial discomfort soon wore off. The only occasion that gave her pause was when they were looking at bedroom furniture. Chris fell in love with the smooth, flowing lines of a four-poster made of rich, dark cherrywood. Logan appeared to favor it as well, and as they lingered before it, the salesclerk persisted in referring to Chris as Logan's "wife." Logan had simply glanced at Chris and smiled, while Chris had felt a rare blush coming on.

She had spotted several pine end tables in a second-hand store that were in mint condition and coordinated rather well with the overstuffed sofa and love seat they'd chosen. By the time Friday rolled around, Logan had managed to amass quite a collection of furniture, most of which had been delivered and stored in

Chris's barn. Chris could only hope that moving day would go as smoothly.

SATURDAY MORNING, exactly one week after Logan had decided to rent the cottage, Chris arrived at Logan's apartment to help with the move. Promptly at nine, Ned showed up to lend a hand. Chris was making sure Annie and her pups were comfortable in the makeshift bed Logan had fashioned from a cardboard box and a blanket, when the two men walked into the kitchen. Ned was a tall, blond man with a ruddy complexion, and Chris liked him on sight. Logan talked often of his friend, and after discovering the lonely life Logan had led, Chris was glad that his relationship with Ned had gone beyond the professional to the personal.

Logan handed Ned the last cup of coffee. "Haven't you caught that burglar yet?" he chided his friend. "I saw in this morning's paper that he's still at it."

"He?" Ned's lips were smiling but his eyes were serious. "It's nice to know someone else thinks this could be a one-man operation. Everyone at the station thinks the robberies are just random occurrences, picking up as usual because of the holiday season. Care to join the boys in blue for a while, Logan? I could use someone on my side of the blanket."

Even though Ned's remark was jesting, Chris noticed the faint shadow that passed over Logan's face. He covered it with a short laugh, but she couldn't help but wonder, and not for the first time, exactly why he had left the FBI. The two of them had come a long way since that first morning at Beth's, but there were times—times like now—when she wondered just how well she knew him. But, as she reminded herself, he had a right to his privacy.

"There was another break-in last night?" She looked from one to the other, suppressing a shiver. She still hadn't quite forgotten the night she'd set off the alarm in her building.

Ned nodded. "A couple of doctor's offices downtown."

"What was taken this time?" Logan hunched down to run a hand over Annie's fur, now soft and gleaming from his care.

"Typewriters, a couple of adding machines, a portable TV. As usual, stuff that's easy to fence." Ned frowned. "This time, though, he cleaned out a couple of petty cash funds, too."

"That's a first, isn't it?" Logan looked up.

"Yeah." Ned's face was grim. "Another reason everybody thinks the same person isn't responsible."

"Could it be a couple of kids?" Chris suggested. "Teenagers looking for a way to get some easy money?"

"Possibly." Ned hesitated. "If these were residential burglaries, I'd be more likely to think it was teenagers, but the damnedest thing is that these are all businesses. We've been getting hit at the rate of at least three break-ins a week for the past month, which is a lot for a city this size. Kids hitting businesses is unusual; most times they'll find out from their friends when someone will be gone, and that's the house they'll hit."

Chris made a face. "Can you tell the criminal mind is more your area than mine?"

They got down to work after that. Logan and Ned headed out to Chris's to begin transferring furniture from her barn to the cottage. Chris had offered to sort through and pack the contents of his cupboards and closets, so she stayed behind in order to accomplish that chore.

Not that there was much to sort through. Logan's cupboards were as neat and organized as only a bachelor's could be. Her own move a year ago had been far less orderly. It seemed she had rummaged and sorted and discarded a dozen times before she finally decided what to take and what not to take. In that, Chris decided she took after her mother.

She grinned at the thought. Her father had always accused his wife of being a pack rat, though he had long since ceased to argue and throw up his hands in disgust; now he merely walked away with a shake of his head. But to Chris and her two sisters, dreary, rainy days had never been boring. They had browsed through the trunks in the attic, preening and parading in the outlandish costumes they concocted from the contents.

And now Wendy was continuing what had almost become a tradition. It had rained one day during the week Chris was home for Thanksgiving, and Wendy had begged to be taken into the attic to explore. And no doubt Josh would soon be begging to join his sister.

Scottie had never even had the chance.

A hot ache filled her throat. Against her will, an image of flailing limbs, baby-soft skin and bright blue eyes burned beneath her eyelids.

Chris sank down on the floor, still clutching an armload of towels. "Oh, Scottie," she whispered. "I still miss you. I miss you so much...."

Long moments passed before she was able to gather her tumultuous emotions and overcome the storm in her heart. When she finally resumed her task, it was with dry eyes and an empty heart.

By early afternoon, she had finished packing all the towels and washcloths from the two bathrooms into several cardboard boxes. There was still room in one of them, so she decided to add the linens from the hall closet. The customary items were all there—stacks of pillowcases and sheets—but when she started to reach for the neatly folded pile on the top shelf, something clattered to the floor.

She instinctively picked up the object and saw that it was a photograph in a wooden frame. Miraculously, the glass hadn't broken.

The photo was of a woman, dressed in brief white shorts and a tank top. It had been taken on a palm-fringed beach. In the background, shimmering blue waters glimmered invitingly. The woman was beautiful and young, with carefree, laughing eyes and long, dark hair strewn over her bare shoulders.

And then Chris spotted the smooth flowing script in one corner: It was signed "To Logan, Love, Denise."

Suddenly Chris remembered the night Logan had mentioned that she was the type of woman to carry pictures of her family in her wallet, while he was a man who hid them away in the closet, as if he wanted no reminders. . . .

Once again her eyes strayed to the photograph. Palm trees. Sun-kissed beaches and jewellike aquamarine waters. Her eyes widened. Florida . . . Miami.

Logan's last assignment had been in Miami. Chris remembered that very distinctly, and a dozen unanswered questions tumbled around and around in her head. Her mind searched quickly over all the conversations they'd ever had. He'd never said he'd been married, nor had he claimed to have been a bachelor all his life either. So who was Denise? His ex-wife? His fiancée? His lover? Was Denise the reason he had given up his career with the FBI? Was Logan a broken-hearted lover determined to make a new start?

She felt a sudden, unexpected pang in her heart. Surely she wasn't jealous, she thought, stunned. Yet she couldn't deny that the thought of Logan with another woman disturbed her.

She had no reason to be upset, Chris told herself, the calm, rational part of her taking over. After all, she and Logan were friends. The fact that they happened to be of the opposite sex meant nothing; their closeness could scarcely be attributed to sexual attraction. To add such a dimension to their friendship—and certainly Logan had never given her any reason to believe he wanted to—would be nothing but a complication. And that, Chris suspected, was the one thing neither of them wanted or needed.

Yet she couldn't help but feel a little guilty when she heard the front door open at precisely that moment. She quickly shoved the picture back where she had found it.

Logan was still standing in the entryway when Chris hurried into the other room. "Hi," she said, forcing a weak smile.

"Hi." He returned her smile, his own not the least bit tentative.

He weaved his way through the boxes and cartons littering his living room. "You've been hard at it, I see."

"About the only thing left is the linen closet in the hall. And the things in the fridge."

"Good," he pronounced. "I'm starving."

"How are you and Ned coming along?" Did she sound overly bright? She hoped not.

"Ned's already gone home," he told her. "We got everything moved out of the barn and into the cottage. We've got furniture shoved every which way and everything needs to be arranged, but I can do that later." He started toward the kitchen. "You hungry?"

"No." Chris shook her head. "I was just thinking, though, since there's not much left to do here, would you mind if I deserted you this afternoon?" The laugh she gave was rather breathless. "I'm like everyone else, I'm afraid. There's less than ten shopping days left until Christmas, and hardly any of it is done."

He glanced up from where he was rummaging through the refrigerator. "Of course not, Chris. You've done more than I ever expected anyway. You'll stop at the cottage later and have a look around, won't you? I can't promise much—" he cast a rueful glance at the brick of cheese he was holding "—but I think I can come up with something for dinner."

Their eyes met briefly, and Chris noticed that for once, he was a little disheveled. Oddly enough, it didn't make him look tougher or harder; instead it gave him a boyish, vulnerable look that made her heart catch.

"Sure," she said softly. "See you later."

Hard as she tried, when she left his apartment she couldn't block the image of a dark-haired beauty from her mind. Was Denise the mystery behind the darkness she so often glimpsed in Logan's eyes?

All of a sudden, Chris wasn't sure she wanted to know.

IT WAS NEARLY FIVE O'CLOCK when Chris finally pulled into the long drive that led to her house. She almost bypassed the cottage, though lights were blazing inside and Logan's BMW was parked near the back door. But she'd promised him she would stop, and she wouldn't go back on her word.

Logan showed her through the cottage enthusiastically and she tried to match his mood, hating to ruin the day for him. An hour later, Chris sat in the living room, her back propped against the sofa, absently feeding Annie a piece of the sandwich Logan had made for her.

Logan surveyed her thoughtfully from the doorway. "You're awfully quiet tonight," he charged gently.

"Changed your mind about having me for your near-est neighbor already?"

"Changed your mind about wanting to stay?" she countered with a smile. It disappeared a fraction of a second later. "I'm not very good company tonight, am I?" She sighed. "If you had any brains, you'd shoo me home."

Logan advanced into the room carrying two mugs of coffee, a bag of cookies tucked under one arm. "I seem to have this soft spot for a pretty lady who feeds Annie the ham from her sandwich."

That she had said just about the same thing to Logan a week ago escaped her notice. Instead her mind homed in on one word. Pretty. The girl in the photo had been pretty, Chris recalled with disturbing clarity. Was that what was responsible for her blue mood? No, it wasn't that, and she knew it.

Logan eased down beside her, placing the mugs and cookies on the end table. "Thanks for the bed for An-nie. I feel like I've neglected her, sticking her in that old cardboard box all week."

"Call it a housewarming present," she told him, her gaze drifting to the dog. The trip to the pet store had been her last stop, where she'd purchased a large wicker basket, big enough for Annie and her pups, complete with a gaily patterned cushion. Annie had settled into her new home and bed as readily as she had taken to the cardboard box in Logan's kitchen a week earlier. She now lay at Chris's feet, her five blind, wiggly pups rooting at her warm belly. Chris didn't know when she'd seen anything so adorable.

"Besides," Chris found herself teasing, "I thought it would blend in perfectly with the decor. Who *is* your decorator, by the way?" It was truly amazing how cozy and homey the cottage had turned out. Except for curtains at the windows and pictures on the walls, Logan had everything in tip-top shape. Despite her mood, Chris had felt a warm pride when Logan had shown her through, and it pleased her to know that he felt it, too.

"Actually," his voice lowered to a conspiratorial whisper, "she comes rather cheap. Offer her a meal, top it off with something that indulges her sweet tooth and she'll do just about anything."

He found himself on the receiving end of a playful punch on the shoulder, and then it was Chris's turn to find herself on the receiving end of a rather vocal protest by a yipping, yapping extremely defensive little creature.

"Good Lord!" Chris exclaimed, laughing while Logan reached out to soothe the dog. "You sure don't need to install one of your security systems here. You've already got yourself a built-in bodyguard."

Logan smiled, although beamed was a much more accurate word, Chris thought warmly. All of a sudden she didn't feel quite so moody as she had earlier. Annie settled back in her basket, though not without casting one last wary glance at Chris.

"You haven't shown me what you bought this afternoon," Logan mentioned conversationally a few minutes later.

"All Christmas gifts, except for Annie's basket," she told him, then hesitated. "Would you like to see?"

"Sure." His reply came readily.

Chris went out to the trunk of her car and quickly retrieved several oversize shopping bags. She had intended to buy something for Logan, but hard as she had searched, she couldn't find anything that satisfied her. Logan came out to her car to lend a hand, and Chris stole a speculative glance at him when she slammed the trunk shut. Should she have asked him to come along?

Whether or not he had his own Christmas shopping done, she had no idea. She had no idea if he even *did* any Christmas shopping for his parents. But knowing how he felt about them, the last thing she wanted was to make him feel guilty.

They both resumed their places on the sofa. Annie looked on as Chris began to pull items one by one from the bags.

There were several pipes and an assortment of tobacco for her father, a warm down vest to wear on his hunting trips in the fall and winter, a much-needed jewelry box for her mother and several pieces of costume jewelry for her as well. Rick's present came next, and then the cashmere sweater she knew Char would love dearly, but whose practical nature would never allow her to buy. For Diane she had chosen an outrageously expensive silk teddy.

Logan smiled at the pink tights and multicolored ribbons she'd purchased for Wendy, but he regarded the Barbie doll and various outfits she laid out with polite—and exceedingly masculine—disinterest. Chris smothered a grin, thinking that his expression proclaimed his bachelor status quite clearly.

But his eyes were soft when she finally lifted one last item from the bag—a huge, cuddly stuffed panda bear. "Aha," he murmured. "That must be for Josh. He's the baby, right?"

She didn't answer.

His gaze was drawn to her face. Her eyes were closed, her thick lashes fanned out like dark, feathery crescents against her cheeks. Her head was bent, and she was clutching the panda bear as if it were her only link to a world that threatened to leave her behind.

"Chris?"

She opened her eyes then, and Logan knew he would never forget the utter agony on her features. She looked stricken, devastated beyond anything he had ever witnessed. She looked as if she desperately needed to cry. But the eyes that gazed back at him were dull and opaque, so unfailingly empty he had to steel himself against the hurt he sensed in her.

He spoke again, his tone very low. "Chris, what's wrong?"

"I don't know why I bought this," she murmured. "It's so much like the other one I bought...." Her voice trailed away. Logan had the strangest sensation she was lost in another time, another place.

"For Scottie?" he asked quietly.

Her gaze focused on his face. There was surprise and puzzlement reflected in the wide hazel eyes that met his. A faint frown etched its way between her slender brows as she relaxed her grip on the panda bear. "Yes," she said slowly. "But how did you know—"

"That first day at Beth's restaurant," he reminded her. "You said you had a son, a little boy named Scottie."

"He's gone now," she said tonelessly.

"I know." He spoke as gently, as reassuringly as he could. "You told me." There was a brief pause. "How long now, Chris?"

His heart caught when he saw the muscles in her throat constrict. He watched her wordlessly, aware of the effort it took for her to speak.

"Two years," she whispered.

He hesitated a moment. "I don't want to pry, Chris, but...how? An accident?"

"No." She shook her head. "Have you ever heard of SIDS?"

SIDS. It sounded familiar....

"Sudden infant death syndrome," she clarified. Her lips parted as she took a deep, uneven breath. "Better known as crib death."

"Crib death," he repeated, stunned. Barring an accident, he'd thought perhaps some childhood disease. "My God," he said hoarsely. "He was just a baby then."

The silence seemed to stretch into eternity before Chris said anything. When she finally did, she sounded so tired, so emotionally drained and weary that Logan fleetingly wondered if he hadn't made a horrible mistake.

"Just a baby," she echoed dully. "Only six months old."

Logan listened quietly as she began to speak, his long legs stretched out before him.

"Sometimes I can think of Scottie without any pain at all," she stated very quietly. "And there are other times when I think of him and it's like there's a knife inside me; times when his memory is so close it's as if I could reach out and touch him."

So close. Close enough to touch . . . Logan felt an icy coldness seep through him. Just like Denise, he realized. Just like Denise.

It was almost a relief to focus on the soft-spoken voice coming from beside him.

"I'd wanted a baby for a long time," she continued, her voice almost painfully husky. "But I still hadn't finished my training yet, and Bill had just started his job."

"What did he do?"

"He was a high school P.E. teacher. At any rate, we decided to put it off for a while. Then we bought a house, and we both thought it was best to get on our feet financially. We were young. We thought we had all the time in the world to start a family.''

Her mouth was curved in a forlorn little smile that caused an unfamiliar tightness in Logan's chest.

''We'd been married almost seven years when I found out I was pregnant. We were both ecstatic. It was like a dream come true when Scottie came along. I had everything I'd ever wanted. A home, a career, a healthy, thriving baby...''

Logan frowned. ''His death was completely unexpected?''

She paused and looked down at her hands. ''It always is. That's what's so tragic about SIDS. A baby dies, a normal, healthy baby, and there's no apparent reason.'' Her voice plunged to just above a whisper. ''I can't tell you what it's like to...'' She stopped, seemingly unable to go on.

A lean hand stole out and caught hers. Logan weaved his fingers tightly through hers, and still he could feel her tremble.

''I'd given Scottie a bath after dinner that night and laid him in his crib for a minute to make a phone call. He fell asleep, and I decided to let him nap for a little while, since I still needed to work on some cases I'd brought home from the office that day. Bill was gone that night, coaching a basketball game.''

Again she stopped, and the sudden quiet that descended was almost unbearable. Logan took one look at her face, feeling as if he'd been punched in the stomach. Her bottom lip was quivering, and her eyes were glistening with unshed tears, but he knew she was trying very hard not to cry. She looked so hurt and defenseless, but so valiantly brave, that he reacted without even thinking, pulling her up against his body and tucking her head in the hollow of his shoulder.

His fingers combed gently through her hair. "Go on," he said softly.

She took a deep, shuddering breath. "I can't tell you how many times I've wondered what would have happened if only I'd gone in to check on him. But I didn't, because I didn't intend to let him sleep long." Logan could tell by her careful tone the rigorous hold she was keeping on her emotions. "Finally after about twenty minutes, I went in to wake him. I picked him up and..."

Her eyes squeezed shut. Logan could almost see the horror of remembrance that battered her. "He looked so—so peaceful, that for a split second, I had a hard time accepting that something was wrong. I called the ambulance. My God, it seemed to take forever! I remember standing in the pouring rain, waiting and hoping and praying. But when it finally arrived and I watched them run into the house, I knew—somehow I knew it was too late."

Her voice broke, and Logan's heart contracted. He felt the pain of her loss as if it were his own...as indeed it was. But suddenly he remembered the night they had met, and the look of sheer, blind panic on her face. It had been raining that night, too, he recalled.

Please, she had whispered. *The siren, the lights...*

Gut instinct had told him then that there was something more to her reaction than being startled by the police, and now he knew.

That night had been an agonizing reminder of an agonizing loss. And Logan couldn't help but think once more of Denise.... But Scottie had been just a baby. Just an innocent, helpless baby.

Christine's hand was still linked tightly with his, resting on his stomach. Logan could see her white-knuckled grip on his fingers; he could feel the tightening of her entire body. For a long time he simply held her close, stroking the honeyed strands that lay loose on her shoulders, over and over and over until he felt some of the tension seep from her body.

"Your husband," he asked very quietly. "Don't tell me he blamed you."

She was silent for so long that Logan experienced a slow, burning resentment toward the man who had once been her husband.

"Bill never came right out and said so," she murmured. "But maybe it was just because I felt so guilty that I unconsciously thought that Bill blamed me."

She drew away from him slowly, and a part of him felt bereft. The role of giving comfort and solace was one that was foreign to him; he had never thought of himself as a tender, compassionate man. But the privilege of holding Christine—and it was a privilege—simply holding her and giving her a shoulder to lean on, was like a gift from heaven. The moment ended far too soon for Logan.

He watched as she tucked her feet beneath her, resting her weight on one arm.

"It was really rather odd," she began, her voice scarcely above a whisper. "Bill was completely torn apart the first few months after Scottie died. For both of us, it wasn't like losing an arm or a leg, it was more like losing half a heart. The first year after losing a child is the most difficult, but it was almost as if it were left to me to be the strong one. Maybe it stemmed from being the eldest child, the one to take charge when my parents weren't there." Her shoulders lifted helplessly. "Or maybe it was because I was the psychologist, the one who was supposed to have all the answers, the one who was supposed to know how best to deal with grief.

"We'd wanted a baby for so long that when Scottie was born, he was all the more precious to both of us.

But it also made losing him all the more devastating. Scottie was barely gone before Bill had everything cleared from his room; he couldn't hear Scottie's name without breaking down.... It was as if he wanted to wipe away all traces of Scottie, as if he'd never been alive. And I—I couldn't stand it! But as the days passed, the easier it became for Bill—" she shook her head, her eyes dark with pain "—and the harder it became for me to talk about Scottie."

"'Physician heal thyself'?" he quoted.

Chris paused. "Maybe," she said slowly, then let out a heavy sigh. "In the long run, though, I think Bill got over Scottie much better than I did."

Logan frowned. "What makes you think that?"

"Six months later, Bill decided he wanted another baby."

"And?" His gaze never wavered from her face; he sensed there was more.

The clock chimed in the corner. Annie nudged a wayward puppy back to her side then settled back to sleep. Chris stared straight ahead, her eyes bleak.

"I wasn't convinced that was the answer." Her voice was flat, completely emotionless. She turned her head to look at Logan. "They say a child can never be replaced by another. Bill swore that was never his intention, but I couldn't help but wonder. I also wondered if perhaps Bill just wasn't able to cope with the fact that he, a big, strong jock, had fathered a child who wasn't perfect."

"That's when your marriage started going sour?"

She nodded. "I can't really say why. But from the time we lost Scottie, everything just seemed to go downhill. Scottie was always such a good baby—so sweet-tempered, not at all fussy. It's hard to accept when a baby simply stops breathing and never wakes up. There *has* to be a reason, right? Was it Bill? Was it me? Or the two of us together?''

She looked down at her hands. "I don't know," she murmured finally. "Maybe we both subconsciously blamed each other. I hated myself for thinking it would have been easier if we'd lost Scottie at birth, but that's the way it was. But to have another child and wonder—day after day, week after week—if it would be the last time I would ever hold my baby...I couldn't do it." Her voice was choked. "I just—couldn't."

Logan's heart twisted. He heard the deep, tremulous breath she drew into her lungs, saw the effort it took to control her emotions.

Long painful seconds passed before Chris was able to speak again. "Whatever the reason," she finished very quietly, "Bill and I just couldn't seem to understand each other anymore. I haven't seen him in over a year, since he moved to Montana."

Once again the room was steeped in silence, and once again her words from only moments before drifted through his mind.

"Losing Scottie wasn't like losing an arm or a leg. It was more like losing half a heart." And well he knew....

He also knew mere words could never make up for such a loss. But he touched her arm gently. "I'm sorry, Chris," he offered quietly. "For what it's worth, I'm sorry."

Her eyes were shimmering, and even as he watched, a single tear trickled down her cheek. She dashed it away, but then she smiled at him, a sweet, beautiful smile that took him totally off guard.

There was still a trace of elusive sadness in her eyes, but there was also such trust reflected there that he felt himself humbled.

This time it was Logan who battled a burning ache in his throat as Chris propelled herself gently forward and kissed his cheek.

"I'm glad I met you, Logan Garrison," she said very softly. "Because I think you're the best friend I've ever had."

A PAIR OF CALLUSED HANDS draped a daintily crocheted afghan across the back of the rocking chair in the corner.

The man stepped back to survey the effect, lines of worry carved into his forehead. He wanted her to like it here. It was important to him, for this time he intended to make certain that she would never leave him . . . like the other one.

But *she* was different. She had proved that, time and again. No matter how tired she was, or how busy, she always had time for him.

And she had liked the flowers. How it had pleased him to see them occupying a place of honor on the corner of her desk.

No, she wasn't like the other one.

But he had never been lucky, a voice reminded him, a voice that took on a taunting, shrewish quality which plunged him back in time.

I hate it here. I hate living in the middle of this god-forsaken wilderness. I hate seeing no one but you for days on end. . . .

But this time he had learned his lesson; this time he would be prepared.

Because nothing would stop him from having her.

CHAPTER EIGHT

"I THINK you're the best friend I ever had."

In the days that followed, Logan often wondered why those words filled him with such conflicting emotions.

From the time he and Chris had met, from the time he had learned how she felt about those she loved, he had somehow thought that Chris would be a very physical person, demonstrating her feelings through sight and sound and touch, as well as thoughts and deeds.

She wasn't.

But learning about Scottie had helped him realize that perhaps Chris was subconsciously holding back, afraid to give for fear of being hurt again.

And now he, who rarely initiated physical contact with another person, found himself compelled by the need to reach out and touch, to stroke and seek and learn. At times that need was almost overwhelming.

Chris was a warm and sweet woman, lovely and desirable. And what about him? Was he simply a man who had been alone too long?

She, too, had known sadness. She, too, had suffered the same, heart-wrenching pain of loss. And she was the purest, gentlest person he had ever known.

He liked her quiet dignity, her calm serenity. He liked the smooth, fluid way she moved, her slender gracefulness. She was so small, so delicately made. He liked the low, soothing tone of her voice, the way the sun picked out the golden lights in her hair. Most of all, he loved the way her eyes lit up her entire face at the most un-expected moments.

It would be easy...so easy to fall in love with her.

But Logan sensed Chris didn't want that from him; she sought a friend, a companion, someone to make her lonely days a little less lonely.

He found it ironic that Chris didn't see him in the same light. But he could hardly condemn her for that. Instead, he was thankful for what she had given him. There was a deeper understanding between them now, an unseen bond that transcended everything that had gone before.

They were two people who had been simply going through the motions of living. She didn't pass judg-ment on his estrangement with his parents, and for that he was grateful. But it surprised him when Chris con-fided that she wouldn't be going home to Boise for Christmas, that she'd sent her presents special delivery. Her sense of home and family was unlike anything Lo-gan had ever encountered; that she was cutting herself off from what she most treasured in life was an opin-ion that he kept to himself. But it was then that Logan realized he and Chris were two people who were still running from the past.

Neither suspected that their days of running were about to end.

THE WEEK BEFORE CHRISTMAS was hectic and ex-tremely busy. But the bouquet of daisies Chris received early Monday morning was certainly the right way to start things off, though again they arrived without a signature on the card.

Logan came to an abrupt halt when he entered her office to pick her up for lunch. "Uh-oh," he said guilt-ily. "It's your birthday and I missed it, right?"

Chris chuckled. "You missed it, all right. It was six months ago."

He glanced at the flowers inquisitively. "What, then?"

"You tell me," she teased, moving across the room to retrieve her coat.

When she turned back to him, he looked completely blank.

"Oh, come on." She laughed. "I know you sent them, Logan. Who else would?"

"You tell me." He lifted his eyebrows, turning her words back on her.

Chris paused in the midst of tightening her belt. "You really didn't send them?" Her tone was both curious and incredulous.

He shook his head, a puzzled half smile on his lips. Chris wasn't sure she believed him.

"Then who did?" she wondered aloud.

"Someone in your family?"

Chris made a face and looped her purse over her arm. "Are you kidding? They're all too practical to send flowers. A plant, maybe. Flowers, no way!"

Logan held the door open for her. "Then maybe you have a secret admirer," he suggested.

Perhaps she did, Chris agreed silently. The flowers had arrived from a different florist this time, and she had Jean call to see if she could track down who had ordered them. All she discovered was that the purchase had been paid for in cash. Despite his denial, Chris wasn't entirely convinced that Logan hadn't sent them, and she enjoyed the arrangement as much as she had the previous one.

Unfortunately, the week ended on a far different note. For the second time that month, one of Chris's patients, a young girl named Lindsay Russell, landed in the hospital, though for a different reason than Tom Chamberlain.

Chris had seen the young girl for only two sessions. Lindsay had been referred by her family physician. She was fifteen years old and anorexic. What had begun as a desire to lose "a few pounds" had become an obsession. She had collapsed in the high school cafeteria and was taken to the hospital where she had been diagnosed as suffering from malnutrition and exhaustion.

As Chris was leaving Lindsay's hospital room later that evening, she was lucky enough to encounter Lindsay's mother in a nearby waiting room. The two women had a long talk about the seriousness of Lindsay's condition and the effort both mother and daughter would have to make to ensure her full recovery.

By the end of their conversation, Chris was relatively certain that Lindsay would receive the emotional support she needed and would soon be on her way to regaining her health. And as she passed Lindsay's room on her way out of the hospital, Chris caught a glimpse of Mrs. Russell sitting on the edge of Lindsay's bed, the girl's thin hand clasped in both of her own.

The scene was still vivid in Chris's mind as she exited through the hospital's double doors. The wind was so vicious and strong it nearly pushed her back inside. Inhaling a stinging mouthful of air, she ducked her head and began to run toward the parking lot. It had snowed in the past hour, and she shivered as the wind pelted icy needles against her nylon-clad legs.

The drive home seemed to take forever. The snow increased its earthward-bound momentum almost as soon as Chris slammed the car door shut. To make matters worse, the wind gusted more fiercely than ever, blowing snow across the road so that it was almost impossible to see.

She frowned when she finally pulled into the long drive, immediately noting that there wasn't a light burning in the cottage. Logan always stored his car in the garage at night, so she wasn't sure if he was home yet. If he wasn't, he would likely be stranded in town.

Her heels crunched on the frozen surface of the ground as she ran toward her back porch. Once there, she fumbled with the key and dropped it twice before her gloved fingers were finally able to insert it in the lock. Inside, she reached for the light switch.

Nothing happened.

"Damn," Chris muttered. "Of all the times for a light bulb to burn out!"

Just then the phone began to ring. She stumbled into the kitchen, sending a bucket flying in the process. Lifting the receiver, she gasped out a breathless, "Hello."

"Tell me, young lady," intoned a familiar male voice. "What does your nose for snow tell you right now?"

"I've been telling you all week it was going to snow." In spite of her aching shin bone, Chris voiced the reprimand lightly.

On the other end of the line, Logan smothered a laugh. "Even *I* knew that, Christine Michaels."

"Christine? You're beginning to sound like my father," she complained. She groped for the light switch in the kitchen, again to no avail. "Logan," she said, moving the receiver to her other ear, "is there something wrong with your electricity?"

"What makes you ask that?" he said dryly. "In addition to your nose for snow, don't you have X-ray vision as well? Or are you sitting in the dark wearing your heaviest coat, too?"

"I think *you're* the one who has X-ray vision." Chris's laugh broke off abruptly. "Oh, no! I forgot the cottage has electric heat. And I just realized my gas won't work either, not without power for the blower. Have you been home long?'' she added.

"Long enough to wish I wasn't,'' came the reply. "I called the electric company already and found out that there are power lines down all over. They don't expect it to be reconnected in this area until sometime tomorrow.''

The temperature had been flirting with the freezing mark all week, but it had taken a rapid plunge tonight. Combined with the fierce wind, Chris didn't even want to guess at what the wind-chill factor might be. She shivered, glad that she'd had the house insulated well last year. Nonetheless, she decided wryly, the temperature in her kitchen couldn't be much warmer than that outdoors.

Once again she heard Logan's voice. He sounded rather sheepish. "What I really called for was to see if you happened to have an extra kerosene lamp, or some candles. My flashlight lasted about two minutes after I got home.''

Chris hesitated only an instant. "I've got a better idea,'' she told him. "It's bound to get a lot colder tonight, so why don't you come here and stay? It's not much in weather like this, but at least I've got the fireplace.''

"Sounds good to me. Anything you want me to bring?''

"Just your sleeping bag.''

A dead silence followed.

"You don't have one, do you?'' She smothered a chuckle.

She heard him sigh. "Chris, I'm sorry—''

"Hey, it's not a big deal,'' she dismissed lightly. "I have one that we can open up in the living room. And

I've got some old quilts stored up in the attic. I won't promise how good they smell, but they should still be usable. Try not to get lost in the snow drifts on your way up, will you?''

"With my luck," came the grimly convicted response, "that's exactly what will happen."

Chris quickly exchanged her skirt and blouse for jeans and a plaid, flannel shirt, topping the shirt with an oversized white shaker sweater. Her ears were cold, though, and she had just pulled a red woolen cap over her head when she heard pounding at the back door.

Flashlight in hand, she ran toward the porch. "My goodness," she laughed on seeing Logan. "You are anxious to warm up, aren't you? I thought the whole house was about to collapse around my head."

"I used my foot," he explained with a lopsided grin, though Chris had already seen why. He was carrying Annie's basket, wrapped in a blanket.

At the sound of Chris's voice, a small velvety brown nose peeped from beneath the folds. "Well, hello there!" Chris exclaimed. "Traveling in style tonight, aren't you?" Annie licked the hand she offered, and Chris glanced up at Logan.

"Why don't you go start the fire in the living room while I hunt up some quilts in the attic? I've got a kerosene lamp already burning on the mantel, and there should be plenty of wood in the holder next to the poker set. The matches are there, too. Later you can go out in the wood shed and get some more logs."

The corners of Logan's eyes crinkled. "Thanks a lot," he called after her. "Now I know why you wanted me here. You just didn't want to get your hands dirty. Maybe you won't get any of the fudge I brought with me after all. And I got it from that candy store downtown that you like so well!"

Halfway up the attic stairs, Chris shook her head and smiled to herself. There were times when Logan appeared as hard as a diamond, but she—and Annie—knew the real story. Logan Garrison, she had learned long ago, was just an old softie at heart.

She returned downstairs five minutes later, several blankets and quilts tucked under each arm. "They don't smell too bad, I guess," she decided. "As long as you like *eau de* mothball." She chuckled. "Frankly, it's not my favorite fragrance."

She dropped her cumbersome burden on the sofa, then turned to find Logan still kneeling before the fireplace. Annie sat beside him. At Chris's inquiring look, the dog thumped her tail and fixed wide brown eyes on her, as if to say "Help!"

"What's wrong?" she asked, crossing the room.

Logan leaned back on his heels. "I can't get it to start," he muttered. He indicated the fireplace with a grimace. "I've used nearly all the matches."

From her vantage point above him, Chris's puzzled gaze traveled from his face to the fireplace. The parted mesh screen revealed that the grate was neatly stacked with logs. For a moment she simply stared, but then she burst out laughing.

"You," she accused teasingly, "really are a city boy, aren't you?"

A thick, well-shaped eyebrow arched. "Meaning?"

"Meaning—" she dropped to her knees beside him "—that you've never started a fire before. You didn't use any kindling!"

"I never claimed to be a Boy Scout," he countered mildly. "I had a place in Denver once that had a fireplace, though."

"Which you never used?"

"Which I never used."

"I can see why!" Dusting her hands together in an exaggerated motion, she cast him a lofty glance from the corner of her eye. "Care to see how it's done?"

"If someone doesn't do it, and it obviously isn't going to be me, we're all likely to freeze to death."

Chris wasn't about to argue with such logic. Still smiling, she rolled several sheets of newspaper from the pile next to the wood holder and inserted them between the cut surfaces of several logs. Logan watched, one strong hand dangling from his knee as she added a handful of cedar kindling. When it was arranged to her satisfaction, she struck a match and held it to the edges of several wads of newspaper.

The fire crackled and roared to life. As the flames leaped higher, Chris carefully closed the wire mesh screen. Turning to Logan, she raised a finger to him in mock reproach. "It's your job to see that it doesn't go out."

"So you've told me," he said dryly, and got to his feet. "You're a hard woman, Christine Michaels, to send a man out on a night like this."

"Better you than me." She held out her hands to the warmth of the flames. "Besides," she added sweetly, watching as he pulled on a pair of gloves, "I started the fire, remember?"

"And *I* didn't," he muttered. "Am I going to have to live this down the rest of my life?"

She grinned and handed him the flashlight. "Not if you let me have some of that fudge you brought."

Logan raised his eyes heavenward. "Is this what's known as manipulative behavior?" He pulled a foil-wrapped square from the inside pocket of his parka and tossed it to her. "I hope it's melted," he added as he headed for the woodshed.

When he returned with a box full of wood a few minutes later, Chris had pushed aside several pieces of furniture to clear the floor in front of the fireplace. Logan set aside the wood as she unzipped the sleeping bag.

"I think we should lay this out first," she told him. "Even with the carpet, it'll be drafty down here on the floor. This should help, though, and we can cover up with quilts."

Logan grabbed one corner of the sleeping bag and pulled it taut. He eyed the red wool cap she still wore. "You can take your hat off now. In case you hadn't noticed, your fire seems to be doing the trick."

Chris stuck out her tongue. "Ninety percent of the body's heat is lost through a person's head. Didn't . . ." She caught herself just in time. She'd been on the verge of saying, "Didn't your mother ever tell you that?" Instead she finished airily, "So don't you dare make fun of me, Logan Garrison. Otherwise I won't let you have any of your fudge."

He assumed a shocked expression. "There's still some left?" He ducked as a pillow came sailing past his head.

Between the two of them, they managed to turn the floor of Chris's living room into an unorthodox but not-too-uncomfortable makeshift bed. They tucked a paisley-patterned quilt across their laps as they sat cross-legged on the sleeping bag and proceeded to polish off the square of fudge. Logan enjoyed seeing Chris lick the remaining chocolate from her fingertips. But he found himself overcome by the urge to seize her fingers in his, raise them to his mouth and finish the task for her. He knew he didn't dare, and so he banished the impulse.

Dragging his eyes away from Chris, he dropped a wayward pup back into Annie's basket. They were more active now, running and playing whenever they weren't curled up sleeping.

When his gaze returned to Chris, he discovered her expression was rather pensive. "What is it?" he asked.

Chris drew her knees up to her chin and wrapped her arms around them. "I was just thinking about all the times Char and Diane and I 'camped out' in our living room." She smiled wistfully. "We used to drape sheets across the furniture so we could crawl under and pretend it was our tent."

Logan's gaze drifted around the shadowed room. Chris had extinguished the kerosene lamp, but the fire blazing in the grate threw light and warmth into the room. Even without the coziness lent by the fire, there was an undeniably homey and unpretentious ambience present. But the one thing that was conspicuously absent was the lack of anything relating to the holiday that was only three days away. No Christmas decorations; no fir boughs on the mantel, no vivid sprigs of holly. No holiday cheer at all. Why, even he had a table-sized Christmas tree displayed in his picture window. Granted, it was rather small and spindly looking, but at least it was real and smelled of evergreen.

It was odd. Damned odd, Logan decided. But this was an observation he thought better kept to himself. "I'd like to meet your parents someday," he said quietly.

Chris turned to look at him. He lay stretched on his side, his head supported by one long-fingered hand. His lean length was tucked into jeans and a light brown crew-necked sweater, and he had pulled a quilt up to his waist. "They'd like you," she returned softly.

Logan was quiet, seemingly lost in his own thoughts. "I'm probably not like anyone they've ever known," he said after a moment.

"So what?" She blinked in surprise.

He merely smiled, but it was a sad, almost derisive kind of smile that tugged on Chris's heartstrings as she thought of the lost, lonely little boy he had been.

"Just because you're a poor little rich kid?" She tried to tease him from the pensive mood she sensed had overtaken him.

"*Was* a poor little rich kid," he corrected.

"Whatever." Her tone was light as she shifted so she could see him better. "Either way, it wouldn't make any difference to Mom or Pop."

Logan would have liked to think that; he liked to think his background didn't make one bit of difference to Christine as well.

"In fact," Chris added, "I know Diane would like you."

"Meaning?"

She watched as he turned onto his back. Linking his fingers over his abdomen, he eyed her quizzically.

"Meaning that Diane has an eye for good-looking men." The words were no sooner out than Chris felt a stab of some nameless emotion. Jealousy? She was reminded of the photo she had found not long ago in Logan's linen closet, but she forced a lightness she suddenly didn't feel. "You wouldn't get in the door without her noticing every last detail."

"Hmmm," he murmured. "Diane sounds... interesting."

There was an almost playful quality to his voice and Chris experienced an irrational fluttering of her pulse. If there was even a chance that he was serious...

"Let me know the next time you head back to Boise and I'll mark my calendar."

She wrinkled her nose. "Be quiet, you! Don't you think it's time we hit the rack?" She wasted no time in tossing a pillow at him, which he deftly caught in mid-air and promptly stuffed beneath his head. A warm contentment began to flow through her, but as Chris slid beneath the blankets, she had a sudden inspiration.

Maybe that wasn't such a bad idea after all. Not introducing Logan to Diane, she assured herself hastily, but going home to Boise. For Christmas, in fact. That way she could keep her promise to her mother, and neither she nor Logan would be alone. The more she thought about it, the more the idea appealed to her.

She would see what Logan thought of it tomorrow. And then, she'd give her mother a call, just to give her a little warning, of course.

A smile edged Logan's mouth when he turned his head a short time later to find Chris huddled beneath the blankets, the blazing red of her cap all that he could see of her.

The silence was altogether comfortable as they each settled into their own thoughts. As always, Logan marveled at how relaxed they were with each other. What he and Chris had was special, unlike anything he'd ever felt for any woman...any*one*, for that matter.

And yet he suddenly felt very empty. He and Chris were so close...so close and yet so far. Again, he thought of how easy it would be to fall in love with her. But he knew he didn't dare. For Chris's sake, he didn't dare.

And the longer he lay there, the more painful that hollow ache inside his chest became.

CHAPTER NINE

SOME TIME LATER, Chris awoke. It seemed like hours had passed, but when she consulted the luminous dial of her watch, she discovered she had slept less than two hours.

The silence of the night was broken only by the storm outside, which raged even more fiercely than before. The wind howled eerily, blasting icy pellets against the frozen windowpanes. A fierce gust whistled down the chimney, sending up a shower of sparks.

Pitted against the frigid temperature outside, the warmth cast out by the fire was piteously feeble. Her toes, tucked into two pair of socks and her warmest pair of boots, felt as if they were encased in ice. Even her nose...but that was why. Her hat had come off. She stretched out a tentative arm in search of it, and an involuntary shiver ran through her.

"Chris?" Logan's voice, low and deep, breached the silence and the foot or so that separated them. "Are you awake already?"

She nodded, sensing his eyes upon her in the dim light. "My nose is freezing!" she complained. "Probably because I lost my hat." Even her laugh sounded shivery.

It was Logan who located it, lodged beneath the corner of the sofa. "Button your coat, don't forget your hat, and don't talk to strangers," he teased, his lips twitching. "Didn't your mother ever tell you that?"

"Thanks." Chris grimaced. "That's exactly what I needed to hear when it feels like we're at the North Pole."

Logan smiled and pulled the hat on her head. At the feel of her hair against his fingertips, he was reminded of the time he'd pulled the pins from the silky strands. He resisted the impulse to linger, to separate and sift through the spun-gold strands of her hair. Reluctantly he pulled his hands back.

Chris rolled over, her back to him. After a moment, she rolled to her stomach, propping herself up on her elbows. "This bed's not as comfortable as it looks, is it?"

His lips twitched. "You like my couch better?"

"Do I ever!" She fluffed her pillow and flopped to her back.

Logan got up to toss several more logs onto the fire. Ten more minutes passed. He glanced over to find Chris huddled beneath the mound of blankets, curled into a fetal position. A warm feeling stole through him. She looked like a child, with her chin tucked to her chest, her red hat the only part of her that was visible to him.

"Still cold?"

"Don't ask," came the woeful response from between chattering teeth.

Logan hesitated only a second. "Come here," he said softly.

There was no time to either protest or question before strong arms reached out to pull her firmly up against a body much longer and harder than her own. But for Chris, second thoughts were the last thing on her mind.

She breathed a sigh of relief almost the instant she came in contact with Logan's warmth. He wrapped her securely in his arms, the action comfortably familiar.

She nestled against him instinctively, curling against him as if it were the most natural thing in the world.

"How's the nose?" he asked presently.

Chris raised her head from the haven of his shoulder. "You're a fantastic nose-warmer," she told him, her voice bubbling with laughter. "It's too bad you can't do the same for my feet!"

"I probably can," he said smugly.

She scoffed. "I suppose you've got some of those new battery-charged socks that are supposed to keep you warm."

"We've already proved that body heat works much better," he told her blandly, "so why don't you take off your boots?"

She managed to slip off her boots without sacrificing much of her newfound warmth. "Now what?" she asked doubtfully, wriggling her still-freezing toes.

"Put them against mine."

Chris stretched her toes downward, then found that he had angled his stockinged feet toward her. "You not only make a fantastic foot and nosewarmer," she confided moments later, "but you make a very good footrest, too."

"Thank you," he returned gravely. "I only hope that's not in the same category as a doormat."

They lay there, steeped in contentment, and it wasn't long before Chris felt warm and toasty and on the verge of drifting off to sleep once more. Her right arm was hooked across Logan's abdomen. He shifted slightly, easing her higher in his arms.

Where minutes before, her fingers had rested against the soft cotton of his sweater, for just an instant they encountered skin. Warm . . . bare . . . hair-dusted skin.

Chris froze. An ember popped. A log shifted and sizzled.

Just that quickly, in the instant between one breath and the next, something changed. It was night. They were alone together. But they had been alone before, many times, she argued silently. Still, she couldn't forget the night-dark intimacy that existed at this moment.

And her fingertips still tingled. The hair-roughened feel of his skin epitomized how completely and utterly male he was.

This is Logan, her mind screamed. *Why, just last week you told him he was the best friend you'd ever had*... and it was true. She shivered again.

But not from the cold.

All of a sudden she felt filled with him, surrounded by him. By his nearness, the musky scent of him that was oh so-familiar—yet not so familiar. It was almost as if they were strangers who had met for the very first time.

A dozen images spun through her mind. She saw him as she had that first night outside her office. Calm. Authoritative. A man whose classically male features denoted both ruggedness and an elegant refinement. She saw him as he had been only two hours earlier, the way the worn fabric of his jeans molded his thighs, the way his shoulders stretched to fill his sweater.

Her heart began to thud. Her eyes strayed helplessly to his face, proudly etched in golden firelight. The rich darkness of his hair lay tumbled across his forehead. Her fingertips tingled. She knew that if she lifted her hand, she would find his jaw rough with five o'clock shadow. And his mouth...sometimes hard, sometimes stern. But it didn't stop her from thinking how beautifully chiseled his lips were....

A strange, dark thrill ran through her. The pounding of her heart tripled. She swallowed and prayed that

Logan wasn't aware of the nerve-shattering awareness that had enveloped her.

She prayed in vain.

It was impossible for Logan not to have noticed the sudden tension that had invaded her body.

"Chris?"

Soft as his voice was, there was an unspoken question in it that Chris just couldn't answer right now. She closed her eyes against it and filled her lungs with air, pretending she hadn't heard.

In the brittle silence that followed, her breathing went from fast to slow to fast again.

Logan's hand drifted to the small of her back, then splayed against the outcurve of her hip. "Chris," he said again, more sharply this time. He held her firm, knowing that something was wrong—very wrong.

Lean fingers touched her jaw. His touch was gentle, but firm in intent. He angled her face to his, and their eyes met. For countless moments they stared at each other, almost painfully conscious of the electric current that seemed to charge the very air between them.

He thought once more that she looked like a child, only this time her eyes were tentative and uncertain. But this was no child's body that lay ripe and firm against his, no child's breast that shaped its sloping fullness against his side. Unable to stop himself, his fingers slid into her hair.

Her throat was parched and dry. Chris wanted desperately to say something, but couldn't. She searched for something cute, something glib, to break the uneasy spell that had sprung up so unexpectedly between them. Her heart thundered in her breast, echoing in her ears with a sound that was almost deafening.

Then Logan's expression changed dramatically. "Go to sleep," he ordered brusquely. His voice matched the hard line of his mouth; she knew he was angry. She could hear it in his voice, feel it in the binding tension of the arms that continued to hold her. Chris had the strangest sensation that Logan was experiencing the same conflicting emotions as she.

Her eyes squeezed shut. This was the first time Logan had ever used such a tone with her. She felt inexplicably near tears.

The seconds dragged into minutes. How much time passed, Chris couldn't have said. She tried to relax, but it was impossible. Her body was stiff and rigid. She could feel it, and she knew Logan could as well. When she could stand it no longer, she tried to ease away from him. But his arm was like a visc around her. No matter how hard she tried, some part of her remained in contact with him. Her hip, her knee. Still, she persisted. She shifted, she wiggled, until finally Logan snapped at her.

"For God's sake, Chris, what the hell is wrong with you?"

Chris swallowed miserably, unable to look at him. In some distant corner of her mind, she realized that her hat had come off again. Finding and retrieving it was the last thing on her mind.

Logan sat up abruptly. "Well?" he demanded.

As if he didn't know.... "I can't do this," she whispered.

"Can't do what?" His voice was cold. "This isn't the first time we've spent the night together. It's certainly not the first time we've been alone."

She sat up slowly. The hand that pushed the hair from her cheeks wasn't entirely steady. "But it's never been—like this." Her voice came jerkily. "This is— different."

Logan's mouth twisted. Different? Because for the first time she had noticed him for the man that he was?

He wasn't blind. Other women found him attractive. What about Chris? But he knew that if Chris had ever once looked at him as a man—a man that she could be sexually attracted to—she had suppressed that impulse as surely as night followed day.

And somehow that only made the matter worse. He couldn't pass it off with a blithe disregard. Something primitive, something savagely male inside, wouldn't let him. Even now, she was pulling away from him, and a fiery red mist of anger swam before him...and even he didn't quite understand why.

"Don't you trust me?" Strong fingers banded around her arm. "I'll admit a month isn't a long time, but we know each other better than some people manage to accomplish in a lifetime."

Chris's mind began to churn. On one level she realized that what he said was true. What she and Logan had shared these past weeks was something she had never achieved with Bill, in all their years of marriage. But on another, completely different level...

His fingers bit into her arm when she remained silent. "Answer me, Chris! Don't you trust me?"

The question only confused her. She stared at him, shaken to the core by the angry glitter in his eyes. This man was a stranger, a stranger she had never seen before. Yet she knew instinctively that somehow she had hurt him, and that knowledge cut into her like a rusty blade.

"I—I think I do," she faltered, raising shaky fingers to her temples. There was so much tension in the air she could scarcely think. "You've never given me any reason not to...."

His grip tightened to a point just short of pain. "What the hell are you so afraid of?" he demanded roughly. "A little kissing? A little petting?"

Vivid, sensual images tumbled through her brain. She saw herself and Logan. Together, with nothing between them but the delicious friction of skin against skin. And his hands, those strong, masculine hands, leaving no part of her untouched . . .

She couldn't move. She couldn't think. All she could do was sit there and stare at him numbly.

"Dammit, Chris, I can't believe you just said what you did. Why, I've scarcely ever touched you, except in the most casual way! But maybe—" his jaw clamped down abruptly "—maybe it's time I did."

For the second time that night, Logan left her no time to protest, no room for denial. Without another word— and before he could consider the wisdom of it —he hauled her into his arms.

Even before his mouth came down on hers, the same shattering awareness that had seized Chris only moments before returned, only this time it was twice as powerful . . . and twice as dangerous.

And this time she knew for certain she wasn't the only one who felt it.

His touch was anything but subtle. Somehow Chris had always sensed that beneath his smooth, sophisticated exterior, Logan was a man who possessed a raw, primitive virility. He kissed her with an expertise that was stark and sensual and left her in no doubt that Logan Garrison was indeed a man of the world. His lips were hard and hungry, bold and daring as he evoked a response Chris was powerless to withhold.

She was trapped between his chest and his legs. Her hands clutched his shoulders, the only solid object in a wildly spinning world. Nothing existed except the heat and hardness of his body against hers, the searing possession of his mouth. Willing or unwilling, he aroused urges in her that were sweet. Confusing. Dangerous but fascinating. Over and over and over he kissed her, until she was breathless and clinging, weak and trembling.

"Tell me you don't want this." The words were a ragged mutter, hot and torrid against the pulse that throbbed wildly at the base of her neck. "Tell me this isn't right..."

She couldn't. Dear God, she couldn't. She could feel all of him against her—the strength and security of his embrace, the full, primal potency of his maleness. He drew back, and she had one terrifying glimpse of fiery cobalt eyes. She opened her mouth, but the dark intensity on his face stopped whatever she might have said.

Every nerve ending in her body vibrated as the zipper of her coat was slowly pulled down, then pushed apart. His hands slid beneath her shirt, and for the first time she felt the touch of his hands on her naked skin. The front clasp of her bra was found and released. Chris nearly moaned aloud. This was everything she had feared...everything she had hoped for. Even before his thumbs skimmed her nipples in a tauntingly evocative rhythm, her breasts were taut and tingling and aching for his touch.

She thought she had died and gone to heaven when his palms slowly and possessively covered both breasts. She heard herself whimper, and her hands came up to clutch the back of his head, the warm skin of his neck. Her fingers slid into the midnight darkness of his hair, but whether her intent was to push him away or pull him closer, she didn't know.

His lips brushed the hollow of her throat, then trailed upward to find the sensitive point at the base of her ear, while his hands retained their gentle possession of her breasts. His lips captured hers once more, and his hands slid around to her back, angling her closer...ever closer. Through the mists of pleasure surrounding her, she dimly registered the full, straining pressure of him beneath her thighs.

Suddenly she tore her mouth from his, wrenching herself away from him so that she almost lost her balance. "No!" she cried, then again, *"No!"* It was the sound of a wounded animal, the desperate cry of a woman unable to believe, unable to accept....

There was a heartbeat of silence. Two pairs of eyes clashed for a never-ending moment, one pair fiercely blazing, the other impossibly wide and confused.

Then a soft, feminine sound, a mere wisp of air, broke the tense, waiting silence. "Oh, God," she whispered brokenly.

Logan felt as if something inside had just died. He watched as Chris turned her head aside. She couldn't stand to look at him. She couldn't stand for him to touch her!

Logan got to his feet. He moved to stand at the fireplace, one hand balled into a fist at his side, the heel of the other resting against the mantel. He could still see Chris huddled behind him, her expression bewildered, her posture so utterly defeated that he felt his heart twist even as something inside him grew hard and brittle as glass.

Slowly he turned to face her. "Sooner or later," he said tightly, "this was bound to happen."

His cool tone stabbed at her. But all Chris could do was shake her head.

"Yes, Chris. We both knew it."

Quiet as his voice was, there was a cutting edge to it that made her lift her head to stare at him. His face was shut down from all expression, but his eyes were so icy and remote she almost cried out. The man before her was a stranger. A stranger she didn't know at all.

But was he? a tiny little voice persisted. This was Logan. *Logan.* Her friend. Her confidant. She couldn't even think of him in any other way. Didn't he see that?

She stuffed her fist into her mouth, as if to still her involuntary cry, but it was too late. "This didn't happen!" she cried desperately, and tore her gaze away. "It didn't! We can just forget—"

"We can't and you know it!" His gaze bored into her. His eyes were so piercing, so penetrating. She could feel the effect of those eyes even when he wasn't looking at her. "Dammit, Chris, you, better than anyone, should know that! Why, to this day, you still haven't forgotten about Scottie!"

Her face crumpled. Logan hated himself as never before. He was so full of conflicting emotions—anger, resentment, fear—that he felt he might burst. His voice was very low when he finally spoke. "I didn't plan this," he said again, "but you should have guessed that eventually something like this could happen."

"No!" she choked out. "We don't have that kind of relationship. Logan, you and I—"

"And what if we did?" he cut in sharply. "There's nothing wrong in needing or wanting someone that way." He swore violently. "We're friends, Chris, damn good friends, and in my mind that's the best way to start out any kind of relationship, sexual or otherwise. We're also two mature adults who are capable of handling anything that might come along."

Mature? Capable? Chris had never felt less sure of herself. But something she *was* sure of was the friendship she and Logan had shared. What they had was precious to her. For the first time in years, she didn't feel so—so alone. She didn't want to jeopardize or lose what they had by taking the chance of adding such a dimension to it. And Logan was right. She was really just beginning to get over Scottie. And affairs of the heart were risky business. She didn't need that kind of complication in her life just now.

Her throat was tight. "I won't deny that there's always been a kind of bond between us. I—I've trusted you with things I've never told anyone . . . how I felt after I lost Scottie. I can't tell you how much it's meant to me this past month, knowing that if I ever need someone to talk to, you'll be there. I—I treasure our friendship, Logan."

Logan knew what the admission cost her. She hugged her knees to her chest protectively, her hands laced tightly together. Even in the dim light, he could see how her fingers strained against each other.

"So do I, Chris." He sounded so bone-weary that for an instant, her heart went out to him.

"Then don't . . . don't spoil it."

His gaze sharpened. "Is that what you think will happen? That our friendship will be ruined if things take a direction neither one of us planned on?"

Her silence was all the answer he needed.

"I don't agree, Chris." He steeled himself against the uncertainty reflected on her face and forced himself to go on. "I think you and I could have something very special. Something neither of us has ever had before. It's not wrong to want someone else, Chris. It's not wrong to need them—" his eyes seemed to see clear into her soul "—in a very basic, human way."

Sex. He was talking about sex. But it wasn't that simple, she cried silently. It wasn't simple at all!

He stood before her. Calm. Powerful. So controlled she wanted to scream. But the chill in the room was nothing compared to the chill in her heart. How ironic it was that while they spoke of friendship, of sharing, the emotional distance between them had never been greater.

She raised pleading eyes on his face. "Don't," she begged. "Please don't say any more, Logan." She drew a deep, tremulous breath, then said carefully. "In spite of what you feel, I think the best thing both of us can do is try to forget this ever happened."

His jaw hardened. "That's it?" he demanded. "Open. Shut. Just like that?"

She nodded, and while he continued to stare at her in tight-lipped silence, she turned aside and crawled carefully back beneath the quilts, unable to face him. A few minutes later, she felt him lie down beside her. She didn't have to look over her shoulder to know that his back was to her.

But deep in her heart, the words she had just spoken rang hollowly. For she was afraid—desperately afraid—that she and Logan had already lost something very precious this night, something that could never be regained.

And so once more, they spent the night together. So close, close enough to touch . . . and yet so far.

IT WAS DOUBTFUL THAT either of them slept that night. Logan caught a glimpse of Chris's pinched, white face and wished to hell he hadn't. The frightened little girl was back and he hated himself for putting that look on her face. But hard as he tried, he couldn't prevent the seething anger that simmered just under the surface, ready to erupt at the slightest provocation.

Neither spoke of the previous night. Neither seemed to do much of anything—except avoid looking at the other.

It was lucky, he decided rather bitterly, that the electricity came back on soon after they got up. He helped put her living room back in order, but he had no doubt that Chris was as glad to see him leave as he was to go.

She didn't go with him to the door, but he heard her whispered "Goodbye, Logan."

It wasn't until later that he realized this was the first time—ever—that Chris had told him goodbye. Every time he thought about it, an ominous darkness gripped him.

Logan didn't fool himself that he could have kissed her into warm, willing submission. In spite of all her secret vulnerability, Chris was a very strong woman. And even if he had broken down her barriers, it would have left him feeling empty. As empty as he had felt these past few days. But the nights were even worse. He closed his eyes, and all he could see was the shattered look in her eyes when she had wrenched her mouth from his . . . and he despised himself for being the cause of her pain.

He knew she was scared. Of him. Of herself. Of her feelings, feelings that she was convinced didn't belong. But he had tasted her response to him, tasted her warm, sweet willingness and reveled in it.

Every time he thought of her, and she was scarcely out of his mind, his desire burned stronger. But along with that was a potent sense of loss, and it was that loss which made him silently despair. He and Chris were more alike than either of them had ever suspected.

That night—that bittersweet night when he had crushed her close to his heart—had opened his eyes as nothing else could have. He'd never been able to explain the vague restlessness that had nagged at him since Denise had died. Even after he'd made the decision to settle in Idaho, it was still there, elusive as ever.

Roots? He'd never had any, not really. Not as a child, not as an adult. But perhaps, unconsciously, he had decided it was time to make a home for himself, a real home, not like the sterile mausoleum his parents occupied on Long Island.

In a sense, he had come here to heal the scars of a lifetime. And perhaps he'd unconsciously been paving the groundwork for something more. For years, he hadn't allowed himself to form any lasting attachments. What was the point? he had rationalized many times. His job was sometimes dangerous; he was often on the move. The only people he'd ever been close to, *really* close to, were Denise . . . and Chris.

But Denise was gone, and Chris was shutting him out.

Over the years, there had been many times when he'd felt as if he were a machine, tuned to another's whim, and not a human being at all. But he wasn't heartless; dear God, there were times he wished he had been!

Meeting Chris had changed everything, and for the first time he realized just how much. Little by little, he'd felt himself learning about the world again, the world he'd never really felt he was a part of. He had learned about living . . . and loving. And for possibly the first time ever, he'd felt as if he weren't viewing life through a filmy curtain of bleak emptiness.

Deep in his heart, Logan had always thought that nothing could hurt more than losing Denise. But right now, he didn't think anything could hurt more than Chris's rejection of him.

CHRISTMAS ARRIVED in a pale, dismal sunrise. The cold spell still hadn't snapped, and the day promised to be as dreary as Logan felt inside. Ned called during breakfast to wish him a merry Christmas, and they talked briefly about the latest robbery. On Friday night an electronics store had been broken into and various equipment stolen.

Logan propped his feet up on the hassock. "That's a different section of town than the others."

"The rest have all been confined to the business district," Ned confirmed. "But it could be just to throw us off."

At his pause, Logan knew there was something else on his friend's mind. "You think it's connected to the others, don't you?"

"The same type of equipment was stolen," Ned admitted. "Televisions, VCRs, video cameras. All items easily disposed of. They could be sold to a fence, to a flea market. Someone could even put an ad in the newspaper with no one the wiser. Items could be sold without anyone ever knowing they were buying stolen property. The hell of it is, I can't get approval from anyone higher up the ladder to put somebody undercover to even check it out! They keep harping on the fact that there's been no set pattern in the robberies, nothing to point to the possibility that one person or one group of thieves could be responsible."

Logan could already see Ned's red, blustery face, but he hid his amusement. "You don't feel there are all that many dissimilarities."

There was a hollow silence. "Yes and no," Ned responded guardedly. "Some have been forced entries—a window broken, a door jimmied; some haven't. I'll admit an employee could have been lax and left a door unlocked, but somehow I don't think that's the case. And it's odd, damned odd, because most burglars aren't content to hit just one place. They'll do the one next to it, and the next after that. You know that building in the square, the one across from Chris's?"

Logan frowned. "The one that was hit twice? The school district offices?"

"That's the one. Ever since that happened, it's bugged the hell out of me. There were other offices in that building. Why just that one? And the stereo shop that got hit on Market Street—there's a computer store next to it. Why only one of them and not both of them?" Ned demanded. "It's also odd that not one of these burglaries has occurred on a weekend. One per night, and it's always been Monday through Friday. There's a connection, I tell you, a connection between all of them. But how in the hell do you justify a gut feeling to someone else when that's all you have to go on?"

Logan smiled grimly. "Sometimes you don't. You simply have to follow through yourself, if you're able."

The other man snorted. "What do you think I've been doing? The trouble is, I could use twice as many hours in a day and twice as many hands."

"This is really getting to you, isn't it?" Logan could sense his friend's frustration. "You know," he said slowly, "I just might be able to help you with this. You mentioned newspaper ads. If you can get me a list of what's been stolen so far, I could check the flea markets and pawn shops and private parties that might advertise in the classifieds. I'd have the advantage of not being connected with the police. Maybe I could turn up something that way. We could even do a little night patrolling on our own."

Ned didn't hesitate long. "You sure you don't mind?"

"Not if it will help catch whoever is responsible for this." He thought of Chris, and the nights she spent working late. He didn't like it, and he'd told her several times. But she'd always brushed his objections aside, reminding him that the janitor was always there, too.

"We haven't taken all that much heat over this so far," Ned went on. "But if things continue like they have, it won't be long before every businessman in town is up in arms. Besides, I can't help but think that eventually this guy—or gang, or whatever—will get bolder. He'll decide to hit a bank or a grocery store, or maybe even a residence, and someone else will be around. And then it won't be long before somebody gets hurt," he finished grimly.

They talked a few minutes more, and Ned finally ended the conversation by inviting him over for dinner. When Logan politely refused, Ned got back at him.

"Better things to do, eh?" Ned laughed. "No need to explain, buddy. Who gets to cook the turkey? You or Chris?"

When Logan hung up, there was a bitter taste in his mouth. He knew Ned meant no harm, but for the first time in years, he regretted spending the holiday alone. He tried telling himself it was no different than most other holidays he'd spent in his lifetime, but the thought was little consolation.

Peering out the front window at Chris's rambling front porch, he wondered what—if anything—she had planned for the day. As far as he knew, she still hadn't put up a tree. Not for the first time, he wondered why she failed to get in the Christmas spirit. He hadn't seen or spoken to her since Friday night, but he knew she hadn't gone home to Boise. It wasn't male pride that had stopped him from getting in touch with Chris these past few days. He knew instinctively that Chris wouldn't have welcomed it. Though maybe he was being stubborn after all, in leaving the next step up to her.

His mouth curled derisively. Who was he trying to kid? If he had any guts, he'd pick up the phone and call her. . . .

At precisely that moment, the phone rang. He picked it up and murmured a "hello."

"Logan?"

"Yes." Every nerve in his body tightened. His grip on the phone was almost savage.

And then something inside him threatened to break apart as he heard a whispered, "I—I just called to wish you a . . . a Merry Christmas."

CHAPTER TEN

IT WAS CHRIS. But her voice was wobbly and uneven, scarcely audible.

"Logan? Logan, please don't hang up on me." She sounded almost panicked.

It took a moment for him to recover from his shock. "Merry Christmas," he returned very softly. "I hope Santa was good to you last night."

She didn't answer, and he knew with that sixth sense that had served him so well over the years that it wasn't because she didn't want to... but because she couldn't.

There was no doubt in his mind that she'd been thinking of Scottie, and he cursed himself for his thoughtlessness.

"Chris. Chris, are you there? Talk to me, Chris!"

An eternity passed before he heard her voice again. "I'm here." Her feeble attempt at a laugh made his heart bleed. "But please don't ask how I am."

His hesitation was marginal. "I want to see you." It wasn't a request, it was a quiet statement of fact, but his voice conveyed his intensity. "Now, Chris. Can I come up?"

"I... I was hoping you would. Bring Annie and the puppies, too, okay?"

"I'll be right there." When he hung up the phone, the relief that poured through his veins was indescribable. But the anxious concern that clutched at him overrode everything else. He quickly located five wayward puppies, dumped them into Annie's basket and draped a blanket over it to keep them inside. Throwing on his coat, he hurried up the long drive. Annie scampered along at his heels.

Chris opened the door the instant Logan stepped onto her back porch. At the sight of her tear-ravaged face, he silently cursed himself. She was wearing jeans and a pale gold cowl-necked sweater. Her skin was pale and colorless, her lashes still spiky and damp. The fragile skin below her eyes looked delicate and faintly smudged with purple. The lost, lonely little girl was back again...but this time she didn't have to be alone.

He kicked the door shut behind him and quickly lowered the basket to the floor. One pup immediately poked its head free and glanced around curiously, but Logan scarcely noticed. His entire being was focused on the woman before him. The smile she attempted fell flat. Logan felt some nameless emotion squeeze his heart.

"You've been crying." Unthinkingly he caught her hand and pulled her closer. "Why, Chris? Tell me why."

Chris tried; she honestly did. But the only sound that emerged was a strangled little cry that sped straight to Logan's heart.

Strong arms closed around her. Even while he savored the heady sensation of holding her once more, Logan closed his eyes and forced his voice past the unfamiliar tightness in his throat. "It's Scottie, isn't it?"

Her head was buried against his chest, deep within the folds of his coat. Yet somehow, he felt her imperceptible nod, the wispy flutter of her lashes brushing the hollow of his throat.

In some far-off corner of her mind, she marveled that he knew her so well, yet she felt compelled to explain. She drew back and gazed up into his lean face. His eyes were compassionate, tender, full of caring—as caring as she had known he would be.

"I was up most of the night," she confessed. "I tried not to think of it, but Christmas is...well, it's not a happy time for me."

"I know." His hand came up to cradle her face. His thumb brushed the dampness from her cheek. "Sometimes it seems as if Christmas was created especially for kids. It's easy to understand why, when you've lost a child, that it's just another painful reminder."

She fought to keep the tears locked tightly inside, but they spilled free and seeped down her cheek. "It's so hard to forget." Her voice caught raggedly. "It would have been Scottie's first Christmas...but he died just two days before."

Logan stared down at her in stunned surprise. But it all made perfect sense. She'd as much as told him so. Two years. She had told him Scottie had been gone for two years, and he had obtusely failed to make the connection between Christmas and Scottie's death.

He knew how unbearable her pain was. He felt it as if it were his own. Shock kept him motionless for a fraction of a second, but then his arms tightened around her trembling body.

"I'm sorry, Chris." Lord, but that sounded inadequate. His hand hovered above her head. He'd never felt so helpless. "I wish there was something I could say." He pressed her cheek against his chest. "Something I could do."

Slowly she raised her face to his. Through her tears, she smiled mistily at him. It was a shaky, tremulous little smile, but when her hand came up to cradle his cheek, Logan felt his heart turn over.

"You're here," she whispered, "and that means more to me than I can say."

He crushed her to him without even knowing it. With a breathless little sigh, she sagged against his chest once more. Her arms found their way around his waist, and she clung to him.

Logan's chest was tight. Chris was so small, and she sounded so damnably pathetic. He experienced a surge of fierce protectiveness, and it was only then that he realized his bruising grip. He tried to relax his hold, but her arms tightened. His hand drifted down her back, soothing and massaging. He continued to hold her, letting her absorb his warmth, his strength.

How long they stood there, their bodies clinging together with a desperate strength, Logan could never have said. But he suddenly realized that for the first time in his life, he felt needed. At the knowledge, every fiber of his being swelled with the powerful emotion that washed over him. Perhaps it was selfish of him, but he had no desire to give up this incredible feeling of closeness.

At length, Chris eased back from him, still bound within the confining circle of his arms. "I must look awful," she murmured.

He searched her face as if he hadn't seen her for years. He thought she'd never looked lovelier, and so he told her.

Chris flushed with pleasure. He was glad when a faint gleam entered her eyes. "Freckles and all?"

She found herself on the receiving end of another long, slow look that made her pulse leap inadvertently. But there was a hint of laughter in his voice as he assured her gravely, "I happen to be very partial to freckles."

The corners of her lips twitched. "It must be an acquired taste."

He matched her smile with one of his own, his gaze never leaving hers. "I think you may be right, Christine Michaels."

Chris managed a shaky laugh, but she found her heart was pounding. Staring into his rugged features, she suddenly found herself reliving that poignantly sweet moment when Logan had kissed her. She had spent practically every waking moment since then trying *not* to remember, but she couldn't deny that his touch had stirred something deep inside her.

Her tongue darted out to moisten her lips. She drew back from him, aware of a twinge of nervousness. "Now that you're here, you'll stay, won't you?"

Gently...oh, so gently, Logan brushed his thumb along the fullness of her lower lip, giving her the time to withdraw if she wanted. He yearned to part and taste the satiny texture of her mouth with his own, but he knew this wasn't the time.

"I will," he said very softly, "but only if you really want me here."

Only if you really want me. Those words were more than a little frightening. But if nothing else, Chris had learned one thing during the miserable weekend she had just spent. She needed Logan...needed him badly. It no longer mattered that their relationship had taken a abrupt and startling direction last Friday night. Logan was a man, a very intense, masculine man, and she had been foolish to refuse to acknowledge that fact. But if she had to choose between having him in or out of her life, then there was really no choice to be made at all.

His breath caught in his throat when she looked straight at him, her eyes clear as gold and just as enticing. "I want to be with you," she said very simply.

Logan's chest swelled. She didn't say, *I don't want to be alone.* After finding out about Scottie, he would have understood her need for support. But she had stated, quite plainly, that she wanted to be with *him*. Nothing could have pleased him more.

He heard her sigh. "The only problem is that I don't have much in the way of food. There's a nice, juicy pot roast in my freezer, but that doesn't do us a lot of good right now, does it?"

He paused consideringly. "It's not much of a Christmas feast," he offered, pulling off his jacket and following her into the living room. "But I've got a couple of frozen pizzas at home that won't take long to thaw."

"Sounds great." She took his coat and hung it in the closet. When she turned back, she paused uncertainly. "Are you sure you don't have other plans?" She bit her lip. "I mean, this isn't much of a way to spend Christmas...."

"Wanna bet?" He chuckled. "It just so happens that there's a Gary Cooper movie on this afternoon."

"There is?" Her eyes lit up. "Which one?"

"*High Noon.*"

"That's one of my favorites!" she exclaimed. "I haven't seen it for years."

But once again, Chris didn't last more than halfway through the movie. Logan glanced up during a commercial break and discovered her eyes closed, her head at an awkward angle on the arm of the sofa. He pulled her feet up on the sofa and covered her with a light blanket. He let her sleep, aware that she was both physically and emotionally exhausted.

She looked very delicate as she lay there sleeping, her features colored by a soft flush. The light from the lamp in the corner winked through her hair, picking out wispy strands of gold in her honeyed hair. A dozen new and nameless emotions unfolded within Logan as he watched her sleep. Giving in to the overwhelming temptation of her mouth, he leaned down and pressed his lips against hers.

She didn't awaken, and he rose with a sigh, thinking that this was a good time to head back to his place for the frozen pizza. On impulse, he decided to bring back his Christmas tree, hoping that it wouldn't upset Chris any further.

The little tree miraculously survived the trip without even a single ornament breaking. He had just finished setting it up in the corner by the fireplace when the telephone began to ring. Chris didn't even rouse at the shrill summons, so he picked up the receiver.

Chris awoke to the feel of a warm hand gently shaking her shoulder. Drowsy and disoriented, she opened her eyes to see Logan's face hovering above her.

A smile on his lips, he held out the phone. "Someone wants to wish you a Merry Christmas."

It took a moment for his words to sink in. When they did, she sat up abruptly, grabbing the phone and trying to restore a little order to her hair at the same time. "Hello?"

"Who does that sexy voice belong to?" a female voice demanded. "Trying to keep him all to yourself, hmmm? But you should know better, Chris Michaels. He sounds like the kind of man to drool over, so tell me—does he look as good as he sounds?"

It was Diane, as bright and lively as always. Chris's laugh was rather breathless as her eyes strayed to Logan.

She made the rounds with the rest of the family. Rick and Char said everyone loved their gifts, and there were some for her still under the tree. Then her mother came on the line.

"It's no secret there's someone there with you, Chris." Chris could almost see the warm glow of satisfaction on her mother's face. There was a brief pause. "I'm glad you're not by yourself today," she added. Her voice was low; Chris knew the words were meant for her ears alone.

Her gaze slid unerringly to Logan, who had moved to stand near the wide picture window. "So am I, Mom," she said softly. "So am I."

"Is he anyone special? Or just a friend?"

For some reason, she couldn't seem to stop smiling. "Both," she answered truthfully.

They chatted for several more minutes. Chris's father was the last to come on the line.

"How are you, Chris?"

All of a sudden Chris felt like a blubbering child. A curious lump rose in her throat at the sound of his deep, gruff voice. "I'm fine, Pop."

"The truth now, daughter."

"I am, Pop. Honestly." She dashed away a solitary tear, and her eyes lit on the tree in the corner. Logan now stood towering over the tiny tree, his hands jammed into his pockets. Suddenly she could have sworn she'd felt the touch of his lips on hers, and not so long ago. Had he kissed her? She discovered that she wanted to think so. He chose that moment to glance at her, and she smiled shakily against the mouthpiece. "I even," she added softly, "have a tree this year."

She hung up a few minutes later, and found Logan on the back porch chasing down an errant pup. She watched his long-fingered hands stroking the soft fur behind the puppy's ear, struck by such gentleness in such a hard-featured man. He seemed a little surprised when he turned and caught her looking at him. The half smile he gave was rather sheepish, but then his expression turned serious.

"I hope I didn't create an awkward situation for you by answering the phone."

"Are you kidding? You probably made my parents' day." It was her turn to be embarrassed. "Besides," she added, "I do seem to have this habit of falling asleep on you...."

"But only during Gary Cooper movies." His eyes were teasing.

Together they went back to the living room. He gestured at the tree. "I hope you don't mind that I brought this." His tone was apologetic. "It's the first tree I've had in a long, long time and...well, it just doesn't seem like Christmas without a tree."

"That, too, probably made my parents' day, which only goes to show that I've been right all along."

"How's that?"

"In thinking you're heaven-sent. Although I think my mother may have said it better."

"Aha! Talking about me behind my back—and to your mother yet!" He cocked an eyebrow. "Will it burn my tender ears?"

"Hardly. Especially coming from my mother." Her smile was warm. "She said maybe I'd found my guardian angel after all."

Chris knelt down by Annie and began idly ruffling her fur. Logan watched, but his smile faded. If only she knew, he thought with an unexpected pang. Her mother's observation was oh, so fitting, for all of a sudden, Logan wanted nothing more than to be granted the privilege of watching over this woman...for the rest of their lives. He could only hope and pray that, God willing, that wish would someday be granted.

The afternoon sped by. They ate Logan's pizza, and no elaborately prepared feast could have tasted better. Afterward, Chris pulled out a huge overstuffed pillow and plopped it in the middle of the living room. On impulse, Logan decided to light the fireplace. Chris teased him unmercifully about doing it right this time, but sure enough, in minutes there was a blazing fire roaring up the chimney. "Not bad for a city boy," she told him, her eyes sparkling.

They sat before the fireplace, the pillow between them, talking and sharing with an easy familiarity that was treasured by both. Neither spoke of their last disturbing encounter in this very room. Each seemed to sense the other's fear, or perhaps unwillingness, to shatter the spell of this time together. Chris got up once, and Logan simply shook his head when she returned with two steaming cups of hot chocolate, liberally doused with whipping cream.

When she eased down to the floor once more, he dropped a small, foil-wrapped package into her lap.

"For me?" Her gaze was wondering as it lifted to his.

Logan nodded. Annie came over to sniff the package curiously, but apparently decided it wasn't worth the trouble. She dropped to the floor, her head on her paws.

"I wonder what it is." Her eyes full of impish delight, Chris lifted it to her ear and shook it.

"I have a better solution," he commented dryly. "Open it and you'll find out."

"But that takes half the fun out of it!" she objected.

Logan leaned back on an elbow. "I always knew you were just a kid at heart, Christine Michaels."

"Christine?" Her brows shot up. "You sound like my father again!"

His eyes rested on her indulgently as she prodded and probed, then finally got around to peeling away the layers of paper and tissue. He held his breath when she finally lifted the oak-framed photograph.

"Why, it's us!" she exclaimed. "That Saturday we spent in Spokane." They had braved the brisk winter chill, and lunched in one of Spokane's many parks. Logan had his camera along, and was idly snapping pictures of several old-growth cedars. An old man had come along and offered to take a photo of both of them.

"I know it's not much." For one of the few times in his life, Logan felt inadequate. "But I just didn't know what to get you."

I know the feeling, Chris thought, recalling the first time she had been in Logan's apartment. *You're the kind of woman who carries pictures in her wallet,* he had told her.

"I love it," she told him, truly touched. "But you know—" she hesitated "—I'd love it even more if you keep it instead."

A slow smile lifted his lips. "I already have one," he said softly. Reaching out, he tucked a stray curl behind her ears. She didn't flinch, as he half expected. Indeed, she surprised the hell out of him when she whispered a thank you and leaned forward. He knew she only meant to kiss his cheek, but he turned his head at the last second so that their lips met instead. His heart skipped a beat when she didn't break the contact. It was a brief, gentle kiss, not at all impassioned, but Logan felt near to bursting with the feelings trapped inside him.

She drew away, then rose and carefully placed the picture on the mantel. "I'll be back in a minute," she promised, and disappeared up the stairs.

When she returned, she dropped a gaily wrapped gift in his lap. "It's not much—" she borrowed his words from just moments ago "—but I didn't know what to get you."

She lowered herself to her knees. Slender hands resting on her jean-clad thighs, she watched him unwrap her gift. When he held up the wood hand carving of mother and child that her grandfather had once given her grandmother, wonder and surprise, and the most incredible look of pleasure, softened his features. Chris felt her throat tighten, and she knew why she had finally decided on this gift for Logan. After their last stormy parting, she'd been so afraid she wouldn't be able to give it to him, and so the moment was all the more precious

But Logan was shaking his dark head, and she saw that he meant to refuse it. "Chris," he began, "I'm not sure I can accept this."

Their eyes met. "Why not?" she asked calmly.

"It's been in your family for years, Chris." Logan was moved beyond words, but still he hesitated. "I'm not sure I should—"

"I want you to have it, Logan." She spoke with quiet insistence, her gaze following the glide of his fingertips as they moved with gentle reverence over the carving. Remembering the first night he had seen it, she had sensed the loneliness in him even then. Though that perception was no longer as sharp, she was well aware that Logan's heart was as battered and bruised as her own.

"You're touching it like you did that the first night," she recalled with a tiny smile. "I can't explain, but it seems right to me that you should have it."

Their eyes met, and Chris experienced an almost giddy feeling of relief. He would keep the carving, and she knew that he would treasure it as she had all these years.

He set the carving aside and reached for the cup of chocolate, holding it between his palms. "This may seem selfish of me, but I'm glad you didn't go home to Boise." He blew upon the surface to cool the steaming liquid. "I thought you might change your mind," he added very quietly.

Chris was silent for a moment. In the empty hours since Friday, there were times when she *had* considered it. "I couldn't leave," she replied, just as quietly, "knowing that you were here alone. But I wish I had, because I'd like for you to meet the rest of my family."

Logan stared at her. The ravaging effect of her tears was gone, and he couldn't help but think how easy it would have been for Chris to simply turn her back on him. Instead, she had stayed, battling her loneliness and bitter emptiness...for him. In his entire life, no one had ever given up anything for him, no matter how small or inconsequential.

And somehow he knew that Chris had just given him the greatest gift of all.

He wanted to tell her how he felt, but mere words failed him. And before he could utter a sound, he felt the touch of her hand on his arm.

"It just occurred to me," she said tentatively, "that maybe there's someone you'd like to call." There was a brief but significant pause. "You're welcome to use the phone."

Logan felt as if the blood had suddenly frozen in his veins. By *someone*, Chris meant his parents. He understood the message she was tactfully trying to convey— that perhaps it was time to breach the rift between himself and his family. His mother had dropped him one of the two obligatory cards he received each year; as usual, she hadn't taken the time to scrawl more than a hastily concocted sentence or two. For just an instant, the old bitterness came crashing back. He got to his feet, aware of her gaze sinking into the rigid lines of his shoulders.

He stared out the window, at the frigid landscape. Darkness was just beginning to fall, cloaking the white world outside with an enshrouding mist of gray.

"There's no one, Chris."

His voice was so low it was nearly inaudible. Her gaze dropped to where his fingers gripped the windowsill. For an instant, she sensed a harshness in him that was utterly foreign to her.

She moistened her lips. "If you're sure..." Her voice trailed off as he slowly turned to face her. His expression was one of bitter resignation, yet she saw pain in his eyes, an ocean of it.

He jammed his hands into the pockets of his cords, his posture stiff. "I know it's hard for you to understand, but it's best this way. My parents and I...at least we know what not to expect from each other."

Of all the times that Chris had wondered at the mystery she sometimes glimpsed in the depths of his eyes, she had never been more conscious of it than at this moment.

When she said nothing, he moved closer, dropping down on one knee beside her. His gaze delved deeply into hers. "You think I'm cold, don't you?"

Cold? He was a loner; she knew it instinctively, had known it all along. And she thought him strong, strong enough to endure a life of loneliness. She also thought him a man who had seen too much, lived too hard, a man whose soul would bear those scars forever. But cold?

Her hand crept into his. "I could never think that about you," she told him huskily.

Even before she spoke, he sought the answer in her eyes, those wonderfully expressive eyes that kept him utterly captivated for a moment. But he frowned when they grew faintly cloudy.

"I didn't mean to remind you of things you'd rather not remember. Especially on Christmas." Her tone was very low. Her gaze slid away. "I hope I haven't ruined the entire day."

"Ruined it?" he echoed incredulously. "Chris, this is the best Christmas I've ever spent in my whole life."

She braved a cautious glance. "Better than the ones you've spent with— with other women?"

That made him smile, at a time when he very much needed to smile. "What other women?" he teased.

Chris bit her lip. "Denise," she said in a small voice. His smile withered.

"She was—special to you, wasn't she?"

Special. How inadequate that sounded. No, he thought. She was more. So much more. He had loved her as he had loved no other.

"Yes." The word was as flat and lifeless as he suddenly felt inside.

Chris ignored the knifelike pain that stabbed at her. She spoke quickly, flustered and embarrassed, and wishing she had left the subject alone. Nonetheless, she felt compelled to explain. She took a deep breath and plunged ahead.

"I wasn't trying to be nosy, but I found a picture of her the day I helped you move." She laughed nervously. "I don't know. Maybe I'm a little jealous, thinking you're on the rebound, but I've often wondered who she is and what she was to you. Your wife, perhaps—you've never said you *haven't* been married . . . or your fiancée, or maybe a—" to her utter and complete shame, she stumbled over the word "—lover..."

Logan listened as if he were in a daze. Denise... his wife? His fiancée? His lover? He might have laughed, if his heart hadn't been breaking in two.

He paused for the space of a heartbeat, and when he spoke, his voice was so low she had to strain to hear. "There's no need to be jealous, Chris. I could never even begin to think of Denise in that way."

Her eyes were locked on his face. It seemed she could almost see the grooves beside his mouth deepen. "But who is she, Logan? Who is Denise?"

A sad, wistful smile touched his lips. "Denise was my sister."

CHAPTER ELEVEN

TIME CEASED TO EXIST. For the longest while, Chris sat stunned, trying to absorb what she had just learned. Since the moment she had found the photo, she had been so certain that Denise had once been his lover.

And then it struck her, and his words spun once more in her mind. She *was* my sister.

A low sound broke from her lips. "Oh, God," she whispered. A cold knot of dread twisted her insides. "She's dead?"

He nodded, the pressure of his hand on hers increased to a bone-crushing intensity. But Chris scarcely noticed. For just an instant, the fire blazed brighter, throwing out golden shafts of hazy yellow light. Chris had one terrifying glimpse of his face before the room was again plunged into shadow. There was pain etched in the lines of his face, a world of it. His expression was drawn and haggard, his beautiful silver-blue eyes so full of empty desolation she nearly cried out.

Her hand was abruptly released, and Chris stared at him helplessly. In her role as counselor, she knew the value of listening, asking questions and interpreting. But her years of training had never prepared her for the loss of her child; she felt just as ill equipped right now. She wanted desperately to say something to ease the anguish she sensed in the man before her. But this was Logan. *Logan.*

"I never knew you had a sister." She held her breath. "Why haven't you ever told me about her?"

"Maybe for the same reason you've always found it so hard to talk about Scottie. Guilt. Pain. A dozen other reasons." He was silent for the longest time. "From the first moment I ever saw you, I've always felt a kind of invisible bond with you. We've never been strangers, Chris. But I think part of that stems from the fact that perhaps we're two people who have learned to live with our guilt. You never deserved to feel guilty, though. I'm not sure I can say the same."

The minutes slipped quietly by. A log fell in the grate; the fire snapped and crackled.

"Tell me about her," she said quietly. "Was she younger than you? Older?" *And tell me,* she pleaded wordlessly, *how on earth you could possibly think you're responsible for your sister's death.*

She thought he would refuse. He angled his body away from hers, still resting his arms on his upraised knees. Chris battled an inner hurt; it was more than just his body that distanced himself from her. His withdrawal was almost tangible. It was as if he had disappeared deep inside himself, and for a fleeting instant she was afraid that she would never again be able to reach him.

Logan couldn't prevent the stark blackness that invaded his soul. For years, ever since he was a child, he had guarded his feelings closely, knowing that to reveal them would only result in further hurt and pain. For long, tense moments he struggled with himself. But perhaps it was time, time to say aloud all the things he had kept inside for so long now.

Just when Chris began to give up hope, she heard his voice.

"Do you think I'm cynical, Chris?"

The question was unexpected. She wasn't quite sure what to make of it. She unconsciously reverted to her role of therapist when she countered quietly, "Do you?"

"I suppose I am." A bittersweet smile touched his lips. "Denise used to say I was born that way. And in a way, I guess she was right."

Chris wrapped her arms around her knees and leaned forward. "What makes you say that?"

"When I was a kid, it always made me angry when I thought about my parents and the totally separate lives they lived. I used to wonder how in God's name they had ever managed to produce a child. I was twelve when Denise was born, and even then I thought it nothing short of a miracle."

Chris had no trouble picturing Logan as a young boy—older, wiser than his years. Alone and unloved, as no innocent child could possibly deserve.

"But that's exactly what she was," he continued softly. "A miracle. Oh, I won't deny that having a baby in the house—and a sister yet—took some getting used to, even though I was only home on weekends and during the summer. At first she was like a toy, another novelty."

The story emerged slowly, sometimes haltingly. Chris soon learned that it wasn't long before Logan discovered that his sister gave without question the one thing that had been so lacking in his life—her unqualified love.

"No one could have been closer than Denise and I, in spite of the difference in our ages. Even when I joined the Bureau, I spent every chance I could with her. Why, she even called me clear across the country to get my approval before she went out on her first date! I grew up helping take care of her, disciplining her, protecting and playing with her...."

Giving her everything he'd never had. Chris's heart began to ache.

"I was assigned to Miami the year she graduated from college. She decided to spend the summer with me. I don't know, Chris. Maybe it had something to do with being fresh out of college; she was so full of hopes and dreams, so... so bursting with life. She had everything all planned out. In the fall she'd get a job, and in the meantime I could see about getting a permanent assignment. And the first order of business, she always said, was buying a house together. A home, a *real* home, because that was something we'd never had. She wanted it so badly. *I* wanted it just as badly for her sake. My parents' money never meant anything to me. It meant even less to Denise. But for the first time in my life, I started to think that maybe she was right. That maybe we really could be happy, in spite of our background, and not *because* of it."

Logan stopped, and Chris stole a glance at him. As her eyes swept over his taut profile, an inexplicable feeling of foreboding washed over her. Her stomach knotted. His face had gone expressionless, and she sensed that it was the only way he could manage whatever it was he was about to disclose. Still, the edge in his voice revealed how difficult this was for him.

"I should have known it was too good to be true, but I was too caught up in thinking about the future to think about the past—*my* past." His voice plunged to a whisper. Chris had to strain to hear him. "Someone had been following Denise—tracking her every move—and no one even suspected, least of all me. She was snatched from her car early one evening just a block away from my apartment."

Chris's eyes widened. "She was kidnapped...because of your parents' wealth?"

"That was my first thought, too. Believe me, I'd never had much use for my father, but at that moment I blamed my parents, thinking that someone had found out she was wealthy and hoped to make off with a fortune in ransom money." His mouth twisted derisively. His tone was hard and filled with self-condemnation. "But it had nothing to do with them at all, Chris. Denise was kidnapped because of me. *Me!*"

An icy chill ran through her.

"There were witnesses who saw a man pull her from her car and into another. Someone copied down the license number of the car, and the police put out an attempt-to-locate on the car. The woman who got the license number also got a good look at the man who grabbed Denise. I knew—" his eyes closed "—I knew the minute she described him who had taken her. And I knew he didn't really want Denise. He wanted me."

"You!" Her lips parted. "But why?"

"Denise was kidnapped by a man named Sonny Rossini." His gaze met hers. "A man I helped put in prison years earlier. He was a hit man for one of the organized crime families in New York. The Feds had been after him for years. It was my first big undercover case—what a coup," he added bitterly.

Chris's shock gave way to a prickly feeling of comprehension. "So this man snatched Denise to get to you."

His eyes flickered. "Somehow Rossini managed to find out where I was living. Denise was just an innocent pawn in a game of cat and mouse. He must have been stalking her. He knew she was my sister. He knew how much she meant to me."

"But if he was in prison... Why was he out? Did he escape?"

"Oh, no. He was out on parole." His tone dripped with sarcasm. "Rossini got a light sentence thanks to my father, who had represented Rossini's boss on numerous occasions. He's clever, dear old Dad." The frigid coldness that entered Logan's eyes was almost frightening. "A master at using anything he can to plant that seed of doubt in the jury's mind. He's slick and cunning, just like the scum he represents."

Chris's stomach churned sickeningly. No wonder Logan despised his father. It was more than that he and his father worked on opposite sides of the fence where the law was concerned. Far more. "And Denise?" She spoke quickly, wanting to have this exchange over with, yet dreading what was to come. "What happened to her?"

"The car was spotted at a house a few hours later. I don't know what was in Rossini's mind. Maybe he wanted an exchange—me for Denise. Or maybe he knew he could draw me out if I knew he had her." A muscle tensed in his cheek. "I knew there would be no bargaining with a man like Rossini. And he knew that I knew. He was clever. Conniving. Cruel. I have never doubted that he'd been planning his revenge from the moment he was sentenced, knowing that someday he'd be free. There's no doubt in my mind that he knew I'd do anything—anything!—to get my sister back."

He stopped, and she was achingly aware of his violent inner struggle. Chris had only to look at his face to realize the hurt and anger and resentment that still roiled away inside him.

"The Miami police had already informed my boss as soon as they knew what they had. I was under strict orders not to do anything on my own, but I did it anyway. The house where the car had been spotted was under observation, and we knew Rossini was inside. I went there and bluffed my way through—told the officer in charge I'd been called in as negotiator due to the special circumstances.

"Rossini may have guessed he was being watched, but the decision hadn't been made yet on what action the police were going to take. They were afraid if they openly evacuated, they'd give themselves away. I figured I'd have the element of surprise on my side. By the time the police realized they'd been duped, it was too late to do anything. I sneaked up to the house and kicked in the door. The first thing I saw was Denise. She was sitting on the floor not three feet away from me." Logan swallowed, and closed his eyes. When they snapped open once more, the pain Chris glimpsed was like a bottomless well. "I'll never forget the look on her face when I burst through the door. It all happened so fast. There was such trust in her eyes. She jumped up and lurched toward me. My God, she was so close, close enough to touch...."

An icy coldness gripped Chris. "And then?"

"God, Chris, I don't know. Maybe I wasn't thinking clearly. Maybe I was just so relieved to see that he hadn't hurt her... All of a sudden Rossini just charged out of nowhere. Before I knew what hit me, he slammed the butt of the rifle in my stomach and shoved me outside and down the porch stairs. I heard a shot—" His voice cracked. When it finally resumed, it was so raw and filled with anguish that Chris felt as if a knife were turning in her breast. "He killed her, Chris. He killed my sister, just to get back at me. Nothing in the world could have hurt me more, and he knew it. He knew it...." The seconds ticked by. "There was already a

S.W.A.T. team in place. When Rossini moved into the doorway, he was taken out by a sharpshooter.''

But Chris scarcely heard. In her mind's eye, she could see everything that had happened...in slow motion, in living color. And she knew that Logan felt he was the one who should have died. There was no need for him to say the words. Chris knew it as surely as she knew that he had suffered every day since.

How she came to be on her knees beside him she never knew. A trembling hand reached out to find his lean cheek wet with tears. ''I'm sorry,'' she choked out. ''For you to have to tell me today...of all days. Why did it have to be *today*? I'm sorry about Denise. I'm sorry I made you go through this....''

Strong arms closed around her and drew her close. Her cheek rested against Logan's, but it wasn't until their tears joined that Chris realized she was crying, too, her throat clogged with emotion. Her heart ached for the lonely little boy Logan had been, the embittered man he had become.

Her body against his unraveled a flurry of emotions in Logan, the least of which were desire and tenderness. He felt humbled by her sensitivity, oddly proud that she cared enough to shed tears over his loss.

He drew back and framed her face with his hands. His thumbs skimmed the glistening tears, wet and warm, taking away the chill of remembrance. ''Don't,'' he whispered. ''Don't cry for me, Chris.''

Her lips trembled. ''I can't help it. You'd already been hurt so much. It's not fair—it's just not fair!'' The words were torn from her. ''You, of all people didn't deserve to be hurt anymore!''

Logan was silent for a time. His arm slid around her back. He eased down to the pillow, taking her with him. She breathed a wordless sigh of relief when she saw that some of the awful bleakness had left his face. Tucked in the curve beneath his shoulder, Chris waited for him to speak.

"Life is rarely fair," he murmured finally. "But it's true that while God takes with one hand, he gives with the other. I won't lie and say that I wasn't bitter and resentful, because I was. I hated myself because I felt I had failed Denise. I'd lie awake night after night, because every time I closed my eyes, I saw Denise. And for months, I didn't care about anyone or anything. Suffering was the only thing that made me feel alive."

Logan turned his head to find a single tear sliding down her cheek. With his thumb, he gently wiped it away, his eyes never leaving hers. "But the world is never constant, always changing. A child falls, he picks himself up; after an earthquake, a flood, we build and renew, we start all over again.... But these past few days of being apart from you has made me realize—it's *you* who has finally given me that sense of renewal, Chris. You've made me feel as if I've just now found a part of myself that I never even realized existed."

Her eyes were wide and glistening. Everything she felt at hearing him reveal the depths of his soul was reflected in the doe-soft warmth of her eyes. Pity was the one thing Logan would never accept from anyone. But Chris didn't feel pity for him. She simply *felt* for him, and there was a world of difference.

He leaned up on an elbow, staring down at her through the shadowed darkness. He wanted to be everything to her. Friend. Protector. Lover. He swallowed, struggling for control of his runaway emotions. "Tell me—" his voice was hoarse "—tell me I'm not the only one to feel this way."

His plea went straight to her heart. If ever there was a time for honesty, total honesty, it was now. "Oh, Logan," she whispered brokenly. "I thought I'd die this past weekend. I was so afraid you were still angry with me!"

"About the other night? The argument we had?"

She bit her lip; it was all the answer Logan needed.

His eyes darkened. "I'm sorry, Chris." His voice was rough with emotion. "I shouldn't have kissed you—"

Her fingers rested on his lips for an instant, stifling whatever he was about to say. "No," she whispered, and all at once she was quiveringly aware of his closeness, the muscled stretch of thigh that paralleled her own. "You were right, Logan. It was bound to happen, and I was a fool for not seeing it sooner. And I was wrong for not wanting it to."

She had never looked more desirable than she did at that moment, her hair loose and flowing over her shoulders. She held his gaze, and in the glow of the firelight, her cheeks were tinged with pink. But her faint shyness only made her all the more bewitching.

Uttering a silent prayer, he reached out a hand. His fingers slid down her cheek, over the curve of her jaw and down her throat. For a heartstopping second, his fingers rested on the frantic throb of her heart. "Then you won't be angry if I kiss you again?" His tone was painfully husky.

"I think I'll go insane if you *don't*."

His head slowly lowered. She sighed when his mouth finally reached hers. He kissed her then, sweetly, tenderly, his lips barely skimming hers. He drew her close but held her as if she were infinitely precious.

Afterward she smiled at him with beguiling innocence. It was the smile of a woman, deep and mysterious. It was the smile of a child, blind and innocent, a child who had not yet learned how to fear. This time when he kissed her, something gave way deep inside him.

His lips claimed hers. Once. Twice. Long and lingeringly.

"Chris," he said into her mouth, and then again. "*Chris.*" The sound carried such torment, such desperate longing that she felt helpless. She and Logan had been through so much . . . so much. In spite of what he had said, could either one of them even *hope* to find happiness again?

But as his lips moved with yearning sweetness over hers, all doubt fled as suddenly as it had made itself known. She was achingly conscious of the heat and hardness of his male body against hers. He was so warm. So strong. And they had both been alone too long.

"Oh, Chris." He released a long sigh, his forehead resting against hers. "That's all I've been able to think about, ever since I kissed you that first time." He eased down to her side, his fingers brushing a wayward curl from her cheek. "I didn't hurt you, did I?" His voice had turned low and urgent. He braced himself above her, staring down at her and demanding an answer.

She knew instinctively that he referred to Friday night. A tremor went through her at the memory. Chris shook her head, her eyes clinging to his.

Above her, he went absolutely still. But inside he was shaking. "The truth, Chris." He remembered crushing her against him, trapping the softness of her mouth beneath his with bruising intensity. "Ever since then I've been afraid that I was too rough, too hard—"

She laid a hand on his forearm, feeling the rigid tension there. "You weren't." She gazed at him, knowing but not caring that everything she felt was exposed in her eyes.

"I want to make it up to you. I want to show you that I'm not as hard as I look—"

That made her smile. "No?" she teased. "I'm not so sure." Her arms slid around his neck, her eyes on his mouth. Tangling her fingers in the thick darkness of his hair, she brought his head down to hers.

Everything was suddenly magnified a hundredfold. The sound of flames licking up the chimney, her breathing and his, the pounding of her heart, the heavy pressure of his chest against hers.

"And if I'm not, I will be shortly." His mouth softened with amusement, but then his expression turned serious. He caught a strand of her golden-brown hair and toyed with it idly. The greedy curl grasped his finger and clung. "This isn't wrong, Chris. What we have is special. Something very special."

A peaceful sense of inevitability swept over her. Something special? Logan was a friend, a man she had come to know and trust. He was all those things and more, and it was just as he had said. It wasn't wrong to want or need someone, and she *did* want him. She also needed him as she had never needed anyone in her life. And soon...soon he would be her lover, because it could be no other way.

"I know that." Her smile was sweet and pure, but she found she was shaking inside as she gathered every ounce of her courage. "Stay with me," she whispered. "Tonight. Please stay with me."

He stared at her endlessly, and she feared he would refuse. But then he laid his palm against the smooth curve of her cheek and smiled, that rare, beautiful smile that transformed his whole face. "I hope there's not a Gary Cooper movie on later," he murmured. His fingers slid lingeringly down her throat.

Her laugh was breathless. "I guess that means you won't let me fall asleep on you this time."

Never before had his eyes been so pure a blue, the color of the morning sky and just as clear. "I may not let you sleep the entire night," he murmured.

His head dipped. She thrilled to the wholly male stamp of possessiveness. She tasted chocolate on his lips, opening her own to the gentle demand of his tongue and shivering at the boldly swirling intrusion. The contact was new. Exciting. A little scary, perhaps, but it was a thrilling kind of fear, like a wild roller-coaster ride that left one overwhelmed but exhilarated.

Her hands gauged the shape of his back, from shoulders to waist. Unable to help herself, she tugged his shirt free from his belt and slid her hands beneath. His skin was taut and smooth. She thrilled to the feel of muscle and bone.

She felt bereft when he finally released her mouth, but he only finished what she had started. His gaze never left hers as he reared back and began to unbutton his shirt. Chris sat up, aware of an odd melting sensation deep inside as she watched him undress. Firelight flickered over lean muscle, gilding his body a muted shade of gold. He was all lean, sinewed limbs, coated with dark brown hair that grew darker and thicker on his chest and abdomen; she experienced a wild urge to slide her fingers through it to see if it was as silky as it looked. She had never seen a more perfect male body. Not, she thought with a giddy inner laugh, that she had seen all that many men unclothed.

She was far from naive, and she recognized that Logan was a strikingly attractive man who certainly hadn't been celibate all of his adult life. He was worldly. Sophisticated. She realized helplessly that undoubtedly there had been other women in his life, women who were skilled and experienced in the art of pleasing a man. Chris's only experience had been with Bill.

Logan dropped down beside her, wearing only a brief pair of men's underwear, and she was suddenly glad. "What are you thinking?" he asked softly.

She gnawed her lip uncertainly, her voice tentative. "You know the other night, when we were talking about Diane?"

He nodded, his gaze riveted to her profile.

Chris's mind was racing. Though she was still slender and trim, she was thirty-four years old. And then there were the five pounds she'd gained last year.... She made a vain attempt at a smile. "Maybe I should have taken you home and introduced the two of you. You might be better off with her, after all."

Something flickered on his face, something hard and swift and decisive. But he must have sensed the source of her uncertainty, because he grasped her shoulders. "You're the one I want," he said with quiet intensity. "*You*, no other."

"But I-I'm not sure you understand." She hesitated. "You see, I've never—"

"Been with any other man but Bill," he finished for her calmly. Before she had a chance to respond, his hand came up to gently turn her face to his. His thumb beneath her chin dictated that her eyes meet his. "Don't you think I know that, Chris?" he asked softly. Even as he said the words, he wished he'd met her fifteen years ago. That he, and not Bill Michaels, had been the first to teach her about love and loving.

The uncertainty slowly left her eyes. "Now," he added, his eyes sliding over her, "do you think we could get rid of this?" He gave a meaningful tug on the hem of her sweater.

Logan felt his heart turn over as her eyes began to dance. "Only if you tell me what *you're* thinking."

It was a challenge he didn't mind complying with in the least. He seized her hand and carried it to his lips. Pressing a kiss into her palm, he murmured, "Only that I've waited a lifetime to meet someone like you."

If any doubt had remained in her mind, it would have disintegrated with his husky declaration. There would be no turning back now, for either of them. Chris sensed Logan's need that this last, final step belong to her.

Her heart was pounding when she pulled the sweater over her head, then pushed her jeans from her legs. All the while, silver-blue eyes watched her, alight with a slow, burning flame. It was the intensity of that flame that set her fingers to trembling, so much so that she had trouble with the clasp of her bra. His strong hands closed over her shoulders and pulled her around so that his lean, hard fingers had access to her back. A single deft movement and the garment was tossed impatiently aside.

His hands were warm as he once again turned her to him. They faced each other, chest to chest, thigh to thigh, only a breath apart.

Never in a million years would she forget the look on his face. It was so incredibly gentle, so tenderly possessive it made her want to cry. She would carry the memory of it deep in her heart for a long time to come.

His hands coasted down her arms, kindling a tingle of sensation in their wake. She felt the heat of his gaze burn through her as he sought the pouting thrust of her breasts. "God, you're lovely," he murmured, eyes intent.

Something inside her melted. Chris was suddenly glad she wasn't standing; her legs wouldn't have held her.

Her gaze touched on the width of his shoulders, the taut hardness of his arms. Except for the dark fur on his chest and abdomen, his skin was smooth and sleek, gilded a gleaming shade of gold by the light from the fire.

Feminine softness yielded to bold, masculine strength as Logan eased her back upon the pillow. His weight braced on his forearms, he rested his forehead against hers. "Are you sure," he asked very quietly, "this is what you want?"

Chris looked into his face and saw all that made him the man he was: his caring, his strength, his sensitivity. She was seldom at a loss for words, but with the depth of emotion that swept over her, she found herself struggling to find the right words. "I don't think I realized it at the time," she told him softly, "but when you came into my life, I needed someone to talk to, someone to share the little everyday things that people sometimes take for granted." She paused. "I needed a friend rather badly, Logan."

There was a heartbeat of silence.

"And now?" Low as his voice was, Chris detected both strain and an uncharacteristic uncertainty in the question.

Her arms slipped around his neck, her fingers knotting in his hair. "And now I need you even more," she whispered.

Logan closed his eyes, wanting to brand this moment forever into his soul. *I need you.* Such simple words, yet no one had ever said them to him before. His eyes flickered open and he smiled at her, his heart so full he thought it might burst. He kissed her breathlessly parted lips with gentle thoroughness, putting everything he felt for her in that one sweet caress. When he drew back, he searched her eyes and saw only pleasure, no shadows or fear.

With a muffled groan, his mouth captured hers once more, fierce and tender all at once. Chris responded with a breathless little sigh, and soon the room began to swirl in a vague dark mist where the only thing that was real was the feel of his hands on her body, stroking, caressing, learning all the secret places that gave her the most pleasure. His endless, drugging kisses, the intimate glide of his tongue against hers, reawakened her to the rhythm of love. Her heart went wild and she reached for him, digging her fingers into the sleek flesh of his shoulders.

It felt just as wonderful to be able to touch him like this. To explore and tantalize and indulge every curiosity she had secretly harbored about his body. The skin on either side of his ribs was soft, as smooth as a baby's. From there she raked her fingers through the mat of hair on his chest, tested the resiliency of muscle and bone. Yes, she thought again, oh, yes... It was even more wonderful to be making love with him like this.

Her fingers clung to his arms as his mouth slid with slow heat down her chest, then pursued a relentless path up the burgeoning fullness of her breast. Her breath caught as his warm breath caressed her. She nearly cried out when his tongue swirled around first one nipple and then the other. A cramping excitement raced through her as he lingered there, lavishing first one nipple and then the other, sucking with a rhythmic tugging that inflamed them both.

It wasn't until she saw his eyes, bright and smoldering with a pale blue flame, that she realized how much he was holding back.

"Lord, what you do to me," he breathed. His mouth was buried at the hollow of her throat while his hands outlined a searing path to catch her hips in his hands. Tenderness and a fierce desire rained down at her as he raised his head to gaze at her. His palms slid under her buttocks and cupped her firmly against the fiery throb of his hardness. His legs parted hers; Chris shivered and arched unconsciously toward his heated strength. Mouths sealed, limbs entwined, their breath swirled and mingled as he slowly filled the warm velvet of her body, claiming all of her with a bold surge of power that robbed him of breath and wrung a cry of surprise and delight from the tempting lips trapped beneath his own.

The outside world ceased to exist. There were only the sounds of their loving, the crackle and hiss of the fire blazing in the hearth before they were swept up in a torrent of passion. And when it was over, Logan gathered Chris against his body, sheltering her, holding her close as they drifted slowly back to earth.

He kissed her then, and her eyes fluttered open. She smiled at him, the drowsy smile of a woman satiated and fulfilled.

And Logan had one last thought before a blessed contentment more pure than anything he had ever known filled his heart and soul. He had been wrong after all. This was more than something special. What he and Chris shared was much more than two people reaching out because of a deep-seated need for another.

This was love.

IT WAS MIDNIGHT, the darkest, most forbidding time in the forest.

But the man in the cabin found the shrouded landscape, the looming shadows of giant fir trees that stood sentinel in the clearing, rather comforting.

He sat in the rocking chair, rocking back and forth, finding the creak as soothing as he did the silence. His callused hands fingering the dainty lace of the afghan, his mind conjuring up visions of the future. He saw her sitting here, in this very chair, the afghan draped around her shoulders to shield her from the cold. And then she would reach out to seek warmer comfort... *his* comfort.

The sound ceased for a moment, and the man tipped his head back. Love was a funny emotion, he reflected. There was once a time when he thought he'd never love again. The other one had done that to him, he reflected. She had fed a burning resentment, made him hate her and yearn for her at one and the same time. Even now, the remembrance made him clench his fist. He had given her everything—everything! All that he was capable of giving. His home. His name. All that he possessed. But it hadn't been enough. Never enough. And how had she repaid him? By walking out on him. By denying him as her husband.

His eyes drifted across the planked wooden floor to the bed in the corner. But it didn't matter, not anymore, for he had found another. His lonely days, and even lonelier nights would soon come to an end.

The creaking resumed. The man smiled. The night continued its lonely vigil, and still the man continued to sit. Smiling and rocking. Smiling and rocking...

CHAPTER TWELVE

EARLY THE NEXT MORNING, Logan watched the woman still sleeping against his side. A thousand new emotions filtered through him as he gazed at her. He felt possessive of her, so possessive it almost scared the hell out of him. What if something should happen to her? To him? To them? He couldn't face the thought of never having her at his side, never seeing her or feeling the softness of her beneath him once more.

Denial of what he felt at this moment was inconceivable, yet for an instant he was stunned. He felt happy. Contented. And—complete. Wholly complete. In his entire life, he couldn't recall ever feeling this way; never dreamed he could be so blessed. He had been protective and loving when he was with Denise. But even then, it was as if there were something missing, the piece of the puzzle that would make him complete, make him happy. Happiness was something reserved for other people, people who led normal, everyday lives, people who didn't suffer the stigma of being the offspring of Robert Garrison.

His eyes softened as they moved over Christine's face, absorbing her every feature—the thick shadow of black lashes resting on her cheekbones, the freckles sprinkled across the bridge of her dainty nose and rose-dusted cheeks. There was an air of childlike innocence about her as she continued to sleep, her lips parted, her hair spread like honeyed silk across the pillow. She looked so fragile and so vulnerable. The restless week-end had taken its toll; there was still a faint smudge of purple beneath her eyes—not that he had helped the matter any. His grin was rueful as he thought of the night just past. They had alternately talked, made love, and talked again, sometimes dozing in between. There had been wonderful, sensual discoveries to be made, and they were eager to make them. It was nearly dawn when they had fallen into a light sleep. Even now, Logan had to curb the tempting impulse to kiss her into wakefulness and renew the magic of the night. Reluctantly he pulled his gaze from Chris and glanced curiously around her bedroom.

The early-morning light bathed the room with a rosy glow. It had been dark when he and Chris had entered last night, and neither one had been interested in anything but the other. Now he looked around, not at all surprised by what he found. There was nothing frilly or fancy about the furnishings; they were practical, homey and down-to-earth, much as Chris herself. The wide double bed was of antique brass, with a long cedar chest at the foot. The accents were of pine and oak, continuing the motif found in the rest of the house.

When his gaze returned to her face, he found her eyes open and looking directly into his.

"Hi," he said softly. He yearned to touch her, yet for a heart-stopping moment, he was unsure of the welcome he would find this morning in her bed.

"Hi," she returned gently, and then she smiled. It was a smile so breathtakingly sweet and beautiful he thought his lungs would burst with the emotion that swelled his chest. "What time is it?" she asked, her voice still husky with sleep.

"Seven o'clock." Logan watched as she ran a hand through her tousled hair. "Are you working today?"

She nodded. "I have a nine o'clock appointment."

"Unfortunately—" he propped himself up on his elbow "—so do I. I'm giving a presentation to the Downtown Merchants Association on keeping their business space secure."

"Certainly a timely topic."

"Mmm."

Something in his tone brought her eyes to his. His expression was rather admonishing. "Why are you looking at me like that?" she complained playfully. "I've been locking my doors lately."

"Only because I've been looking over your shoulder."

"That's not true!" She stuck out her tongue, then half rose, leaning back against the pillow, careful to keep the blankets tucked over her naked breasts.

"So modest already?" He couldn't resist teasing her. "You certainly weren't last night."

He enjoyed watching the slow blush that heightened the soft bloom in her cheeks, not entirely unaware that Chris was remembering the touch of his hands on her breasts, the heated fullness of him inside her. "A woman who still blushes." He sighed. "You are a rare breed indeed, Christine Michaels."

Chris's lips twitched. Though she tried to summon a righteous indignation, the feeling just wouldn't come. "And you," she accused without rancor, "are enjoying *making* me blush."

He leaned over and kissed the tip of her pert nose. "I think that waking up with you is the perfect way to start the day. I also think that I'm even more partial to freckles than I originally thought."

"Why," Chris asked dryly, "do I have the feeling there's more?"

"Because there is." She felt him smiling against her lips. "You *do* have freckles in the nicest places, you know." Before she could utter a protest, he had yanked the concealing blanket from her. "Like here—" a lean finger traced the upward swell of one breast "—and here." It traveled to the other.

"And I suppose you see what no one else sees." Her voice was threaded with amusement.

"Took the words right out of my mouth," he murmured. He raised his head to gaze at her before pulling the sheet up, but not before he'd dropped a kiss on each pink-tipped breast.

His lips curved into a wicked, suggestive smile, and it hit Chris right in the pit of her stomach just how ruggedly good-looking Logan was. His dark hair was appealingly tousled, lending his rugged features a boyish look in spite of the dark shadow on his jaw. Her pulse quickened.

But at the same instant, Chris also realized something else, and it was this which caused a well of tenderness inside her. She'd never seen Logan so relaxed and complacent, and suddenly Chris knew that Logan had been right after all. Oh, so right. What they had was special, and good, and she had no regrets about the night they had just spent together. When Logan pulled her into his arms, she went willingly and eagerly, rubbing her cheek against his shoulder, savoring the strength of his arms around her, the sound of his heart beating steadily beneath her ear.

Last night had paved the way for them to talk—really talk about everything Logan had gone through—the heartache of losing Denise and his resentment of his parents. They had spoken of it one last time as they lay before the fire, and it was then that Logan told her of his sister's funeral.

"My father scarcely said a word to me," he had recalled, his voice gritty with suppressed emotion, "except to say that he thought it was time I came home. And my mother...oh, she dabbed her eyes at all the right moments. But I couldn't help but wonder why they'd even bothered to come."

Chris had done her best to try to console him. "Some people find it hard to express their grief," she murmured.

His expression was shadowed. "Maybe," he conceded after a lengthy silence. "And maybe they do miss her—hell, I don't know." His jaw was hard as he stared into the dancing flames. "But nobody could miss her the way I have."

His grip on her naked shoulders was unyielding, but when he turned her mouth up for his kiss, it was slow and lingering and meltingly tender. And Chris was heartened by the feeling that, at long last, Denise's memory had finally been laid to rest.

It was while this thought was running through her mind that Logan laid a possessive hand on her abdomen. "You realize," he said with quiet emphasis, "that last night changes things between us."

Chris didn't pretend to misunderstand, nor could she look away from his penetrating gaze.

His eyes searched hers. "We can't go back to the way things were before," he added, his voice pitched very low. "We can't erase what happened." She heard him take a deep, unsteady breath. "Nor do I want to, Chris."

"No," she murmured, then fell silent for a moment. Even if she wanted to, she couldn't forget. The feelings she and Logan had for each other were too strong, too intense...and too new. She could make no promises or guarantees, and she wanted no false promises from Logan. Nor could she hide the truth from herself any longer. Her need for this man far outweighed any fears she might have had. She could only take things one day at a time, and hope that it was enough.

Her hand lifted to his face, shaping the jutting forcefulness of his jaw to her palm and loving the abrasive texture of the night's growth of beard. "I think," she told him softly, "we can go one better. Friends—and lovers."

He raised her chin with a forefinger, looking deeply into her eyes. Her heart turned over at the heartfelt emotion she glimpsed on his face. When he slowly lowered his head and kissed her mouth, Chris lost herself in the infinite gentleness of his touch, achingly aware that it was more than just a kiss. It was a gentle acceptance of everything he had just stated, everything she had offered, everything they had shared last night.

He reluctantly released her mouth, then smiled directly into her eyes. "Can I rephrase what I just said a few minutes ago?"

She slipped her arms around his shoulders, admiring with her fingertips the smooth flow of muscle, the heavy satin texture of his skin. "And what was that?"

"That waking up with you is the perfect way to start the day."

"And what would you rather say?"

His hand trailed gently over the slope of her shoulder. "Making love with you is the perfect way to start the day."

Her laugh was low and provocative. "But you don't know that yet, do you?"

He bore her back upon the pillows. "No," he agreed huskily. "But I think I soon will." Very slowly he pulled the sheet to her waist, staring at her velvet-tipped bare-ness with an unrestrained mixture of hunger and reverence. "God, you're pretty," he muttered intently.

"Pretty?" Her breath caught as his fingers strayed beneath the sheet and sought the smooth hollow of her belly, straying relentlessly downward. He stopped just short of her tender threshold. Her laugh was shaky. "So are you, Logan. Pretty hairy."

He merely smiled. "Aha," he murmured. "Is this some kind of word association game you psychologists like to play? Are you trying to pick my mind, Dr. Michaels?" Even as the words passed his lips, he had a thought: she had already stolen his heart.

Her pulse leaped at the fiery gleam in his eyes. Already there was a welter of excitement building inside her. "Only if you're willing," she parried breathlessly.

"Oh, I'm willing." His chuckle vibrated against her mouth as he nudged her bare breasts into the dark forest of hair on his chest, relishing the hazy glow of invitation on her face. "Would you like to see just how willing?"

He gave her no chance to respond as his mouth met hers again, his tongue mating with hers in a soft, fleeting caress. His fingers teased the quivering erectness of her nipples; he traced a flaming line lower to skim soft, vulnerable flesh. The intimacies grew bolder and more daring, the kisses longer and longer, urgent and more fierce until their mouths were fused together as if he needed the very essence of her for life itself. Logan needed her, as much as she needed him. At the realization, Chris felt something give way deep inside her. Their bodies arched together, seeking and straining with a reckless passion more powerful than anything they had ever known before.

Her legs shifted. Logan gasped as his fiery hardness brushed her irresistible feminine warmth. His eyes drifted closed as he settled within the silken prison of her thighs, groaning his pleasure as her body surrounded his. She was so tight. So smooth. His fingers tangled in her hair. His mouth sought hers with an almost frantic urgency as his body surged boldly against hers again and again, faster and faster, their loving as tempestuous and torrid as their joining last night had been gentle and tender. It was an outpouring of their deepest needs and desires... and, Chris confirmed, the perfect way to start a day.

THERE WAS A LOVELY ARRANGEMENT of white daisies and yellow carnations waiting for Chris when she arrived at her office later that morning. Strangely enough, the bubble of enthusiastic pleasure she expected didn't come. As usual, the card was unsigned. Jean shook her head and rolled her eyes heavenward. Chris summoned a smile and continued on into her office.

Jean's voice stopped her. "Aren't you going to take those with you?" Her voice reflected surprise.

Chris shook her head. "Let's let everyone enjoy them for a change."

Jean looked at her oddly, but said nothing.

Inside her office, Chris hung up her coat and sat down at her desk. She found that her hands were shaking, and she hid them in the pockets of her skirt to still their trembling.

Flowers again. This was the third week in a row. Why, suddenly, did she have the feeling that they weren't from Logan? It hadn't mattered that he'd denied it. She'd thought it was just a game. But now...

The message had been the same: "For a very special lady." If Logan had sent them, surely the message would have been more . . . romantic, perhaps. Or affectionate. Or even playfully secretive! But if he hadn't ordered them, who had? It was a question that was both puzzling and disturbing. An acquaintance? A patient? They were an extravagant item that not many could afford to send on a weekly basis.

Logan didn't breathe a word about the flowers when she spoke with him on the phone later that morning, and by then Chris had decided her reaction had been silly. Besides, with helping Ned investigate the robberies, Logan had enough on his mind without these mysterious flowers. And if they weren't from him, she didn't think he'd be pleased that someone else was sending her flowers. Maybe if she was lucky, they wouldn't come again.

In spite of the rocky beginning, it proved to be a productive workday. Tom Chamberlain had an appointment late that afternoon, and almost from the moment he walked into her office, she sensed a change in him. Though he had been doing much better, Chris had been afraid that the holiday might reverse the progress they had made. She was pleased that Tom seemed much more relaxed than she'd ever seen him, even happy.

She soon discovered the reason for his satisfaction. "I've met the most fantastic woman," he confided halfway through their session.

"Oh?" Her chair creaked as she leaned back, waiting for him to elaborate.

He appeared to hesitate, but only for a moment. "She works in my office building. I've known her for a while—just a passing acquaintance—but it turns out she's recently divorced, too. We've got quite a lot in common."

"Sounds like a good way to get the ball rolling," Chris observed. "Did you spend Christmas with her?"

He shook his head.

"How about your kids?" She probed very gently.

Tom shook his head again. "They spent the day with their mother."

Chris watched him closely, waiting for the familiar bleakness to enter his eyes, but it never came. "Did that bother you?"

"A little," he admitted. "But at least I'll have the boys this weekend."

She smiled. "Going to introduce your lady friend to them?"

He laughed. "I think it's a little soon for that. But to tell you the truth, Dr. Michaels, I think she and I are going to be seeing quite a lot of each other."

Chris was glad, for his sake. A female friend might prove just the impetus Tom needed to pull himself up once and for all. She only hoped that Tom took things slowly. The last thing he needed was to fall for another woman too hard and too fast, and end up substituting one heartache for another. His divorce had been traumatic, and he was only just getting over the hurt. Nonetheless, she felt confident enough about Tom's progress to change his weekly appointments to every other week instead.

Chris had lectures several nights that week, and Logan spent a lot of time running back and forth to Spokane where he'd been hired as a security consultant for an upcoming business development. Consequently they had little time together over the next few days, but they planned to welcome the new year with a quiet weekend together. Just thinking of it made Chris shiver with excitement.

But that was before Char called Chris at her office Thursday morning.

"Hi!" Her sister's voice rang out bright and cheery. "I'll bet I'm the last person you expected to hear from so soon!"

"I did just talk to you a few days ago," Chris teased. "Are you calling for all the gory little details?"

"About the man who stole you away from the rest of us?" Chris could almost see her grinning from ear to ear. "Seriously, though," Char added after a moment, "how *was* your Christmas?"

Chris sensed a different, silent question in her sister's voice. *Were you really okay,* she seemed to be asking, *or was it just a front for the rest of us?*

"I had," she answered softly, "the most wonderful Christmas I've spent in a long, long time."

"Thanks a lot!" Char's effort at a disdainful sniff didn't quite succeed. "But that reminds me—I suppose you're expecting me to ask when I get to meet this lucky guy you deserted us for."

"Something tells me it's coming," she murmured indulgently.

"Actually—" Char's laugh sounded almost apologetic "—it may be sooner than you think. You see, Chris, I'm calling to plead on your tender mercies—"

Chris's lips twitched. "I've been told on numerous occasions that older sisters don't have any."

"Then call it a favor to your poor, overworked brother-in-law," Char retorted promptly, "who has this once-in-a-lifetime chance to spend the last three-day weekend of the year alone with his wife tucked away at a ski lodge up near the Canadian border."

"The poor man," Chris returned. "Give him my sympathies, will you?"

It turned out that Char was calling to ask Chris to take care of Josh and Wendy for the weekend. "I'd ask Mom and Pop," Char went on quickly, "but they already have plans to go out on New Year's Eve with several other couples. I know this is sudden, but Rick just found out last night. Rick's boss had reservations for three nights—he'd planned to go hunting. But he has the flu, so he thought we might want to go up in his place. It's been ages since Rick and I have had a whole weekend to ourselves, and I thought as long as we'd be driving almost past your doorstep anyway..."

Chris hesitated only a second. She couldn't refuse; she couldn't hurt Char like that. "I'd be glad to take them, Char," she told her, allowing no time for second thoughts.

"Are you sure you don't mind?" Char asked. "I know Wendy will be thrilled to see you again. She's always asking when Aunt Chris is going to come visit again. And Josh is such a good baby. I know he won't give you any trouble—"

"Whoa!" Chris was aware of the anxiety in her sister's tone. "It's really no problem," she assured her firmly. "You and Rick deserve some time alone together. And it'll be good to see Josh and Wendy again," she continued, proud of her even tone. "We'll be fine, Char, really." And somehow, she knew that they would be. Herself, Wendy, Josh...and Logan. Oh, yes, Logan.

They made arrangements for Char and Rick to drop the kids off early Friday evening and stay until Monday. Chris told Logan of the phone call when they left her office together later that night. "You don't mind, do you?" she asked. A blast of frigid air greeted them as they exited her building, the light from the street-light spilling down from overhead.

They stopped beside his car. Logan's eyes had taken on an unholy gleam. "Which sister is this?" he asked, arching a roguish eyebrow.

Chris dug her hands into her pockets. "Char. Married. Two kids. A husband." She sent him a meaningful, sidelong glance, her own eyes full of impishness. "A *jealous* husband," she added.

He heaved a sigh, slipping the key into the lock. "Too bad," he murmured, his tone deceptively innocent. There was a brief but significant pause. "I was hoping it was Diane."

Chris responded by attempting a well-aimed jab at his rib cage. Logan counter-attacked by hauling her into his arms for a warm, thorough but definitely unchastising kiss that left her breathless and giddy.

But suddenly Logan raised his head, succumbing to a feeling that wouldn't be put aside. Someone was watching them, he thought curiously.

Hard, precise footsteps echoed on the pavement nearby.

His eyes narrowed. His muscles tensed as he searched the darkness. A door slammed. An engine roared to life. There was the sound of squealing tires.

Watching him, Chris tried not to be alarmed. "What is it?" she asked quickly.

He scanned the shadows a moment longer, then caught her gaze. "Nothing, I guess." He smiled at her and tucked her hand into the crook of his arm. "Let's go home."

THE MAN'S FIRST REACTION was one of disbelief. He found it almost impossible to believe that *she*—so sweet, so loving, so giving—could have done this to him.

Hours later, the cabin door crashed violently open. He stood there, silent and frozen in the chilling darkness and felt his soul fill with an all-consuming anger. A fisted hand shot out and grabbed a crystal vase, a vase he'd bought for her. The next moment he was staring at its shattered remains, feeling as if his life were breaking apart before his very eyes.

And only one thought ran through his mind that entire sleepless night. Betrayed. Betrayed by a woman . . . yet again.

CHAPTER THIRTEEN

AT THE PROSPECT of Logan meeting Char and Rick, Chris found she was as nervous as a teenager bringing home her first date for the inevitable parental inspection and introduction. It struck her that it was as much for Logan's sake that she wanted him to be liked and accepted, but it did nothing to lessen her fears.

She might have known her worries were for nothing, however. There was no mistaking Logan's possessive manner when Char and Rick pulled into the drive Friday night and piled out of the car. Chris and Logan stood on the back porch, his hand riding casually on her waist. She recalled the conversation they'd had over dinner less than an hour before.

"Would you rather that I left before Char and her husband arrive?" he'd asked rather offhandedly. "It's no problem," he added quickly. "Especially if it's going to make things awkward for you."

Chris had looked at him, surprised that he'd even asked. "Don't be silly! I want you here," she protested. Then her eyes began to dance. "Even though I know you're pining away because it's Char and not Diane who's coming."

"If I'm pining away, it's definitely not for Diane." And with a slow, burning gaze, he let her know exactly what he meant, which made it all the more surprising when his expression again became serious. "Do you have any idea," he asked very quietly, "how much I want you?"

It was the one thing in the world she wanted to hear—the one thing she *needed* to hear—yet Chris unexpectedly found she couldn't meet his intense gaze. The easy camaraderie between the two of them that had existed all week transcended all that had gone before. But there had been a few times, times like right now, where she was still a little awkward over their transition from friends to lovers.

She managed a smile. "I was beginning to wonder," she murmured, still not meeting his eyes. Though he had touched her, kissed her, held her, they had yet to spend another night together.

A lean hand reached out to capture her chin. With a finger beneath her chin, he brought her face up so that their eyes met. For the longest time he simply watched her, his gaze keen and penetrating, but dark with an emotion she couldn't quite fathom. Chris sensed that Logan was feeling his way as carefully as she.

He tested the texture of her lower lip with his thumb. It was soft, so soft he wanted to press his lips on hers and forget the outside world existed. And he wanted to confess...oh, so many things. Yet deep inside, he knew the time wasn't yet right. What he felt for Chris was more than physical. Far more. But everything they had was still so new and so tenuous. The last thing he wanted was to upset the delicate balance between them. She needed time to adjust; he needed to give her that time.

"I want what's best for you, Chris. The last thing I want is to push you." He appeared to hesitate, yet in that all-seeing, all-knowing way that he had, he seemed to divine exactly what was on her mind. "Believe me, if I haven't made love to you again, it wasn't because I wanted it that way," he finished huskily. "I just thought it might be wise for a few days."

There was an intimate quality to his voice that reminded her of the way he had whispered warm, sweet praises in her ear. And the thought of him holding his desire in check, for her and her alone, wasn't only touching. It was exciting as well.

"You're what's best for me," she said softly. "Don't you think I know that?" Her hand came up to cover his; she pressed a kiss into the warm roughness of his palm. "I need you, Logan."

His expression became so tender it made her throat tight. "And I need you." His chair scraped back and he pulled her into his arms. "Lord, how I need you!" he had muttered hoarsely, his lips taking hers with an almost desperate urgency.

Now, standing beside Logan on the back porch, Chris slipped her hand into his. His fingers closed about her own, solid and secure. And then all else was forgotten as Wendy charged up the steps. "Aunt Chris! Aunt Chris! Me and Josh get to stay here with you! Mommy's gonna bring us back a present, too, 'long as we're good."

Chris caught the four-year-old up in her arms. She was laughing when she met her sister's vibrant brown eyes. "Bribery already?" She shook her head dryly. "I never thought I'd see the day."

"Bribery?" Char wrinkled her nose, her foot on the top step. "I'll have you know, Dr. Michaels, that the word used nowadays is compromise."

Chris, still chuckling, reached out to hug her sister. Rick, carrying Josh, was the last to clamber onto the porch. Chris linked her arm through Logan's and made the introductions all around. She had barely finished when Wendy, who had scampered off in the direction of the kitchen, reappeared.

"Who are you?" she asked with unabashed candor, staring up at Logan.

Logan found a pair of wide brown eyes curiously examining his long length. An embarrassed Char opened her mouth, but before she had a chance to say anything, Logan spoke. "I'm Logan," he replied with an easiness that somehow surprised Chris. "And you're Wendy, right?" His eyes began to twinkle. "You don't look like a 'Josh' to me."

Wendy giggled. Char, visibly relieved, began to smile, but that was before her daughter posed the next question to the tall stranger.

"Mommy said this is where Aunt Chris lives. Do you live here, too?"

Char looked horrified at Wendy's frankness. Rick had transferred Josh to his mother's arms and had just opened the screen door to retrieve the luggage from the car, when his head whipped around and his eyes widened. Chris bit her lip to keep from laughing.

Logan dropped down to the little girl's level. He pointed toward the direction of the highway. "I live in the house down there. The one right after you turn in the drive." He glanced warmly up at Chris. "I'm going to help your Aunt Chris take care of you and your brother this weekend."

"You are?" If a four-year-old could chortle, then Wendy did so. "Are you gonna change Josh's diaper? Daddy doesn't like to," she went on. "Whenever he does, Mommy says he complains about it so much she'd rather do it herself."

Char closed her eyes and sagged against the door frame. "You sure you're up to this?" Her eyes traveled from Chris to Logan and back again. "By the time

Monday rolls around, she'll know everything there is to know about both of you—and even a few things you didn't know yourself."

Chris chuckled and stepped over to take Josh from her sister's arms, the action appearing far more casual than it really was. In truth, she was still a little fearful about Josh rekindling Scottie's memory.

"Go," she commanded her sister, softening the words with a smile. "Have a blast, don't feel guilty and don't worry about any of us." Soft, baby-fine hair tickled her chin. She glanced down to find that Josh had ducked his head and was fingering the buttons on her blouse. As if sensing her thoughts, he lifted his head. Wide brown eyes blinked up at her, and he grinned unexpectedly. Chris felt something melt inside her, and she brushed the soft downiness of his hair with her lips. Still smiling against his head, she lifted her gaze to Char. "Go," she repeated. "We'll be fine. All of us."

And at that moment, Chris had no doubts in her mind at all.

NOT UNEXPECTEDLY Wendy was wound up from the trip and the excitement of staying with her aunt. It was after eight, but Chris decided not to hustle her off to bed right away. She had set up one of the spare bedrooms for both Wendy and Josh, and Wendy was delighted when Chris told her she could unpack her suitcase and put her clothes into the bureau drawer. Chris and Logan exchanged amused glances as Wendy fastidiously fulfilled the task, her small chest filled with self-importance.

It wasn't long, though, before Josh began to fret. Chris changed him into his night diaper and zipped him into a fluffy blanket sleeper with brisk efficiency, a little amazed at how quickly the skills returned.

She warmed Josh's bottle, and sat down in the rocker near the fireplace. Wendy had settled into a corner with her favorite doll, and the room was quiet and cozy.

The baby eagerly reached for the bottle and pulled the nipple into his mouth, attacking it vigorously. Logan's half smile was indulgent; then his eyes flickered up to Chris.

There was a rather odd expression on his face, something she couldn't quite fathom. "What is it?" she asked softly.

He reached over to switch off the lamp near her. "Just thinking."

She raised her eyebrows. She watched as he leaned forward, resting his hands on his knees and linking his hands together. "So I see," she said with a faint smile, quickly dismissing the vague impression that he was stalling. "About what?"

He was silent for a long time. "I was just thinking," he murmured finally, "that you're a natural mother." His gaze never wavered from hers. It wasn't as if he were challenging her; it was more like he was testing her reaction to his words.

It was the kind of statement that didn't require a response, but Chris found herself floundering anyway. The way he was looking at her made her heart beat faster. She felt suddenly warm. Desired and desirous. She also wished desperately that she had the power to read his thoughts, but something warned her that would be heading toward dangerous ground.

And how right she would have been, for at that moment Logan could think of nothing he'd like better than to see Chris with a child at her breast, *their* child, nurturing the life that they had created. The thought was totally unexpected, almost alien, for Logan had never considered having a child of his own. His parents' shortcomings, and his own vulnerabilities had seen to that. He couldn't deny the surge of possessiveness that shot through him. But what would Chris say if she knew of his wistful imaginings? He wished he could believe that she would be pleased. That he couldn't caused a painfully acute tightening in his chest.

"Did you nurse Scottie?" He watched her face go from vaguely disturbed to slightly embarrassed. Her eyes lowered to the child she now held in her arms. Josh's mouth worked the nipple more slowly. His lashes had begun to droop.

Her smile slipped a notch. She steadied it, then nodded slowly, the tip of one finger picking up the bubble of formula at the corner of the baby's mouth. "I was home for three months with him," she said softly. "When I picked up my practice again, it was only part-time so I was still able to nurse him." He sensed her struggle before her eyes made the return trip to his. "That's quite a question coming from a man who's been a bachelor all his life."

Logan smiled slightly. "I'll admit I've never been around kids much. But I think I do know a little about nature, and breast-feeding seems to really be in vogue again." He inclined his head toward Wendy, still absorbed in her dolls. "I wonder," he murmured, "who'll get the privilege of telling this young lady all about the birds and the bees? Mom or Dad?"

Wendy's head shot up at that moment, and left them in no doubt that her hearing was indeed very keen.

"Mommy already told me about the birds and the bees," she announced matter-of-factly. "And the grass and the worms, too." With that, she jammed a hat over her doll's curls and went back to her own business.

Logan glanced over at Chris and found her choking back a laugh. It seemed Wendy couldn't have picked a better moment to lighten the intense atmosphere. "I think," he predicted dryly, "this promises to be quite a weekend."

He switched on the hall light when Chris rose to take Josh upstairs. Jean had a friend with an old but still serviceable crib, and Logan had put it together for Chris just last night. When Chris emerged from the spare room, he was waiting for her in the hall.

"Don't close the door," she said quickly, spying his hand on the door handle. His heart twisted at the urgent plea, and he silently cursed himself for being so unthinking. Josh was only a month older than Scottie had been when he died, and he'd done enough reading on SIDS to know that it usually afflicted infants less than a year old. Although only a single wall separated Josh from Chris, he knew of the unspoken fear present in her.

Wendy, who appeared to have a limitless store of energy, was still bright-eyed as ever when they returned downstairs. Her eyes lit up like hundred-watt light bulbs when Logan mentioned getting home to Annie and her puppies.

"Puppies?" She was fairly jumping up and down. "Your dog has puppies?"

He nodded, his eyes on Chris. She was smiling at Wendy's enthusiasm, but he could see how tired she was. "Tell you what," he said to the little girl. "If you go brush your teeth and get ready for bed now, I'll bring Annie and the pups up tomorrow."

That succeeded as nothing else would have. Chris shook her head. "Bribery," she pronounced with a grin.

Logan took a cue from the absent Char. "Compromise," he contradicted with a gleam in his eyes.

While Wendy was in the bathroom, Chris saw him to the front door. Her arms slipped around his neck. "I wish you could stay," she whispered.

His gaze drifted toward the stairway. He couldn't see Wendy, but he could definitely hear her. "Something tells me your niece is wise beyond her years already."

"Some excuse." She made a face, and Logan was glad to hear the note of amusement in her voice. "But you're right." She sighed. Nuzzling the warm hollow of his throat, she breathed in his warm, heady male scent.

His hand cupped her chin. "There'll be other times," he promised softly.

Chris felt an odd pang as she watched him walk away, his tall form swallowed by the darkness. *I hope so,* she prayed fervently. *Lord, but I hope so.*

CHRIS'S BACK DOOR was thrown open by a pajama-clad four-year-old early the next morning.

"Did you bring the puppies?" Wendy demanded.

Logan chuckled and pointed to the basket near his feet. Wendy squealed and would have rushed onto the porch in her bare feet if he hadn't quickly pulled the basket inside.

"Can I have this one? No, this one!" By the time Logan had stomped the snow from his feet and closed the door, she already had two squirming pups in her arms, one tan and one white. Annie was every inch the protective mother as she sat on her haunches, her front paws braced apart, her dainty ears lifted in silent question. Logan gently removed the white puppy and replaced it in the basket, then carefully showed the little girl how to hold the other.

She beamed when a small, rough tongue lapped her cheek. "Can I take him home?" she repeated. "Does he have a name yet?"

Logan chuckled. "Him is a her. And no, she doesn't have a name yet."

"Can I take her home?"

He hesitated at her hopefulness. "I don't mind, Wendy. But raising a puppy takes a lot of time and a lot of work from everyone in the family. When your mom and dad get back on Monday, that's something you'll have to ask them."

"I will," she promised, looking not the least bit bothered by the prospect. "I'm gonna call her Brownie."

Logan gave a mental sigh and hoped he hadn't raised her hopes too high. "Where's Aunt Chris?" he asked the youngster.

"Upstairs." Wendy beamed when the puppy she was holding licked her cheek. "Givin' Josh his bath."

Taking a bath with Josh would have been a more apt description. Chris was kneeling at the side of the claw-footed tub, still in her nightgown. The thin jersey was plastered to her skin, leaving nothing to the imagination...and Logan's imagination was having a field day. She had wisely pulled her hair back with a ribbon, but a trickle of water ran down her cheek. He longed to kiss it away. And he promised himself that he would—another time. For now, he was too busy enjoying the tantalizing glimpses of ivory-colored flesh.

It seemed like hours to Chris before she finally lifted a protesting Josh from the bathwater. Wrapping his slippery, wiggling body firmly in a towel, she rose and turned toward the door. She stopped short at the sight that met her eyes.

Logan was leaning against the frame, his arms crossed over his chest. His expression was ripe with amusement, his eyes glinting with a thoroughly male appreciation.

Warm color suffused her cheeks. "How long have you been there?" Why she even bothered with the question, she had no idea. His indolent stance suggested he'd been there for some time.

His smile widened. "Long enough," he murmured.

If her arms hadn't been full of a squirming, lively baby, Chris would have taken great pleasure in wrapping the nearest soggy towel around his neck. Instead, her eyes began to dance with an unholy gleam.

"Here," she said, and thrust Josh into his arms. His startled look was gratifying. "Why don't you take Josh into the spare room and keep an eye on him for a minute while I go get dressed."

The urge to dawdle was tempting, but Chris pulled on slacks and a sweater, washed her face and brushed her hair in less than five minutes.

Also for the second time in five minutes, she stopped short at the sight of Logan. He was on the edge of the twin bed Wendy had slept in, a bare-bottomed Josh sitting on his lap. With Josh looking up, one tiny hand exploring the hard contours of Logan's mouth, and Logan looking down, they appeared to be taking each other's measure, and each appeared quite pleased with the result.

"Some help you are," Chris chided. "Why isn't that young man dressed?" She picked up the towel that had been draped around Josh, then went in search of a diaper and clothes for the baby.

Logan scarcely noticed. He gestured helplessly with one hand while holding on to Josh with the other. The span of his hand nearly encompassed the baby's back. "He's so—so small," Logan marveled aloud.

Wendy chose that moment to walk into the room. "That's 'cause he's just a baby," she pronounced flatly. "Haven't you ever seen a baby before?"

Chris chuckled and reached for her nephew, patting Josh's naked bottom meaningfully. "Now I can see why you were with the FBI for so long. You *do* like to take chances, don't you?"

Wendy was busy rummaging through the contents of Josh's diaper bag. "Uh-oh, Aunt Chris." She looked up with concern. "Mommy forgot to put Josh's toys in."

Logan looked as worried as Wendy, but Chris merely shrugged. "We'll find something for him to play with."

Later that morning, Chris set the baby on the kitchen floor with several pots, pans, lids and a wooden spoon. Logan clearly thought she'd gone insane. Chris had the impression he'd have liked to go down and buy out the nearest toy store, but he changed his tune when Josh played with his makeshift toys for nearly an hour.

Nor had Chris ever seen Logan laugh as hard as he did when Wendy decided she wanted to make *pup*cakes after lunch. Luckily it didn't take Chris long to figure out what she meant. It was while chocolate cupcakes were baking in the oven that Wendy topped that one.

"What are we having for dinner, Aunt Chris?" she had asked.

Logan had laughed at her stricken look. With so much going on in her usually quiet household, Chris had completely forgotten about dinner. But it was Logan who came to her rescue. "We could go out," he suggested.

Wendy looked thrilled. "To a restaurant that serves water?" She began to bounce up and down. "Can we, Aunt Chris? Can we go to a restaurant that serves water?"

Logan was startled. Chris could almost hear him saying, Don't Char and Rick ever take this child out? Even Chris was momentarily stumped until Wendy added glumly, "The only place we ever go is McDonald's."

Logan lifted her onto his lap. "Then we'll go out for dinner." He tweaked her nose. "To a restaurant that serves water." How he managed to keep a straight face, Chris was never certain.

But even while it warmed Chris clear to her toes to see the way he responded to the two children, it was also a rather poignant reminder of just how much had been missing from Logan's life. It was almost with a sense of guilt that Chris acknowledged that her home life—her relationship with her sisters and her parents—was something she had always taken for granted. It hurt to realize how lonely Logan must have been, especially once Denise was gone. It hurt unbearably.

Wendy also took quite a fancy to Logan. It was Logan to whom she came to dress her Barbie dolls. Logan who took her ice-skating on the pond behind the house. Logan who allowed her to "help" paint Chris's utility room and back porch. She insisted on wearing an old cast-off shirt of his that dragged the floor, and Chris lost count of the times he stopped to patiently roll up Wendy's sleeves. She *knew* that neither one of them would forget the evening Wendy spent rummaging through Chris's cast-offs. She had paraded before them in outfit after outfit, hems dragging, necklines and sleeves plunging precariously low. But top honors went to the bra she'd put on backward, straps looped around her neck to keep it in place.

Then there was Josh. Logan though it was hilarious when Josh braced his tummy on the back of the sofa, eagerly making tiny handprints on the steamed-up picture window. He shared Josh's delight when playing with a crumpled up paper sack.

On Sunday afternoon, Logan fed the baby his bottle. Josh fell asleep on his shoulder, and when Chris peeked half an hour later, Logan hadn't moved to place him upstairs in the crib. The sight of his hands, so big and dark against the baby's soft plumpness, kindled a feeling that was part pain, part pleasure. He still hadn't moved when she checked an hour later, and Chris didn't pretend to misunderstand what kept him there in the rocker with Josh in his arms. Long ago, she'd spent too many afternoons rooted to that very chair, savoring the warmth and closeness of a tiny body, loath to put Scottie from her.

Yes, it was just the four of them that weekend. Cozy. Intimate. So much a family, it nearly broke her heart.

New Year's Day was crisp and clear and very cold. Nonetheless, early that afternoon, Logan took Wendy ice-skating one last time at the pond. When Josh woke up from his nap, Chris decided to brave the cold herself. After bundling Josh into his snowsuit, she shrugged into her warmest coat, a navy-blue hip-length jacket. She couldn't help but think of Logan's reaction as she pulled on a pair of bright red mittens and a pair of ear muffs.

Josh squinted his eyes against the glare of the winter sun. It had snowed the night before, leaving the world bright and glistening. The pond wasn't far, but it was hidden by towering spruce and stately firs. Chris trudged along the path, silently admiring the frozen scenery, inhaling the pine-scented air. Soft, powdery snow clung to the pines, occasionally sifting to the ground, helped along by the brisk breeze.

The landscape was brilliantly colored, breathtakingly clean and fresh looking. Chris loved the pleasant climate here in northern Idaho, from the delightfully gentle spring of the year to Indian-summer autumn with its vivid hues of gold and russet. But there was nothing like the sparkling white, blue and green canvas of sky and earth on a sunny winter day.

Josh bounced along on her hip, absorbing the new sights and sounds contentedly. He gave a grunt of recognition and stuck out his mittened hand when he caught sight of his sister skimming the ice, her braids and muffler flying along behind her. She was really quite good, but then Char had started her on skates when Wendy was only two.

Logan was nowhere in sight. Chris clamped her teeth against the icy bite of the wind and wrapped her arm more tightly around the baby. When she neared the edge of the pond, she opened her mouth to call out to Wendy. But a startled gasp was the only sound that emerged as a hard pair of arms snaked around her from behind. Chris had time only to inhale a stinging mouthful of air before she found herself pulled against a solid form, her mouth covered by hard, masculine lips that drove all other thought from her mind. The kiss was brief and warm, but so thorough it sent shivers racing down her spine . . . and not from the cold.

Releasing her, Logan's mouth relaxed into a grin. The next second, though, he had pulled off his leather gloves. After blowing into his hands, he rubbed them together briskly before replacing his gloves. "I don't see how Wendy can stand it," he said, his eyes on the little girl. Wendy had spotted Chris and was coming toward them at full speed. "I'm freezing out here," he complained.

Wendy arrived just in time to hear his last words. "That's 'cause you don't have a hat on," she informed him loftily.

"Well, well." He raised his eyebrows. "I can see who she's related to. Does she have a nose for snow, too?"

"It's a little early to have developed just yet," Chris answered him solemnly, then laughed when he jammed his hands into his pockets. "How come you're not out there on the ice with Wendy? You wouldn't be so cold if you kept your blood moving."

Logan greeted this observation with a growing smile. "I don't have any ice skates," he said softly, then paused.

Chris read the gleam in his eyes all too clearly. She couldn't resist teasing him. "Then maybe we should see about getting you a pair. When's your birthday?"

"February tenth. I think, though, that we're straying from—"

"February tenth!" she echoed. "Why, that's perfect. If we're lucky, we'll still have ice thick enough to skate on then!"

"Good." His smile deepened. "As I was saying, though, I think I know something that'll keep my blood moving—" he took Josh from her arms, set him on the blanket he'd been sitting on, then reached for her once more "—and it isn't ice-skating."

This time when he pulled her close and took possession of her mouth, it was a long, leisurely exploration that set Chris's senses swimming. A pair of small hands tugging on both their arms finally broke them apart. "Hey," Wendy shouted delightedly, "you guys smooch like Mommy and Daddy!"

Logan rested his forehead against Chris's. "My Lord," he complained, trying hard to smother a laugh but not quite succeeding. "She doesn't miss a thing, does she?"

Hazel eyes twinkled up at him. "Could it be—" she glanced around as if they were being watched, then lowered her voice to a conspiratorial whisper, "—that

Rick and Char have a future FBI agent on their hands?''

They headed back to the house soon after, but this time it was Chris who bore the brunt of his teasing when she admitted that it was too cold even for her.

Logan carried Josh on the way back, giving Chris the opportunity to study him without his being aware of it. He wore jeans and a sheepskin jacket, the fleecy collar pulled high against the icy nip of the wind. To Chris, he'd never looked more attractive or captivating, his lean cheeks ruddy with cold, and delicate flakes of snow glistening like crystal in his windblown hair.

A heady, powerful emotion surged through her. He was so tall. So inherently masculine...and he was hers. *Hers.* Suddenly she wanted desperately to believe that.

There'll be other times, he had said, less than three days ago. But all of a sudden, Chris wasn't so sure. There was a nagging doubt deep in her breast, and she couldn't prevent the terrible sense of foreboding that swept over her. She reached for him, her grip almost frantic as she clasped her fingers around his elbow. He glanced down at her in surprise, but when she managed to keep her smile glued in place, he said nothing.

Char and Rick had just pulled into the drive when they got back to the house. There was a rather noisy reunion between parents and children, then Logan held his breath after Wendy ran inside to proudly display the puppy. The discussion proved to be a short one; the kids' gear and one tan puppy were toted to the car. Char rolled her eyes when the two men stayed beside the car, glancing between Logan's BMW and the new station wagon Rick and Char had recently purchased.

''Man talk,'' Char sighed. ''Wait and see if I'm not right. Unless I say something, Rick will still be standing right there an hour from now." She shook her head expressively. "And they talk about women!"

It turned out that Char was right. Fifteen minutes later, the two men were still outside. In the kitchen, Char consulted her watch before pulling on her coat once again.

Near the screen door, Char gave Chris a long, thoughtful look. "You know," she said softly, still studying her sister's face, "I'm glad we left the kids here. Now I can see that you really are okay."

Chris pulled her sweater closer around her. "I told you I was," she reminded her.

Char grinned sheepishly. "But now that I've seen for myself, I *know* that you're okay. Besides, you know me. I was always the doubting Thomas among the three of us." She inclined her head, indicating Logan. "He's good for you, Chris," she said simply.

Chris silently and wholeheartedly agreed, but *good* somehow seemed much too inadequate a word to use.

Happy as she had been to see her parents, Wendy shed what seemed like buckets of tears at leaving Chris—and Logan. *Especially* Logan.

"I don't know when I'll see you again," she sobbed, flinging her arms around Logan.

Logan lifted her in his arms, chucking her gently beneath the chin. "Hey," he chided gently. "This isn't goodbye, you know. I'll see you again, Wendy."

Goodbye. At his use of the word, Chris felt an odd pang. Her throat tightened as she looked on.

"Promise?" Wendy raised her head and looked directly at Logan. "Promise you'll be here the next time I come to stay with Aunt Chris?"

Chris understood his slight hesitation completely. She sensed his eyes on her, but found herself unable to meet

his gaze. The next second she heard his voice, low but
sounding very sure of himself.

"I promise," he told the youngster, then smiled.
"Now *you* make sure your Mom and Dad bring you
back—soon."

When Rick finally turned the car in the opposite
direction, Wendy was dry-eyed, her face wreathed in
smiles as she continued to wave until they were out of
sight.

Chris remained where she was, battling a ridiculous
urge to cry. The car had long since disappeared from
view when an arm draped heavily across her shoulder.
The smile she directed at Logan was faint but genuine.
"Something tells me," she murmured, "that you've
conquered another female heart."

He neither agreed nor disagreed. Though his lips were
curved, there was an air of the utmost seriousness about
him as he steered her back into the house and into the
kitchen. He sat her at the table and pressed a warm cup
of coffee into her hands before pulling another chair up
to hers.

His eyes fastened on her with a gaze of penetrating
intensity. "Your niece," he said finally, "is quite a
charmer. She's almost as much of a delight as her aunt.
But much as I think Wendy will one day make some
man very lucky," he added softly, "I'm afraid my heart
is already taken."

There was a heartbeat of silence. In the seconds that
followed, Chris's heart began to thud. For one crazy,
mixed-up moment, she felt as if she were being torn in
two by a heartrending mixture of hope and fear.

Because she knew what Logan was going to
say...even before he said it.

CHAPTER FOURTEEN

BUT HIS FIRST WORDS weren't quite what she expected.

"I've always envied you your home, Chris. It's everything I've always wanted—" his mouth formed the tiniest of smiles "—but it's only lately that I realized it."

Her eyes clung to his. *Don't,* she wanted to cry. *Please don't do this to me. I'm not ready for this.*

"You have the best of both worlds, city and country," he went on. "The orchard, the barn, the pond . . . It's a great place." There was a heartbeat of silence. "Especially for a family."

Her hands were shaking so that she could scarcely hold the cup. She managed to set it on the table, unconsciously twisting her hands together and forcing a laugh past the tightness in her throat. "Are you trying to get me to sell out, Logan?"

She didn't know that Logan was fighting hard to keep his hands at his sides. He finally settled for pulling both her hands within his. At the touch of her icy-cold fingertips, a slow curl of dread began coiling in his stomach. Logan ignored it. He'd come this far, and he wasn't about to turn back now. Instead he shook his head and twined his fingers tightly through hers, as if he could infuse his heart, mind and body into hers.

"Do you have any idea how much you mean to me?" The look he gave her was devastatingly penetrating. "You've made me believe in things I never thought existed, Chris. Things I thought were forever beyond my reach."

With every word, with every breath, his voice took on a new intensity she'd never heard before. Her gaze was welded to his, drawn and held there by a force she was helpless to deny. She couldn't look away even if she wanted to.

He lifted one of her hands. His lips brushed across her knuckles. "I love you, Chris," he said, his voice very low. "I love you and I want you to marry me."

The silence that followed was nearly unbearable. Chris looked at Logan and saw all that made him the man he was: his strength, his caring, his sensitivity. His eyes had never been more silvery-blue, placid and serene on the surface, but shielding an intense, complex man that perhaps no one would ever completely understand. But there were no secrets between them now, nothing but emotions that were poignantly sweet...and painfully honest.

She couldn't shake the sensation that her whole life hinged on this one precarious moment. And perhaps she even resented him for it, for Logan was a man who had always planned his every move with cautious intent. His life had often depended on it. But in her own way, Chris was just as careful and precise as he was.

"Oh, Logan," she whispered, and there was a world of torment inside her. "Much as I want to, I can't." Her voice caught. "I just can't." Her eyes squeezed shut, only to flicker open again an instant later. His hands released hers, but she scarcely noticed. Every fiber in her body was focused on his face, and she almost cried out at the change in his expression. It was as if she could see him disappearing deep inside himself, and she hated herself for causing it.

Yet when he finally spoke, his voice was as raw as she felt inside. "Why, Chris? I know we haven't known each other long. Six weeks is—"

"That's not it," she denied. She shook her head firmly. "I felt close to you right from the start. And the last month has only made me realize just how strong that feeling is." She bit her lip, faltering beneath his relentless regard.

"I know you care for me, Chris." The edge in his voice revealed his frustration. "At least a little."

She took a deep, tormented breath. "More than just a little," she confessed unevenly. "Much more."

The silence spun out between them. Logan thought blackly that this whole thing must be a nightmare. Had he finally found happiness only to have it slip through his fingers once more? He couldn't fight the invading darkness that swept through him.

It was Chris who broke the brittle silence. "You don't understand, do you?"

He shook his head, his voice was cold. "No."

"Believe it or not," she whispered, "it's you I'm thinking of, though I'm not sure I can explain."

"Try," he said tersely.

The smile she attempted was an abject failure. "I know that we're good for each other. But did you ever think that maybe we met at a time when we both needed someone? If and when the day comes that you want someone else, I don't want to stand in your way."

The muscles in his jaw were rigid. "That won't happen." He dismissed her presumption curtly.

"But how do you know that?" Her hands spread helplessly. "How do you know that tomorrow, or a year from now, someone else won't come into your life? I know you, Logan. You'd feel honor bound to stay with me, and that's the one thing in the world I couldn't stand!"

His gaze flickered over her. She was so lovely. So vibrant and expressive. But she looked utterly defenseless as she sat before him, her hands linked before her in a gesture of uncertainty. And it was because he knew just how vulnerable she was that he hated himself for what he was about to do.

"I know what I want, Chris." He stared at her, painfully aware of the upheaval going on inside her. "I'm not an overeager adolescent who thinks the world revolves around sex. You and I already have something that few other people ever achieve. In my mind, there's nothing more solid than a relationship based on friendship and trust."

There was an awful pain in the region of her heart. "Then don't force me to make a decision I'm not sure I'm ready to make," she implored. "Not long ago, you said you wanted what was best for me. You said... you said you wouldn't push me."

His jaw hardened. His face was a mask of sheer determination, his eyes an endless well of pain. "Is that what you think I'm doing?" His voice was gritty with suppressed emotion. "Pushing you?"

"Aren't you?" She struggled against the awful tightness in her chest. *Please don't let me cry,* she pleaded to herself again and again.

The atmosphere in the room was stifling. This was agony for her. Logan knew it, and he wanted to stop it, but he didn't know how. "I've waited a lifetime for someone like you," he stated quietly. "I've waited a lifetime for *you*." The look he turned on her was so deep and intense, Chris felt as if she'd been turned inside out. "I think I've waited long enough."

With a tiny moan, she laid her hand on his jaw. Her fingers moved across the skin stretched tightly over his cheekbone, the lean roughness of the hollow below, as she sought desperately to ease the taut lines around his mouth.

"Don't you think I know that?" she whispered. It was sheer torture to hear the words aloud, but she knew that the truth, no matter how difficult for both of them to face, had to be spoken. Yet everything she had said—everything she was about to say—was like pouring salt on a raw, open wound. She swallowed, unable to go on for several long, agonizing seconds.

"I saw you this weekend with Josh and Wendy," she whispered unsteadily. "I saw how you looked at them, how you touched them. I saw the yearning in your eyes, a yearning maybe you weren't even aware of. And what I want, more than anything in the world, is to see you happy. Because you, more than anyone I know, deserve that chance. You deserve everything you've never had. A home. A family. Children who will love you as much as their mother does." Her throat was raw from the effort it took to breathe, to speak. "And if I could give that to you, I would. But I can't...and I'm not sure I'll ever be able to."

The anguish on her face was like a knife in his chest. In some crazy, mixed-up way, he knew that this was all tied in to her loss of Scottie. Though his conscience was reading him the riot act, he refused to acknowledge the plea in her eyes, not understanding it, suddenly not wanting to. He knew only that he was hurting as he'd never hurt before, and no matter what she said, some-how...*somehow* they could get through it.

He was on his feet, dragging her up with him. "It doesn't matter, Chris. The only thing that matters is us. We belong together, Chris. You know it and so do I."

He seized her shoulders and crushed her to him. "Tell me you don't want me," he said roughly. "Tell me you don't need me." He took her mouth in a searing kiss, parting her lips with a desperation born of a fear he was afraid to give in to.

They were both trembling when he finally wrenched his mouth away, and then each battled to control the fierce tide of runaway passion. They stood there in the middle of the kitchen, Logan's arms taut with need, Chris with her head resting weakly against his chest.

Chris was the first to stir, but the instant she raised her head, Logan captured one of her hands and guided it to his cheek. She opened her mouth to speak, but he never gave her the chance.

"Marry me, Chris. I won't lie and say that having a family doesn't matter." His eyes searched hers. "But I think that what we have is worth every little bit of heartache and more. Marry me, and we'll work the rest out later."

Everything she felt was exposed in her expressive features: the starkness of wanting, the desire she made no effort to hide. It was with a defeated resignation that he recognized the wordless resolution in her eyes. She was strong, he relented silently. In her own way, stronger than he.

His hand fell away from her. Through a haze of pain he heard her voice. "I can't," she whispered, her voice shaking. "I just can't. But that doesn't change what I feel for you. I want you to know that I—" her voice finally broke "—that I love you."

His eyes drifted closed. Logan wished like hell that he could walk away. A tiny voice inside urged that it would be easier now than later.

His eyes flicked open to stare directly into the cloudy depths of hers. "I know you do, Chris." He didn't bother to hide his bitterness. "But you're wrong if you think that makes this any easier for me."

He despised himself for the pain he was inflicting. He watched as her eyes flitted away, watched her swallow deeply and struggle for control of emotions he sensed were scattered in every direction.

"I need . . . some time," she whispered at last. "Will you give me that, Logan? As much time as I need to think about this?"

"And in the meantime?" He saw her flinch and despised himself further for his harshness.

Her eyes were wide on his face. "In the meantime, we'll just have to go on as we are. I'm sorry," she faltered, "but that's the best I can do."

His jaw tensed, but he nodded reluctantly. The concession was more than he had expected, but he couldn't stop himself from thinking bleakly that all the time in the world wouldn't change her mind.

He would have left then, but suddenly he heard her voice, a mere thread of sound . . . and betraying her as nothing else could have.

"Please, Logan, don't go. Don't leave me alone again."

Slowly he faced her once more. There was the unmistakable sheen of tears in her eyes, but her throat worked convulsively to hold them back. Logan's heart twisted.

They were no more than three feet apart, but the distance between them had never been greater. Yet he couldn't leave her. Not like this. Never like this.

Exactly who took the first step, he was never certain. Her arms slid around his waist, and she sagged against him weakly. Logan rested his cheek against her shiny hair. How many times, he tormented himself silently, would he hold her like this, wondering if it would be the last?

He gathered her more tightly against him, holding her as if he were afraid he would never see her again, never hold her in his arms. And that was exactly how he felt. For beyond the here and now, he wasn't sure that Chris would ever belong to him again.

HOW HE GOT THROUGH the next few days, Logan was never sure. He held Chris in his arms; he touched her and made love to her. But there was a part of her that she kept separate from him, as though she was afraid to give too much of herself.

As if that weren't enough, on Monday night someone broke into a bookkeeping firm, bypassing the alarm system his company had installed just one month earlier. He was at a loss to explain how it could have happened, but he did have a business reputation to protect. He sent the control panel back to the manufacturer to have it checked, but he had a hunch it wasn't an equipment failure; that someone was clever enough to have gotten by the system. That same night, an attorney's office was also hit.

At midnight Tuesday a man was assaulted and robbed at an automatic bank teller.

The next evening, there was a scathing editorial in the newspaper lambasting the police department for its "appalling lack of action and inability to protect the property and citizens of the city." Who, the editorial concluded, would be next?

Ned was convinced the burglar he'd been tracking was responsible in both instances, and Logan was inclined to agree. The loss of property wasn't the only concern. As Ned had predicted, someone had been hurt, and it was time the rampage ended. Whoever was responsible, whether they were random robberies or the result of a gang working together, they had to be stopped.

Logan was just as frustrated as Ned. He'd checked out the pawn shops and sale ads in the paper, but he'd come up with nothing.

In the meantime, the police had stepped up night patrols. Ned asked Logan to ride with him during the shift Wednesday night. Logan felt a little guilty, but maybe it would take his mind off Chris. Still, he didn't like the idea of leaving her alone the entire night, so he agreed to ride with Ned until midnight, but only after Chris had promised to keep the house locked up tight as a drum.

It was a quiet night. Most of the shops downtown were closed, and the people they encountered had a legitimate purpose for being on the streets. Even the police radio crackled and buzzed with only a handful of calls being dispatched, none of them critical.

Eleven-thirty found the big police cruiser rolling slowly down an alleyway between two sets of buildings, spotlighting back entrances and windows, looking for anything out of the ordinary. Ned pulled out onto the street, and Logan's eyes drifted to the service station on the corner. The pumps and service bays were blazing with lights. In the still silence of the night, they seemed stark and glaring.

The sign in the window said CLOSED.

His eyes narrowed. The instincts that would forever be a part of him surfaced abruptly. "Ned, what time does that gas station usually close?"

A frown crossed the other man's face. "Eleven, if I'm not mistaken."

"Then I think you'd better stop." Logan's voice was sharp. "Something's not right here."

Ned wasted no time in pulling to the curb. The two men jumped from the car and ran toward the service station, eyes darting, ears straining, all senses attuned to anything that might signal danger.

The small building was unlocked. Inside, the prone figure of a man was stretched on the cold tile floor, still and unmoving. There was a dark splotch of crimson on the back of his head.

Logan dropped to his knees beside him. He could hear Ned on the radio summoning an ambulance. He gently rolled the tall, gangly figure over, onto his back.

The pale face Logan found himself staring at was that of a boy, perhaps seventeen or so. His lashes fluttered open. He started to sit up, then fell back with a groan. "My head . . ."

"It's all right. There's an ambulance on the way." Logan's voice was firm and reassuring as he pressed a handkerchief to the oozing wound on the young man's head. Beneath the cloth, he could feel a lump the size of a golf ball.

Ned hunched down on the floor. "Can you tell me what happened, son?"

The attendant shook his head, still dazed. "I don't know...I remember serving a customer—he drove away and I came inside to close up. The door opened and I turned—" he grimaced "—that's the last thing I remember."

"Someone came inside?"

"I—I think so."

"Man? Woman?"

"A man, I think."

"Did you see what he was wearing?"

The boy squeezed his eyes shut for a second. "Not for sure," he muttered. "All I saw was a flash of brown moving toward me. I—that's all I remember."

The ambulance arrived then with a whirl of lights and sirens. Ned saw the injured man safely onto a gurney. By then, the station owner had arrived. The motive for the assault was clear—the contents of the till had been stolen.

Ned's expression was set and angry when they finally headed back to the station. "I've got a bad feeling about this," he muttered. "First that attack at the teller machine last night. And now this." He shook his head. "I've been afraid this might happen. This guy's getting bolder, all right, and I don't like it. I don't like it at all."

Logan didn't answer. He thought of Chris all alone, miles out of town. In spite of all the tension between them, he was suddenly anxious to get back to her.

LOGAN WASN'T THE ONLY ONE who was miserable that week. Hard as they tried to pretend otherwise, Chris was aware that after the night Logan had asked her to marry him, things just weren't the same. When they were together, they were almost painfully polite to each other, but neither seemed able to do anything about it. Only in the silence of the moon-shrouded night, when they clung together in the warmth of midnight fires, were they able to lose themselves in the heat of passion and find the contentment and fulfillment they both needed so desperately.

But with the inevitable dawn, all was as it had been before. Both of them reverted to their polite, careful facade. It was as if with the rising of the sun, it was time for each of them to retreat into their own private shell, while pretending that everything was as it should be and knowing that nothing would ever be the same again.

Chris hated it. She missed their closeness, the long talks they had shared, talks spiced with teasing and occasional quiet moments of silent understanding. Now their time alone was filled with a guarded wariness. Their brief respite of happiness had been shattered, and she had no one to blame but herself. She even found herself wondering bleakly if it wouldn't be better for both of them if they simply made a clean break.

Together... yet separate. They were like intimate strangers, strangers who loved with all the passion and fury of a raging tempest. And yet Logan's presence was everywhere. In her car when she drove to her office in the morning; in the kitchen when she washed the dishes; in the bathroom, where the smell of his aftershave lingered—he hadn't slept at the cottage at all this week.

She could have screamed with hurt and frustration every time she glimpsed the shuttered mask on Logan's face. She understood Logan's feelings; she understood why he was so cool and distant. She had hurt him unbearably with her refusal to marry him, but she knew it could be no other way. She had never felt so helpless. She was trapped by her own fears, trapped by her love for Logan—and there was no way out. Heartbreak lay in every direction.

The first Friday of the new year she made an attempt to bridge the gap between them. Her last appointment of the afternoon canceled, so she decided to make an early day of it. She hurried home, put Logan's favorite dish in the oven—lasagna—and headed for the shower.

She had just put the finishing touches on the table when Logan walked in the door, lines of exhaustion carved around his mouth. He looked so tense and on edge that her heart went out to him. He scarcely spared a second glance for Annie and the pups, who danced around his heels, and merely nodded when Chris told him that dinner wasn't quite ready.

She found him on the sofa a few minutes later, his head tilted back, his long legs sprawled out in front of him, his arm thrown over his eyes. He'd discarded his jacket and pulled off his tie. His shirt was open at the throat, revealing a rough tangle of masculine hairs. There was such an aura of raw and elemental vitality about him that merely looking at him caused her mouth to go dry.

Sensing her presence, Logan shifted his arm and stared at her.

Chris held out the tall glass she carried in her hand. "You look like you could use a good stiff drink."

"Amen to that." Sitting up, he took the drink from her. Their fingers never touched. "What is it?"

"Bourbon and water."

His brows lifted a fraction, registering mild surprise. "You've been holding out on me, I see."

Their eyes met and held. Chris still stood before him, feeling rather awkward. There was no sign of welcome on his face; indeed, she could find no trace of any emotion at all. "Don't you want it?" she asked finally.

Lean, dark fingers curled around the glass. Logan started to bring it to his lips, then stopped abruptly. His gaze never left hers as he set the drink aside. "Not just yet," he said softly. "You don't like the taste of it, do you?"

She didn't catch his meaning until his eyes dropped to her mouth. Chris had never been much of a drinker, even socially. The fifth of bourbon he'd accused her of hoarding was one she'd had tucked away in the cupboard for longer than she could remember.

"No." She shook her head, her voice oddly breathless.

A hard hand came out and caught hers. Logan pulled her down beside him, and then his other hand slid under her hair. Warm fingers curled around her nape. Looking straight into her eyes, he tugged her gently forward.

His lips grazed hers lightly...oh, so lightly, just barely making contact, the merest butterfly caress. It was a kiss that was scarcely a kiss at all, yet Chris had never felt more possessed. She relaxed for the first time in days.

"Now," Logan said, smiling slightly as he withdrew. "I'll have that drink."

He complimented her on the meal. Chris glowed at his praise, like a newlywed who had cooked her very first meal for her husband. At the thought, something inside her froze, but she firmly shoved the disturbing thought aside, unwilling to do or say anything that might break the tenuous peace of the moment.

They spoke briefly of the events of the day. Chris soon discovered the reason for Logan's look of strain when he'd arrived home. Last night, someone had broken into a dental office downtown, getting past one of his security systems—the second one that week. Needless to say, the dentist was up in arms, while Logan struggled to find out why the system had failed.

"Ned's burglar?" Chris speculated aloud.

"Could be," he agreed. "There was almost five thousand dollars' worth of office equipment stolen. Ned came out to take a look, but there was no sign of forced entry."

"That's par for the course?"

Logan hesitated. "Not always, and that's what's giving Ned such a headache. He still thinks all the robberies that have occurred lately are related, but he has nothing but gut instinct to tell him so. Personally," he added, "I'm inclined to agree."

"Maybe the one last night was an inside job," Chris suggested. "One of the dentist's employees."

His smile was grim. "That's what I thought, until I was informed in no uncertain terms by the dentist that it was impossible. His daughter works as his receptionist and bookkeeper, and his wife is his assistant." He mulled for a few seconds. "All three of them swear the system was armed when they left last night. There's no sign that it malfunctioned, so we have no choice but to believe it did, even though it seems in perfect working order now. If it didn't—" he hesitated "—then whoever broke in *knew* the place was alarmed, and knew just how to get around it."

A sudden thought struck her. "You don't think it could be one of your employees, do you?"

His expression was grim. "I was very careful who I hired, Chris— checking up on backgrounds, contacting references. But I'll admit the thought has crossed my mind." He sighed. "Two in one week. Any more like this and I may find all my clients doing business elsewhere."

The conversation drifted to other topics. Logan's eyes followed Chris as she carried their plates to the sink. "What's the occasion anyway?" he asked. "You fixed my favorite dish and used your best china. If I didn't know better, I'd think you were trying to butter me up. Or is this a subtle way of telling me I'm going to have to get used to my own cooking again?"

Wiping her hands on a dish towel, she made a face. "You happen to be a very good cook and you know it."

"Then why the special treatment?"

Light as his tone was, there was an underlying seriousness to the question. Chris experienced a pinprick of hurt at his lack of faith in her, but she ignored it and decided to concentrate instead on the truth.

"There doesn't have to be a reason," she replied softly, "when you want to do something for someone you love."

Something flickered in his expression. It was gone so quickly, Chris wasn't certain what to make of it. For the longest time, Logan said nothing. Then he held out his hand. "Come here, Chris."

She went, on shaky legs.

"Chris." He drew her down onto his lap. "Chris, about these past few days—"

"Shhh." She pressed her fingers against his lips, loving the feel of his hard mouth. "All I need to know is that you're not angry with me."

His hands tightened on her waist. Disappointed, yes, he thought. But not angry. "I'm not." He sought to ease the anxious distress that darkened her eyes.

She began to toy with the collar of his shirt, her gaze confined to the hollow of his neck. "Are you sure?" Her voice was very low.

"Positive." He combed through her silky hair with his fingers.

The wispiest of smiles lifted her lips. "I'm not so sure," she whispered back. "You didn't send me any flowers this week. I mean, what's a girl to think when a man has sent her flowers once a week for three weeks in a row. And then the next there's nothing...."

His fingers in her hair stilled. Chris raised her eyes to find him staring at her oddly. Suddenly she had her answer to the niggling question in the back of her mind these past days, and she didn't think she liked it.

Logan gave her a long, searching glance. "I didn't send flowers, Chris. I told you that before."

She bit her lip. "I know," she said in a small voice. "But when they came again the next week—*last* week— I thought maybe you were trying to be coy or funny..."

But that wasn't Logan, and she must have known it all along. At the realization, an eerie sensation ribboned up her spine.

"They didn't come this week?"

"No."

"And you have no idea who they're from?"

She shook her head, suppressing a shiver. "Jean and I thought it was funny at first, but they've always come from a different florist. We didn't have any luck finding out who ordered them."

"Was there a card?"

"A card but no signature. It always read, 'To a very special lady.'" She rose and poured the remainder of her coffee in the sink. She turned slowly, wrapping her arms around herself as she did.

To a very special lady. Certainly that didn't sound threatening. It didn't even sound overtly suggestive. Yet some sixth sense warned Logan otherwise, and for a fraction of a second, Chris looked rather frightened. He decided to dismiss it as lightly as possible.

"It's probably nothing," he said with a shrug. "They could have been from a patient who has a crush on you. Or *had* a crush," he added dryly, "since they didn't come this week."

A patient? Chris thought of Tom Chamberlain. During his last session, Tom *had* mentioned his interest in a woman. It was all he'd been able to talk about, in fact. She wasn't convinced that woman was herself, but she certainly wasn't afraid of Tom.

She let her breath out slowly, unaware she'd been holding it. "You're probably right," she murmured.

"I wouldn't worry about it if I were you." Logan rose and pulled her into his arms. But in spite of his words, he couldn't check the notion that there was more to this than an unknown admirer sending flowers to Chris.

He tipped her face to his, and Chris let the warmth of his kiss envelop her. After the strain of the past days, she was only too willing to turn herself over to him, mind, body and soul.

THE STARS HUNG LOW and brilliant in the night sky. The air was cold and fresh. But invisible in the black shadows just off the highway, a mud-colored van was parked, hidden behind a looming stand of pine trees.

The man inside the van had a clear, unobstructed view of the house that sat back from the roadside. He had seen the dark BMW pull up in the drive. He had seen the dark stranger enter her home.

And now a single light upstairs flicked on . . . and off again a moment later.

A cold and deadly rage filled his soul. It wasn't fair! It wasn't fair that *he* had her. No one . . . *no one* . . . could love her like he did. What was it, he fumed silently, that kindled such fickleness, such faithlessness, in the women destined to belong to him?

The rage soon passed, mollified, he supposed, by the knowledge that soon—it was only a matter of days now—she would be his. He would give her one last chance to prove herself.

He wanted her to be content with him. Happy, as he would be happy. It really didn't matter if it were here. A hundred miles away, or a thousand. He really didn't care. All he wanted was her. In his arms. In his bed.

When they were alone, when they were far, far away, he would teach her to love him. He would teach her that it was better to live simply, needing nothing but each other. And he would see to it that she never looked at another man again . . . no matter what it took.

In the meantime, perhaps a slight warning was in order. He still had those lovely daisies he'd bought with such hope in his heart, though they were far from lovely now. And perhaps it was time she realized just who she belonged to, for when she was his, it would be for always....

He found he was smiling, a refrain playing in his mind that he thought of often these days. *From this day forward . . . in sickness and in health . . .*

His forevermore. Through life . . . and death.

CHAPTER FIFTEEN

THEIR UNSPOKEN TRUCE lasted through the weekend, and nothing could have made Chris happier. She and Logan slept in Saturday morning, spent the day puttering around the house, the night alternately dozing and making love. If there was a certain sadness in Logan's eyes—if the easy familiarity between them wasn't as natural as before—she wasn't quite willing to acknowledge it. Their need for each other was sharper, more intense than ever before. They didn't speak of the future, nor the past. They were together for the moment and that was all that mattered; she refused to tempt fate further. Chris was so wrapped up in the two of them that she scarcely gave a second thought to the mystery of the flowers.

But that was before she arrived home Monday night.

It was dusk, that peculiar hour of the day when time hung suspended, when all was quiet and hushed. The countryside was an eerie, almost ominous shade of gray. The thin half-light seemed to waver, reluctantly yielding to the darkness, which slowly cast its shadow.

Her briefcase in one hand, Chris slammed the car door shut and walked to the front porch to retrieve the evening paper. As usual, it was lying on the bottom step. She seldom used her front door, but tonight, for some reason, she happened to glance up the wide, wooden stairs.

Her eyes widened, fixed on a point almost level with her eyes. An icy cold washed through her. There was a huge bouquet of limp, dried up daisies in front of her door. They'd been thrust into a filthy, muddied aluminum pail. Dozens of crushed, lifeless petals littered the gay "welcome" mat. It was then that she saw the pretty envelope poking out from the wilted mass, so dainty and pink it was almost obscene. Her name was printed in neat, block letters across the front.

Her briefcase and the newspaper were forgotten, dropped from nerveless fingers. She didn't have to look at the card to know there would be no signature. It was with a debilitating sense of inevitability that she numbly ascended the steps and reached for the envelope. Her hands were shaking as she read the message. "A gift for my lovely lady... love awaits you."

How long she stood there, Chris never knew. The next thing she was aware of was the sound of gravel crunching on the drive behind her. She spun around wildly, a gasp escaping from her lips.

It was Logan, an easy smile softening the harshness of his face, a greeting already coming from his lips.

He broke off at the sight of her ashen face and shocked expression.

"Chris. Chris, what's wrong?" Logan stepped up to her and seized her arm at the same time. Already his eyes were making a quick but thorough reconnaissance of her front yard. She knew the exact moment his gaze settled on the flowers; his grip on her arm tightened to a point just short of pain.

Chris took a curious sort of comfort in it. At least it was real, and it had the welcomed effect of causing the icy numbness inside her to recede. For just an instant she had the craziest urge to burst into tears.

"These were here when you got home?" His hard gaze was still trained on the flowers.

"Yes." Even to her own ears, her voice sounded pathetically thin.

Logan's eyes narrowed and swung back to Chris. A spasm of regret crossed his face; he hadn't noticed his bruising grip on her arm until that moment. Uttering an impatient exclamation, he pulled her body into his protective embrace. A finger under her chin guided her eyes to his. "Are you okay?"

She was suddenly ashamed of her weakness. "I'm fine," she said, though even in her own mind she sounded overbright. "Maybe I should feel flattered with all the attention I've been getting lately. I've never had so many flowers in my life," she tried to joke.

Logan said nothing. He merely watched her in that silent, piercing way that he had, which revealed more clearly than words that she wasn't fooling him.

"Don't look at me like that," she muttered. "It's silly to make such a big deal out of this. So someone has a rather warped sense of humor. I'm not a coward and I'm certainly not going to act like one."

She bent to retrieve her briefcase and the newspaper from the ground. When she faced him once more, there was a faint, almost challenging set to her small chin. Logan shook his head as she turned and headed for the back door. While he admired her spunk, he wished she would show a little more caution.

His hand closed over hers just as she thrust the key into the lock. "I'm going in first," he ordered firmly. "You stay here."

Her eyes flashed up to his face, and she opened her mouth. For an instant he thought she would argue. Then she nodded, her expression sober.

"No more surprises?" she asked when he came back out.

"No." He wasn't about to let down his guard just yet, though.

For all her bravado, Chris was strangely quiet while they prepared dinner. The last thing Logan wanted was to frighten her out of her wits, but once again her words echoed in his mind. There was more going on here than someone displaying a warped sense of humor. It was something—his mind balked at forming the word—something almost sinister. What kind of twisted mind, he wondered, would pull a stunt like delivering dead flowers? It was creepy. *Damn* creepy.

"Chris," he said when they sat down to the table. "I think it might be wise if you're extra careful these next few days. A little more aware about where you go, who you see. And if anything happens out of the ordinary—"

"Logan—" she scarcely gave him the time to finish "—you seem to be forgetting where you are now. This is Coeur d'Alene, Idaho. Most of the people that live here don't even bother to lock their doors at night. So don't you think that maybe—just maybe—you're overreacting a little?"

She was calm, almost too calm. He watched as she busied herself with her tea. "You can't ignore this, Chris." His tone was very quiet. "There's something happening here, and until we know what it is—"

"I'm not convinced it's all that serious." She took a deep breath, concentrating on her tea. "A little odd, I'll admit."

Logan leaned back in his chair, a humorless smile lifting his lips. "So it's not bothering you?"

"No." She made the reply with a lift of her brows.

"Is that why you just put four teaspoons of sugar in your tea?"

For Chris, it was the spark that set the fire to burning. "For heaven's sakes," she snapped, "you act as though someone's about to drag me off the street and kidnap me!"

Something flickered in Logan's eyes and Chris realized she had unthinkingly reminded him of Denise. It didn't matter that it was unintentional. More than anything she wished she could recall the words.

"Oh, God," she said faintly. "I didn't mean to—"

"It's all right." His tone was curt. There was a taut silence as he rose to refill her teacup.

Utterly miserable, she felt rather than saw him replace the cup on the table. He made no move to reclaim his chair. She sensed his eyes on her bent head. When she could stand the brittle tension no longer, she raised her face, unaware of the naked anguish reflected there.

"I'm sorry," she whispered, fighting back the hollowness in her chest. "I honestly didn't mean to have it come out like that."

His eyes fell to the hand she had unknowingly stretched out. He squeezed her fingers for the merest instant, then with a low exclamation he pulled her up and into his arms. Chris clung to him.

"I wouldn't be so worried if I didn't care about you." His fingers combed through her hair. God, caring didn't even begin to describe what he felt for her, and they both knew it.

"I know." She rubbed her cheek against the smooth cotton of his shirt.

"You think I'm making a mountain out of a molehill." His sigh whispered above her bent head. "But did you stop to think that someone, responsible person or no, had to find out where you live in order to leave those flowers on your doorstep? I know why they weren't taken to your office. They'd have been too damn conspicuous."

Logan could see that was something Chris hadn't considered. "Are you saying I *know* this person?" She blinked.

"Possibly."

"Then maybe it *is* a joke."

Logan's arms tightened around her, and Chris could sense the sudden change in him.

"No. No, Chris. I can feel that something isn't right here. There's something weird about this. And I don't like it. I don't like it at all."

She went pale, and Logan gave a low, muttered curse. "Dammit, Chris," he began, "I don't want to scare you—"

"Try a little harder." The trace of unlikely laughter in her voice did nothing to make either of them feel more at ease. She paused, then looked up at him. "You think these flowers are from the same person as before?"

Logan nodded.

Chris bit her lip. "Why? Why would someone do this?"

He released her and began to pace the room. "I don't know," he muttered, more to himself than to her. "Maybe you're right and it's nothing. Or—" Suddenly he stopped.

Chris held her breath, certain there was more. "Or what?"

He turned to face her, his face grave, his hands jammed into his pockets. "Or maybe someone has a fixation on you," he said slowly. Chris could almost see the wheels turning in his head. "And maybe, something has happened to disillusion whoever has been sending them."

"Hey, who's the psychologist around here anyway?" She tried to smile but her lips felt stiff.

Logan's gaze found hers. "You don't have any patients who would do something like this, do you?"

A twinge of guilt went through her as she thought of Tom Chamberlain. "That occurred to me, too," she admitted. "It's not unheard of for a patient to read more into his relationship with his therapist than what's actually there. There are times when there's a fine line between dependence and independence. Sometimes a patient can feel that we're the only friend they have. Or it could be gratitude." Tom, again, she thought with a pang. She had seen him just yesterday, and although he'd gone on about his "friend," she was almost certain he wasn't behind this.

Logan watched her closely. "Maybe at first," he countered quietly. "But not now. The flowers didn't come for a week," he reminded her. "And then today..." He shook his head. "If someone is obsessed with you, and if there's any kind of symbolism involved, I'd say it has to do with anger. Or frustration perhaps." It might even be a warning, he wanted to add, but didn't.

Chris scarcely heard. Her mind had homed in on one word—obsessed. That sounded so violent. "They weren't from a florist this time."

"No," he agreed. "But what reputable florist would deliver dead flowers? And what sane person would make such a request in the first place and not expect to raise a few eyebrows? No," he murmured, rubbing his chin thoughtfully. "Something tells me that whoever is behind this is smart, smart enough to want to avoid any questions. Maybe that's why he kept changing florists in the first place."

Perhaps it was his choice of words—what *sane* person. A shiver ran through her. Logan had said it was only a feeling that made him believe there was something odd about this whole episode, and suddenly Chris couldn't deny she had that very same feeling. Trying to act as calmly as possible, she got up and began to clear the dishes from the table.

"What I'd like to know," Logan wondered aloud, "is where this nut got so many daisies in the middle of winter in the first place, if not from a florist."

"We don't know that," she pointed out.

"No." Logan's expression was set. "But I'm sure as hell going to find out."

Chris dropped the handful of dishes in the sink, a frown etched between her brows. There was something familiar about that phrase—flowers in the middle of winter—that tugged at the fringe of her consciousness. She could have sworn someone had said that to her not long ago, but for the life of her, she couldn't remember who. "Maybe he has his own greenhouse," she said finally.

Logan watched as Chris reached for a towel to dry her hands. "You're certain you have no idea who's behind this?"

Her lips tightened as she correctly read the warning signs in his eyes. "There are such things as a patient's right to confidentiality—and professional ethics," she stated quietly. "I won't have you or anyone else, including your friend Ned, trying to snoop around in my files, or subjecting any of my patients to an inquisition." Her chin tilted almost challengingly. "Not without some proof."

Ethics be damned, Logan thought grimly. There were times, times like now, when not everyone played by the rules. He kept his peace, silently picking up the towel Chris had discarded, thinking that nothing could stop him from doing a little checking himself—without Ned.

When they were done with the dishes, Logan laid a hand on Chris's shoulder and guided her toward the living room and into the chair next to the fireplace. Startled, Chris looked up at him when he moved to pick up his coat from the chair. "You're staying tonight, aren't you?"

An unexpected pain twisted his heart. How he hated the quaver in her voice, and the anxiety she couldn't quite hide. He wasn't sure what was responsible for it— her unease about the flowers or the tentative state of affairs between the two of the them. But her gaze slid away from his as if she couldn't stand to see the wrong answer written in his eyes.

He carefully placed his coat in the front closet, his intention all along. A ghost of a smile lifted his lips as he walked back to her. "Is there a Gary Cooper movie on tonight?" With slow deliberation, he switched on the TV, pulled her over to the sofa and settled her head on his shoulder.

She smiled up at him, and his heart ached as he saw her heartfelt relief. Movie or no movie, she was asleep within minutes, emotionally exhausted, he suspected.

For her sake, he hoped she was right; that the flowers tonight had been nothing more than a sick joke. But even as the thought filtered through his mind, a prickly sense of foreboding washed over him. He had the strangest sensation, almost a premonition, that a trap had been set. And someone was ready and waiting for just the right time to place the wheels in motion.

The only question was when.

EARLY THE NEXT WEEK, Logan contacted the florists who had made the first few deliveries to Chris. He didn't think he would have any more luck than Chris and Jean, but he knew he wouldn't be satisfied until it was done.

The first two floral shops he contacted didn't keep a log of deliveries beyond a day or two. The third had a record of the delivery, but the person who had ordered the arrangement remained a mystery. The order had been from a walk-in customer, paid for in cash.

Compounding his frustration were several phone calls that came through to Chris's that week. He happened to pick up the phone, and the minute he answered it, the line clicked dead. It happened once on Tuesday, and twice on Wednesday and Thursday. Logan carefully queried Chris without managing to alarm her. She had received no similar calls at the office. Coincidence? Logan didn't think so. He had the strangest sensation that someone was checking up on her—or him. Perhaps both of them.

He tried his damnedest to talk Chris into letting him install an alarm system—nothing elaborate, but a system that would protect the perimeter of the house, signifying any attempt to open the windows and doors.

She flat-out refused. Logan was well aware of her reasons; he didn't think he'd ever forget her stricken expression the night she'd tripped the alarm at her office. Still, he was a little irritated with her stubbornness.

But then something happened that wiped everything else from his mind. He was awake early that Friday morning. It had been exactly one week after Chris had received the wilted daisies, and he'd spent a long, fitful night. In spite of the woman who lay sleeping dreamlessly beside him, Logan was filled with that same prickly sense of unease, and after the phone calls last night, it was sharper than ever.

Logan got up and showered. When he'd finished, he woke Chris, who headed for the bathroom to begin her morning rituals. Clad only in a pair of slacks, the towel slung carelessly over his bare shoulders, Logan prowled the room restlessly. Chris had dropped her purse on the edge of the dresser, and he didn't even realize he'd bumped it until it fell to the floor, scattering the contents at his feet.

He hunched down with a grimace and began to shove various items back inside. Wallet. Compact and brush. But his frown turned to mild curiosity when he picked up a small, flat, daintily pink container, absently flicking it open as he rose and sat on the edge of the bed. Comprehension was slow to dawn. He found himself regarding a dispenser of tiny white tablets, half of which were missing.

Birth control pills.

He felt as if every bone in his body had been broken. He felt duped. Cheated. He was unable to control the deep, angry despair that slipped over him. He should have expected it, he thought with a cynical twist of his lips. After all, he hadn't seen to that particular responsibility. And didn't every woman have the right to protect her own body? *Protect!* God, how he suddenly hated that word. But the knowledge did little to assuage his bitterness. Both realizations were like slow poison eating away inside him.

The rush of water in the shower ceased, but Logan never even heard. He remained where he was, a still, silent figure on the bed.

"Whew! Boy, am I glad it's Friday!" Chris's low, sweet voice drifted to him as she swept from the bathroom, a terry cloth robe wrapped around her. "I have to work late, though. I've got dictating to catch up on and I thought I'd do it tonight so we'd have the weekend free.''

She moved past him, reaching out to brush back the silky-rough strands of hair that had fallen on his forehead. A hand like a vise clamped around her wrist, imprisoning her, thwarting her, stopping her cold.

"Don't," he whispered, and somewhere in that low, rough sound, she sensed rather than heard, a million layers of hurt.

Her eyes fell to the pill pack he still held in his hand. The oppressive silence that followed seemed to darken the sunlit room.

Chris felt her mouth go dry. She swallowed sickly and forced her gaze upward. Logan met her look of pained resignation with eyes that blazed like raging blue fire.

Drawing on a courage she hadn't known she possessed, Chris took a deep, fortifying breath. "I take it you have something to say." She was proud of her even tone.

Logan got to his feet. He towered over her. Tall. Strong. Forbidding. His gaze never wavered from hers as he tossed the pill pack aside. It clattered across the dresser, then fell to the floor.

His eyes pinned hers remorselessly. When he finally spoke, his voice was deceptively quiet. "You might have told me, Chris."

Her spine stiffened. "I didn't need your permission," she countered. "Nor did I think it was necessary. The last thing I wanted was to provoke any more friction between us. Besides, it's not as if we're—"

"Married?" He nearly spat the word. "We both know why, don't we?"

Chris felt the color drain from her face. She hadn't meant to say that. She hadn't meant for him to find the pills, afraid of what was happening right now. That Logan would take it all wrong; that he would take it as some kind of rejection. But all that was pointless now. She stared at him wordlessly.

"I suppose you thought it didn't concern me?"

His coolness stung. "*You're* not the one who would get pregnant!" she retorted.

His lips formed a thin, straight line. "That's a cop-out and you know it, Chris."

And she did. Pregnancy was a responsibility Logan would assume every bit as much as she.

"What did you expect me to do?" she responded tightly. "You certainly didn't take any responsibility! What was I supposed to do?"

Logan was angry. He was hurt, and suddenly something within him snapped. "And just what do you expect *me* to say?" he demanded. "That I was wrong for not bringing it up sooner? All right, I admit it. I'm guilty. I should have, but I didn't. I suppose I realized you were using *some* means of protection, but I wouldn't let myself think about it. Maybe I didn't *want* to think about it because I didn't want to have to deal with it!"

Or perhaps, without even realizing it, he'd wanted her to get pregnant. Because that would have given him an edge, a tool to bargain with. Oh, hell, who was he trying to fool? He wanted her in every way possible. He wanted to bind her to him forever, and he didn't care how it was accomplished.

But it was not to be. It was not to be, and everything inside him cried out his hurt and outrage. The atmosphere was stifling. He could feel Chris staring at him; he could sense her confusion and bewilderment. He dragged a hand down his face and summoned every ounce of self-control he possessed.

"Would it be so terrible," he asked very quietly, "to have a baby? My baby?" His eyes never left her face. "You were perfectly willing to have a child with Bill. But I'm a different story." Even as he said the words, he knew he wasn't being fair. He was striking out at her, like a wounded, desperate animal. "You said you wanted time, Chris. And I've given you time. But I think you've already made your choice."

"I . . ." Chris floundered helplessly. The conflict inside her was so strong she felt she was being ripped apart. "Please," she implored desperately. "Just let me explain."

"You don't have to explain anything to me, Chris." His voice was flat. Emotionless. Deep inside, he knew what prompted her fear of becoming pregnant again. It had to do with losing Scottie. Perhaps, being a man, he couldn't fully understand it. And much as he despised himself for it, at this moment he simply couldn't find it in himself to make the effort.

The hard bitter lines on his face were back, lines she had hoped never to see again. They were harsher, deeper than ever.

Chris stared at him. She felt torn in two, sliced cleanly in half. And his lack of expression didn't conceal the stark hollowness that had swallowed him.

"You can't know what it's like," she said raggedly, and the pain in her heart brought agony to her voice. "You can't know what it's like to hold your son's body in your arms, hoping and praying that it's just a horrible nightmare. That he's not really cold and limp—that he's not really dead!—yet knowing that nothing on earth can ever bring him back." She lifted a hand to find her cheek wet with moisture. "I'm scared, Logan. I'm scared that I'll have another baby like Scottie, and

I can't take the chance it will happen again. I can't live with that kind of fear."

There were tears streaming down her cheeks. Logan ached to take her in his arms, to soothe her with lips that healed and arms that sheltered and protected. But she had no way of knowing that in his own way, he was just as vulnerable as she. His emotions were just as raw and exposed; he felt he'd been stripped bare and lashed to the bone.

"I know that, Chris." His voice was soft, almost whimsical. "And that's why I won't ask you to." He walked across the room, pulled a shirt from the closet and shrugged into it. He turned back to her, his posture coldly dignified. He gave her a curiously wistful smile. "But tell me, Chris. Where does that leave us? And where do we go from here?"

And then he did something that neither of them ever expected.

Without another word, he walked out on her.

CHAPTER SIXTEEN

CHRIS COULD REMEMBER only one other day that had brought so much heartache. But somehow she survived it through sheer determination, through a carefully maintained facade in front of her patients and Jean. If Jean sensed that something was wrong, she said nothing. But she dawdled after Chris's last appointment, long after she'd switched the computer off. It was well after five o'clock before she appeared in the doorway. She closed the blinds, shutting out the rest of the world . . . but not shutting out the bleakness in Chris's heart.

"Lord, but it's dark in here!" Jean started to switch on the overhead, fluorescent lights.

Chris stopped her. "I'll get it in a few minutes, Jean."

"Working late tonight?"

Chris nodded.

"Do you want me to stay, too? I can—"

"There's no need," Chris said softly.

"Then how about if I go get something for you to eat?"

"I'm fine, Jean. I won't be here long enough to bother."

Her secretary looked doubtful. "If you're sure," she began.

"I'm positive." The smile Chris adopted made her face feel as if it had shattered into a million pieces. "You go on home. I'll see you Monday morning."

But long after Jean left, the room remained dark. The darkness was curiously comforting and reassuring. She felt like a child who had discovered a secret hiding place where no one could find her; where she could create her own little dream world and live happily ever after.

But dreams sometimes became nightmares, and happily-ever-after fantasies were for children. Reality was all around her. When she finally got up to switch on the light, all the thoughts and fears she'd managed to hold back throughout the day came crashing down around her. Carl entered her outer office to empty the trash and vacuum the carpet, but Chris was scarcely aware of him. This morning's ugly scene with Logan remained in her mind. And it was then Chris knew she had some choices to make and some hard, hard thinking to do. What did she want for herself? For Logan? For the two of them?

She wanted what they'd had before. She wanted them to be friends and lovers and everything in between. At the realization, she leaned her elbows on her desk and covered her face with her hands. A deep despair swept through her.

They simply couldn't go on as they had been. On the surface, both she and Logan seemed content and happy. But it was like a smooth, deceptively thin layer of ice, for beneath there was danger, and so much hidden tension, that sooner or later, one of them would break.

That had happened this morning.

She couldn't leave him. She couldn't even think of going on without him. Yet she wasn't sure she could stay with him either. He would grow to resent her—he resented her already. And someday he would leave her.

But would he? a tiny voice prodded. Would Logan knowingly hurt her?

It occurred to Chris that in spite of their different backgrounds, their values were the same. They both believed in commitment, commitment to each other, to love and life. Only through faith and belief in each other could they achieve that goal.

Logan had believed. *She* had been the one to doubt, the one who dared not trust, the one to have such little faith in herself. And she was beginning to think she had made a horrible, horrible mistake by failing to place her trust in herself, and in him.

A slight rustle at the door caught her attention. Chris looked up to find Carl hovering there, dressed in his usual drab brown shirt and pants.

"I was just about to leave, Dr. Michaels. I thought I'd check and see if you were ready to go home for the night."

Chris roused herself from her trance. Home? she thought dispiritedly. To what? To an empty house? To a long night and an even lonelier tomorrow without Logan? She knew better than to expect him to be waiting for her. But there was no point in staying here either.

Sighing, she rose from her desk, sending Carl a halfhearted smile. "Thanks. I guess it is time to call it a night, isn't it?" She collected her coat and they left the building.

The night air was bitter and cold. Her cheeks stung from the fierce wind. Head down, Chris began to hurry toward her car.

Through the thickness of her coat, she felt a hand grip her arm. She jerked her head up to find Carl's gloved fingers curled around her upper arm.

"Carl!" She was too surprised to resist, thinking he'd made a mistake as he began to pull her along. "Carl, wait!"

They moved several more steps, then stopped in the alley between two of the buildings. The darkness was black and absolute. Chris was barely able to make out the hulking shape of a van parked a few steps away.

"Carl," she began again. "My car is over there—" She never got any further. Carl stepped in front of her, his head turned at an angle so that a gauzy sliver of light captured his face. He was smiling. *Smiling!* Chris had only a fraction of a second to translate the full import of that smile. He murmured something that made no sense; it sounded like "forgive me."

And then a crashing blow caught her on the chin. Stunned, she staggered backward, and the world went dark.

LOGAN'S MOOD was anything but tame that day. He canceled his appointments and proceeded to shut himself in his office. He wasn't particularly proud of himself when Karen, his bookkeeper, walked in with a question about next month's payroll. He'd snapped at her, and she left looking like a frightened rabbit. With a sigh, he walked out and apologized to her. He then decided if he wasn't fit company to be around, he might as well remove himself. But he couldn't go home— either to the cottage or to Chris's. And so an hour later he found himself on the highway, heading toward Spokane.

Twenty miles or so from Coeur d'Alene, he happened to glance over toward a rambling, dilapidated wooden building off the side of the road. There was a sign in front of it: "Nelson's Auction Yard—We Buy and Sell—Sale Every Saturday."

Logan braked sharply and veered off the highway. Rolling to a stop, he tapped his fingers against the steering wheel, aware of a vague, nagging sensation in the back of his mind.

Between him and Ned, they'd made the rounds of the flea markets and second-hand stores in Coeur d'Alene trying to track down the property stolen in the recent burglaries. But neither one had contacted any auction services. He'd almost driven past this one. He stared at the chipped wooden siding a moment longer before he pulled his keys from the ignition.

The door was ajar, so he walked in without knocking. He found himself standing in a room jammed full of furniture and various odds and ends. There were kitchen dinette sets piled high, tabletop to tabletop, chairs thrust beneath. Half a dozen sofas were lined against the far wall. Next to them was an assortment of ancient looking garden tools.

A burly, heavyset man looked up from behind the cluttered counter. "Looking for something in particular?" He stuck a cigar in his mouth.

Logan walked over and placed his hands flat on the counter. He let a smile crease his face. "I am," he said pleasantly. "Portable televisions, VCRs...electronic equipment."

The man gave a loud guffaw. "Stuff like that goes out faster than it comes in."

"I see." Logan let a steely glint enter his eyes, his tone deceptively bland. "That must make you rather eager for more of the same." It wasn't a threat; it was more a subtle warning to talk—or else.

The cigar came out of the man's mouth in a flash. "You a cop?" In spite of his suspicious tone, he didn't seem overly concerned or alarmed.

"Just call me an interested party."

The cigar was crammed back in. Logan found himself being examined from top to bottom. Then, apparently satisfied with what he saw, the man said, "So. You're looking for TVs. Video equipment. Cameras, maybe?"

"Maybe." Logan's eyes narrowed. "Can you come up with any?"

The other man shook his head. "Not right now. But first I want to get something straight. I make an honest living here. If someone comes in here and wants to sell me so much as the shirt off his back, I'm gonna find out where it came from." He stared Logan right in the eye. "That's why I turned down a tidy little profit just last week."

Logan knew he was onto something here; he could feel it.

"A guy came in here last Tuesday," the man went on. "He had all kinds of fancy video equipment. Cameras. Recorders. You name it, he had it. He wasn't in here five minutes before I showed him the door."

"Why's that?" Logan remembered that an electronics shop had been hit last week. Was it coincidence that a man had shown up here the following day? He didn't think so.

"Why?" The man gave a gusty laugh. "Because everything he had was hot! No way am I gonna start running stolen property through here—I never have and I never will."

"But how do you know it was stolen?" Logan persisted.

"How else? I felt it right here." He slapped his belly.

Gut instinct. For the first time that day, a faint but genuine smile lifted Logan's lips. Ned and this man would get along famously.

"Did the guy give you any trouble when you told him to leave?"

"I thought he might," the man admitted. "But he probably decided I wasn't worth the trouble. My guess is he could unload his stuff further down the road in Spokane, no questions asked."

True enough, Logan concurred silently. "What did he look like?"

The man rubbed his chin. "I'm afraid I'm not much good at faces. He was tall. Blond. That's all I really remember." He pondered a moment longer, then snapped his fingers. "He was wearing brown, I remember."

"Light or dark?" Logan tried to prod his memory. "Tan or—"

"'Fraid I just can't say for sure. It was some kind of uniform, though. Sort of like the ones deliverymen wear."

That was all the man remembered, but Logan thanked him and returned to his car. Granted, it wasn't much, but at least he'd have something to report to Ned. He'd give him a call as soon as he got home.

Home. The word kindled thoughts of Chris. He'd picked up the phone in his office to call her a dozen times today, each time slowly replacing the receiver in its cradle.

He had no idea what to say to her. He couldn't lie to her. Any apology he might have made would never ring true, and she'd have seen right through it. Nor could he pretend the ugly confrontation between them this morning hadn't happened. He was still smarting from it, hours later.

Was he being selfish? Insensitive to the needs of a woman whose scars had yet to heal?

He remembered with painful clarity what she had said the night he'd asked her to marry him. *You deserve everything you've never had. A home. A family.*

And if I could give that to you, I would. But I can't, and I'm not sure I'll ever be able to.

Couldn't? Or wouldn't? His fingers tightened on the steering wheel. He had told her then that it made no difference. And until this morning, when he'd faced the cold, hard facts—that he might never bring a child of his own into this world—he'd thought it really didn't matter.

But it did. Dammit, it did.

He had told her that somehow—*somehow*—they could get through this. But he was beginning to wonder. Would it be as Chris had predicted? Would he feel cheated?

He had felt cheated this morning. He *still* felt cheated. But he couldn't deny how right they were together, and he didn't want to. Deep in his heart, he knew that he and Chris could be happy together, just the two of them.

They could be happier still if they were married. With a family of their own.

On and on the battle waged, first one way and then the other. His headlights bounced eerily off her house as he turned in the drive. There were no welcoming lights burning in the window, but he knew he wasn't yet ready to face her. He decided to spend at least the next few hours at the cottage.

The inside of the little house was chillingly cold, since he hadn't stayed there for quite some time. Once he'd turned up the thermostat, he pulled off his coat and headed toward the living room. Even before he walked through the doorway, his eyes had begun to stray toward the small curio cabinet against the far wall. Inside it was the wood carving Chris had given him for Christmas. Next to the carving was the photograph of the two of them, the one the old man had snapped for them in Spokane. It had been such a wonderful, laughter-filled day, he recalled wistfully. He flipped on the light, then came to an abrupt halt, stunned at what he saw.

The glass in the tiny cabinet had been smashed. Jagged shards were strewn across the carpet. He picked his way carefully among the mess, relieved to note that nothing else seemed to have been damaged. The carving didn't appear to have been touched. Then, drawn by some strange, compelling force, Logan reached for the photograph.

His blood ran cold. Chris smiled up at him, but the other image in the photo—*his* image—had been slashed to shreds with some sharp object.

Just then there was a loud pounding at the front door. His face hard, Logan moved to throw it open.

It was Ned. His breath frosty, he rubbed his hands briskly together in front of him. "Looks like we've got another storm headed our way," he said cheerfully. "Hope you've got something to warm up a poor—" He broke off on seeing Logan's tense expression. "What's up?" He quickly stepped inside and closed the door behind him.

It didn't take long to tell the other man about Chris's unknown admirer and the flowers she'd been receiving. Logan put on a pot of coffee while Ned listened intently. The other man made a low, impatient sound when Logan told him about the wilted daisies. He withdrew a small plastic bag from his pocket—the kind used for gathering evidence—and dropped it on the table, then pulled something out and held it to the light.

"Does this look familiar?"

Ned was holding what appeared to be a corner torn from a tiny gift card, the kind used by florists. It was dirty and muddied, but Logan could just make out the intricate scrollwork near the edges. "I can't be certain," he said slowly, "but that looks a lot like the card that came with the dead daisies."

"I thought so." Ned replaced the card in the tiny plastic bag. "I've been making the rounds to all the florists in the area myself the past few days."

Logan frowned questioningly.

"You knew a convenience store was robbed Monday night? Someone knocked out the clerk, tied him up and stole all the money from the till."

He nodded.

"He was discovered the next morning when a customer came in. We found this card—what there is of it—near the cash register."

"And it happened the night before?" Logan's eyes narrowed. "That was the night Chris came home and found the daisies."

The police lieutenant nodded. "There are only two florists in town who carry cards like this, and I just came from one of them. I was frustrated as hell when I left. They use them all the time and it seems they're a favorite among customers. But on the way out, the owner made a crack about taking on another case and finding out who gave her daughter such a hard time the week before. Apparently a man came in the day after New Year's, bought all the daisies they had and wanted more. Nothing else—just daisies. She said he was pretty damn irate when they couldn't get any until the next day. He scared her daughter so much she won't work in the shop anymore."

The day after New Year's . . . something drummed at Logan's brain. That was the week Chris had thought he was angry, the week she had discovered for certain that he wasn't her secret admirer after all.

"Chris didn't get any flowers that week." Logan's eyes sought Ned's. "I know this sounds crazy, but whoever bought those daisies could have intended to deliver them, gotten angry for some reason and let them sit for a week—"

"Long enough for them to wither up and die," Ned finished grimly. He was silent for a few seconds, then he looked at his friend. "You want to hear something that *really* sounds crazy? Last week was the week our friendly neighborhood burglar decided to get a little bolder. The service station attendant was robbed; the man was assaulted and robbed at the automatic teller. Then Monday, this convenience store was hit."

"And someone has gotten through two of my security systems." Logan's fist came down on the table. "Dammit, Ned, you're right. Maybe it's a gang— maybe it's only one man—but they're all connected together. I don't understand how it ties in with Chris and whoever has been sending her the flowers, but at least we may have a clue." Quickly he told his friend what he'd learned at the auction yard.

Ned wore an odd expression. "A brown uniform? You know," he murmured, "the service station attendant thought that the man who hit him wore khakis— shirt, pants and belt. When I talked to him later, he said the outfit was a little like the uniform he wears. We thought it might be someone he worked with, or possibly someone who quit or was fired. And as the man at the auction yard mentioned, deliverymen wear uniforms, too."

"And so," Logan said slowly, "do custodians. Building janitors."

"That's just what I was thinking," Ned said. "Which explains why no one ever heard anything, or saw anything unusual. The forced entries could have been just a ruse. Maybe this guy broke a window or two just to throw us off the track. And it's the perfect out," he finished grimly. "No one suspects the janitor because he's *supposed* to be there after hours."

"It also explains how he managed to get by the security system. No one thought twice about the janitor having access to it." Logan's voice was taut. "And I'll lay you ten-to-one odds the same custodian has contracts at all the businesses that have been hit lately—" But suddenly his skin prickled eerily. Something elusive hovered at the fringe of his consciousness.

Logan surged to his feet and lunged to the window. Chris's house was still dark as a tomb.

"My God," he muttered. "Chris is working late tonight. The building is usually empty by six. The man at the auction yard said the guy who was in last week was tall and blond. I've seen the janitor at Chris's building. He's tall. Blond. If we're talking about the same man, he could be with her right now!"

"Now wait a minute." Ned grabbed his arm. "You said he's infatuated with her—"

"Obsessed," he ground out tightly. "I'm telling you he's obsessed with her."

Ned grimaced and waved a hand. "Either way, I don't think he'll hurt her," he began.

"But he knows about me." Logan grabbed the photo lying on the counter. "Dammit, he knows about me. And we both know what jealousy can do to a person. A crime of passion, Ned. It happens every day."

Ned was already on the phone, tersely giving orders to send a unit to Chris's building. But Logan insisted they head for the building themselves.

When they arrived at the square, the police cruiser was already there, and Logan felt a gut-wrenching fear as he had never known before. He could see Chris's car was still parked in the lot. There was a light burning in her office.

And there was no sign of Chris.

CHRIS REGAINED CONSCIOUSNESS slowly. Something rough chafed the tender skin of her cheek. She was numb all over, stiff with cold. There was a dull pain on the side of her jaw, and for the life of her, she didn't understand why it hurt so much. And then her memory returned with a sickening rush.

The roughness against her cheek must be a blanket. Beneath it, there was a cushioned softness. She was lying on a bed, she realized. She was numb because she was tied up, hands in front of her, her feet crossed and bound securely at the ankles. Her jaw hurt because Carl had hit her...Carl! Where was he? Alarm skittered through her. And where was she? The darkness around her was almost suffocating. Had he dragged her off to some dark, dank basement where no one would ever find her? Wherever she was, the chill felt as if it had penetrated clear to her bones, despite the protection of her coat.

A hysterical laugh bubbled inside her. She was cold because she had no hat. *Oh, Logan, Logan where are you?*

She wasn't alone. Her head swiveled toward the strange creaking that came from just beyond her. A ghostly figure detached itself from the wall and floated toward her.

It was Carl. Her eyes adjusted to the darkness and she saw him strike a match. He lit a kerosene lamp and a halo of gold filled the corner. She saw that she was in a small, one-room cabin, sparsely furnished, jarringly primitive, the walls and floors roughly planked.

It was Carl who had been sending the flowers, all along. And she should have known. *Flowers in the middle of winter.* She'd been so certain someone had said that to her, but it had been the other way around. That night in her office when she had been wistfully wishing for spring was suddenly crystal-clear in her mind. She had said that to him.

Why? Why had he done it? And why had he brought her here?

She watched uncertainly as Carl came toward her, suddenly not sure she wanted to know the answer.

She struggled to a sitting position. She almost flinched when a hand reached out to help her, but instinct warned her it wouldn't be wise.

He touched her cheek. His fingers moved caressingly over her bruised jaw. "I'm so sorry I had to do that." His eyes were filled with regret. "If I had been absolutely sure you would come to me willingly..." He sighed. "I'm afraid I had no other choice."

A shiver ran through her. A blanket was immediately tucked around her shoulders. His thin hands looked like claws, sharp and clinging. But her imagination was running away with her.

Chris wet her lips. "Why have you brought me here, Carl?" Thank God she didn't sound nervous.

"Why?" His eyes reflected his astonishment. "You ask why, love?"

Love? Dear God, what had she done? She'd been nice to him. He seemed so odd, so lonely, that she'd gone out of her way to speak to him sometimes. There was no reason for him to think it was anything more, but there was something frightening in the way he was looking at her.

He got up and began to fill the pot-bellied stove in the corner with wood. Chris's gaze swept frantically around the tiny room, seeking a way to escape. But there was only one door.

Carl came back to sit beside her. "You know—" his tone was conversational "—you've changed since you left me, Wanda."

Wanda? The hair on the back of her neck stood up. He held a small photo in his hands, and he kept looking from it, to her face, and back again. Chris's eyes came to rest with a horrified inevitability on the woman in the photo.

She was small. Very petite, with chestnut hair. She bore a striking resemblance to Chris.

Bile filled her throat. Chris choked back a sound of sick terror. She was alone with Carl. Somehow he'd managed to twist her identity with a woman named Wanda, and she didn't even know where they were.

"Where are we, Carl?" It was a miracle that she sounded as calm as she did.

"Why, we're home again." He shrugged. "I know it hasn't changed much, but you know me. I always did prefer to keep things simple."

She held out her hands, forcing a smile. "Couldn't you untie me, Carl?" Her tone was cajolingly sweet. "This rope is hurting my wrists. And it's cutting into my ankles."

He seemed to consider a moment, then bent over before her to free the rope around her ankles. She stared at his shoulders, aware that the wooden door was no more than two feet away. She was on the verge of jerking her knee up under his chin, but he straightened before she had a chance. Chris held out her wrists, but he frowned at her thoughtfully. "Not just yet, Wanda," he murmured. "Much as I love you, it may take a while for me to learn to trust you again."

Mingled with the adoration in his eyes was something else, something that sent an icy fear swirling in the pit of Chris's stomach.

"I know you need some time." Carl squatted down beside her. "I know how much you hate it here, how isolated you always felt. But it will be better, I promise." His eyes began to gleam. "Remember how you always said we never had enough money to buy you the things you wanted? Well, I've got plenty of money now." He laughed delightedly, "And it was so easy."

Chris stared at him. She'd have bet her last dollar that his business didn't bring in all that much money. A nagging suspicion began to form in her mind, but she tried not to sound accusing. "Where did the money come from, Carl?"

He looked immensely pleased with himself. "I'll tell you later, love. When I'm sure I can trust you not to go to the police."

She feigned hurt. "I wouldn't do that to you, Carl. Surely you know that?"

He stood up so suddenly that she flinched. She had reason to when she saw the fiery flame in his eyes.

"I know no such thing! You walked out on me two years ago, Wanda." His voice lashed into her. "Did you think I'd forget that? The way you were always lusting after other men? You're my wife, Wanda, and this time I won't let you forget it."

He whirled around and stomped across the room. His movements almost vicious, he began thrusting chunks of cedar into the pot-bellied stove.

Chris had begun to get a very clear picture of what this man's life had been like. Carl's wife had left him, unable to tolerate the lonely, frugal existence imposed on her. It was pathetic, even a little sick, but Carl was hopelessly caught up in the past, unable to accept that his wife had deserted him. Her deception had driven him over the edge.

Chris's thoughts were a frantic jumble. Playing along with him was getting her nowhere. He'd gotten her hopelessly tangled in his mind, confusing her with the woman who had once been his wife. Carl was an emotionally deranged man, but somehow she had to get through to him that she was not his wife.

Outside the wind howled. Through the window she could see a curtain of snow falling heavily.

Carl finally turned around. She could feel his eyes boring into her. He continued to stare at her wordlessly, and she raised her head to meet his gaze levelly.

"Carl." She adopted her most forceful, authoritative tone of voice. "Carl, my name is not Wanda. If you'll just think for a minute, you'll know I'm telling you the truth."

He smiled, but it was a smile that sent chills up her spine.

"I am Dr. Christine Michaels, Carl. I'm a psychologist. You're the custodian at the building I work in."

Nothing. He didn't even appear to have heard.

Chris gritted her teeth. "Listen to me, Carl. My name is Christine Michaels. Dr. Michaels. You are not in love with me and I am not in love with you. I'm in love with someone else. A man named—"

"Him!" He spat the word; the smile vanished. "I know who he is, and if it weren't for him, we could stay here. I won't have you looking over your shoulder at him, do you hear? So we're going to do what you always wanted. We're going to leave here. You'll forget him, just like you forgot all those other men. We could go to Montana. Did you know I grew up there? It was a lot like this. My daddy and I had a cabin deep in the woods. Why, with everything I know, we could survive for months and months without ever seeing a soul. Just the two of us. My daddy always said that the only thing a man needed was a woman. And now I have you again, Wanda. Just like before. You're still my wife. You'll always be my wife...."

"Carl, I am not going anywhere with you!" Chris jumped to her feet, unaware that she was screaming until his eyes locked with hers.

"It's him, isn't it?" His lips parted to reveal the feral gleam of teeth. "It's him you want—not me at all. That leaves me with just one thing to do then. I'm getting rid of him."

He snatched the shotgun that hung on the wall. It was old, with dull, gleaming metal and aged wood, but Chris suddenly had no doubt that it was in perfect working order.

She opened her mouth, but before she could say a word, Carl had whirled and shoved her down onto the mattress. There was a deadly look on his face as he grabbed a coat from a hook on the wall, the shotgun gripped tightly in his hand.

At that moment, without warning, the door crashed open. Logan stood in the doorway for a split second, his head and shoulders a ghostly silhouette against the snow-lit sky.

What happened next was like seeing a movie in slow motion. Carl's back was to the door when it burst open. Chris jerked herself up in time to see him pivot, the butt of the shotgun raised and hollowed against his shoulder. A fierce gust of wind tore in through the open door. The kerosene lamp flickered and then the room was cast into darkness.

It all happened in a fraction of a second; there was no time for a warning. There was no time to do anything but watch helplessly as a burst of red spurted from the gun.

CHAPTER SEVENTEEN

THERE WAS AN ANSWERING SHOT. Or was it only an echo in her mind? Over and over again that horrible sound seemed to explode in her skull.

She was crying, she realized. Deep, soundless sobs that racked her body and sent silent tears streaming down her cheeks. All around her there was a flurry of activity, a blurred jumble of shapeless forms. Her eyes squeezed shut as a desolate wave of despair swept over her; she was desperately afraid of what she might see.

Then there was a hand on her cheek, stroking away damp tendrils of hair with infinite gentleness. Her wrists were freed. Strong hands closed over her shoulders and pulled her upright. She felt the touch of warm lips on her cheeks, her eyelids, her temples. A soft, fuzzy-sounding voice whispered her name.

He was alive. Logan was alive.

She reached out blindly. Hard hands caught her to his chest, while tears poured from her eyes. Over and over she whispered his name as she clung to him.

"Shhh. Don't cry, don't cry." The tone that soothed her was one of melting tenderness. She didn't deserve it—she didn't deserve him.

Masculine voices drifted all around them. Tall figures darted back and forth. Chris dimly recognized Ned. Carl was lying on the rough floor, his wrists handcuffed behind him. She took one look at him and shuddered.

She buried her face in the hollow of Logan's throat. "Oh, God," she choked out. "When I heard that shot, I thought he had ... and you were..." She couldn't say it. She couldn't even *think* it. "It was Carl," she whispered. "The janitor in my building. It was him all along. He sent the flowers...."

"I know." Logan wrapped her close once more, shielding her, soothing her, comforting her...as well as himself. At length, he eased back so that he could see her face. "Chris," he said, willing his voice not to tremble, "he didn't—"

She understood immediately. Her fingers tightened on his arms, but she shook her head quickly. "He didn't touch me. And he—he really didn't hurt me either."

The frozen tension slowly seeped from his face. The wind swept in a cloudlike swirl of snow, and they both shivered against its bite. Chris reached up to trace the lean hollow of his cheek. "You don't even have a coat on," she chided gently.

He pressed her hand to his lips. "I had a good reason."

She didn't pretend to misunderstand. She was aware concern for her had driven all else from his mind. But this horrible night was nearly over, and suddenly she knew that everything was going to be fine. Logan had been right all along. Whatever problems they had could be worked out. And she was going to try—Lord, but she was going to try.

With a soft sigh, she pressed her face against the curve of his shoulder, savoring the feel of his arms around her. Her head lifted a second later.

"You know," she murmured, a trace of the impishness he so loved in her lighting her eyes, "as long as you have a birthday coming up, maybe I should think about getting you a hat, too. Maybe you'll start taking better care of yourself.''

That's something I think I'll leave to you, he decided silently. His lips twitched faintly as he said, ''I thought ice skates were the first order of business for my birthday.''

No, she thought fuzzily. The first order of business was something else entirely. But there was time for that later. For now, she was only too willing to give herself over to him. His warmth, his familiar scent was like a benediction straight from heaven.

''Let's go home,'' she said softly.

NED SAW TO IT that the time they spent at the police station was brief, and for that Logan was grateful. He took Chris home and they talked for a while about Carl. Her hand gripping his tightly, he told her how he and Ned had pieced the puzzle together, finally figuring out that the city's notorious burglar and the man obsessed with her were one and the same.

Chris finally drifted off to sleep, cradled in his arms like a baby. Logan knew what an ordeal the day had been for her. First there had been that damnable argument this morning, and then the madcap nightmare tonight. He held her for a long, long time, stroking her back, listening to her even breathing. Sleep proved far more elusive for him.

Two o'clock that morning found Logan sitting in the living room, an untouched cup of hot cocoa beside him. It had been difficult for him to leave Chris—on several different levels, he decided wryly, thinking how careful he'd been as he'd eased from the tangle of silken arms and legs. But there was still so much turmoil going on inside him. He needed some time to think.

How he loved her. With every heartbeat, he wanted her more. He loved her more. But he had no idea what the morning would bring; he wasn't sure he wanted to know. Neither one of them had mentioned their argument this morning, yet he knew it weighed heavily on both their minds.

It was hell knowing Chris loved him, too. She found excuses to touch him—adjusting his tie, slipping her hand into his as they walked, reaching out for him in the quiet of the night. But she had only said the words that one time, and he desperately needed that reassurance from her.

He shuddered as he thought of what had nearly happened tonight. It was his worst nightmare come to life all over again. There were no words to describe the clawing fear he'd felt when he'd seen Chris lying helplessly in the cabin. So close. Close enough to touch and yet so far. So much like Denise it nearly killed him inside when he thought of what might have happened.

He wished he could believe the worst was over. Where Carl was concerned, it was. But for him and Chris... He believed in the two of them. He wanted her to believe in the same way, and he wanted it so much it hurt inside.

With a heavy sigh, he leaned his head back wearily and closed his eyes.

He didn't hear her come in. He didn't even realize she was awake and in the room until he felt her hands on his shoulders.

"Couldn't sleep?" he asked softly.

Even though she knew he couldn't see her, she shook her head. "I woke up about an hour ago. I couldn't go back to sleep and I . . . I was just thinking," she ended lamely.

Logan twisted slightly to catch a glimpse of her face. Her expression was uncertain. He sensed her need for him not to look at her just yet. "About what?" he asked.

There was a huge lump in Chris's throat. It was an effort to get her voice past it. "About us. I think maybe we need to talk."

His fingers came up to cover hers where they rested on his shoulder. He rubbed his thumb absently over the back of her hand. "It doesn't have to be now, Chris."

"It does," she countered, her voice very low.

He smiled slightly. "Now or never? Before you change your mind?" His tone was light, but she recognized the guarded wariness in the question.

"I won't change my mind." She swallowed. "There's so much I want to say, so much I need to say that I—I don't even know where to begin."

Logan sensed her helplessness. "I'm not going anywhere," he murmured.

His tenderness nearly made her come undone. She loved him so much, and she had almost thrown it all away. "Oh, Logan," she whispered. "Can you ever forgive me for what I've done to you?"

He started to shake his head. "It doesn't matter," he started to say.

"But it does. It does!" The words were torn from deep within her. "I cringe inside whenever I think of how selfish I've been." The pressure of her hands on his shoulders kept him where he was for a moment, but then he twisted so that he was able to grasp her wrist and pull her around the end of the sofa. She came willingly enough, but her eyes refused to meet his.

"Chris," he said very softly. "There's no need for you to torment yourself like this. I know what you're going through."

She was quiet, and when she finally lifted her eyes, her tremulous little smile caught at his heart. "I know you do. But just because you're willing to let me off the hook doesn't mean I am." She paused. "Do you remember the night you asked me to marry you?"

Dear God, how could he forget? Before him, her fingers plucked one another, over and over, betraying the strain she was under. He ached with the need to touch her, to strip away the prim little robe and nightgown she wore and explore the warm, sleep-scented hollows of her body.

"I thought I was doing the right thing, for both of us," she said unevenly. "I said—and I really believed—that it was better if we simply went on as we were. No pressure. No demands. No commitments. I told myself I was doing it for you, but *I* was the one who was afraid of being hurt. And I never really considered just how selfish I've been—" she hesitated "—until yesterday morning. But I know now that I can't go on trying to protect myself, when everything I've always wanted is at stake."

Logan held his breath, scarcely daring to hope. To even breathe.

"I remember you said once that you envied me my home. My family." Her expression was wistful. "Strange as it sounds, I think I've always envied my parents. They have the kind of marriage that only comes along once in a lifetime. And I—I want that for me. I want it for *us*." Her voice began to shake. "I want to wake up in the morning and see your head on my pillow. I want to see a dark-haired little boy on your lap, the spitting image of his father. I want to hear you laugh at the trail of tiny footprints across the kitchen floor I've just waxed. I want it for me—" she choked back a sob "—every bit as much as I want it for you."

Her eyes were huge and glistening, so full of longing that they seemed to eclipse the rest of her face. He could feel her before him, quivering. She had come to him, freely, without question, and he could ask no more of her.

Except one thing. He cradled her face in his hands, looking deeply into her eyes, as if he could see through her...straight into her heart. But his quiet tone betrayed him. "Do you love me, Chris?"

The question fell into a hushed void. She held his gaze endlessly, tears standing out in her eyes. He was everything to her.

Her hand crept up to cover his. She pressed her lips to his palm. "I love you," she whispered, "more with every breath I take."

His heart contracted with the pure, sweet pleasure that pierced him. He caught her to him, holding her with arms that were fierce and tender and hungry and gentle all at once.

Chris buried her face against his chest. "I love you," she cried softly. "And if you can find it in your heart to ask me again to—"

Firm lips swallowed her husky whisper. "I'm asking right now," he said hoarsely after taking her mouth in an achingly tender kiss. "Will you marry me, Chris?"

"Yes." Her whispered "yes" turned to a sob as heart and eyes finally spilled over. She flung her arms around him. "Oh, yes!"

A rush of joy swept through him, so profound and intense he felt dizzy. He carried her upstairs and began the pleasant task of making slow, sensual love to her.

And when they finally came together in the age-old cadence of love, he found a fiery warmth. A healing softness. A haven from the bitter past, a promise of the future...and a lifetime of everlasting love.

EPILOGUE

A FULL MOON hovered in the darkness, surrounded by an eerie halo of silver. Hazy gray clouds streaked across the sky, occasionally obscuring the moon's brilliance.

Far below, high on a hill at the end of a dead end street, stood a house. It was large and homey looking, flanked on three sides by a wide porch. Twin patches of light gleamed from a pair of narrow windows, dappling the shrouded landscape outside.

Inside, a lone figure stood gazing reflectively into the night. Tall in stature, lean in build, the man was simply dressed in dark slacks and a long-sleeved sweater.

Logan Garrison smiled slightly, still staring into the distance at the twinkling of bright, multicolored lights that provided such a stark contrast to the cold and lonely night. Boise, Idaho, like the rest of the world, had welcomed the holiday season with open arms.

It was Christmas. A time for mistletoe and magic, for joy and loving, for angels and miracles.

His eyes drifted to his father-in-law. He was sitting in the living room, peacefully dozing in his recliner, the evening news forgotten. A jumble of newspapers lay scattered at his feet. Beside him, his wife had just picked up a pair of knitting needles. Logan's eyes grew soft as he regarded the couple he now called Mom and Pop.

Through the simple privilege of his marriage to Chris, he had been blessed with far more than he had ever imagined. A home. A family. A wife whom he loved more with every day that passed. Logan didn't think it was possible for any man to be as lucky, or as happy, as he was.

And then the day had come when he'd lost his heart yet again, this time to a pair of honey-haired little girls. Even now, his heart swelled with pride as he thought of his daughters, both with eyes as blue as a storm-washed sky.

Just then the sound of several high-pitched giggles reached his ears.

Four small children were thoroughly engrossed in playing house. Wendy and the twins, who had celebrated their second birthday in October, were all decked out in the latest cast-offs from Elaine's wardrobe. Three-year-old Josh wasn't the proverbial man-of-the-family just yet, though. Glancing over, Rick wore a look of pained resignation. Much to his father's chagrin, Josh was just a little too engrossed in the contents of his sister's purse.

Bedlam again reigned supreme in the Jordan household.

At the ruckus, Paul Jordan's eyes drifted open. "Can't a body get any sleep around here?" he grumbled good-naturedly. "You kids are about as quiet as a basketball team!" And with that, he sent a pointed look at his three daughters, who were so engrossed in catching up on all the latest news that they never even noticed. For the life of him, Logan couldn't understand why. Chris, Char and Diane had spent three whole days here at Thanksgiving "catching up." But he grinned nonetheless.

It was much later, lying in the double bed his wife had spent countless nights in, that a warm, feminine voice sighed in his ear, "This was the best Christmas ever, wasn't it?"

Logan smiled. "You said that last year," he reminded her.

Curled in the haven of his arms, Chris pressed a kiss against his collarbone. "Did you like your present?"

He thought of one gift he'd received last year—not one, but four red knit stocking caps. One from Chris, one from Paul and Elaine, and one from each of his sisters-in-law. He didn't mind being the butt of their humor, but this year Chris had given him a rather unique Christmas present.

Very gently he hooked his fingers under her jaw. "You don't mind another baby so soon, do you?" She had told him that she was pregnant just this morning.

There was a radiant glow to her features. "It's a little late for that," she laughed. "But I may cut my practice down to three days a week. Besides, Heidi and Julie will be almost three by then."

There was a soft, faraway look in Logan's eyes. He was thinking about how awed and humble he'd felt while Chris was carrying the twins, knowing that he'd been an equal partner in creating this miracle of life. As he'd expected, though, the first year hadn't been easy. Logan knew that Scottie was on Chris's mind many times when the twins lay peacefully sleeping. But it had been while she was pregnant that she'd decided to start a support group for others who shared her hidden fears, for parents who had also lost children to SIDS. There was even a couple who came from as far away as Twin Falls for the monthly meetings.

Yes, the twins' birth had wrought miracles in more ways than one. No one could have been more surprised than Logan when his parents showed up on their doorstep to see their month-old granddaughters. His father had stayed two days, his mother a week·—phenomenal, in Logan's eyes. There were some tense moments for all of them, and Logan knew he would never truly understand his parents. But he'd begun to think that, in time, there could at least be a measure of peace between them. And to Chris's delight, he'd begun to consider opening up a law practice.

Logan sighed and tightened his arms around her. He bent to brush her lips lightly, possessively. "Do you mind if we wait till we get back from Washington before we tell the folks about the baby?" They planned to leave the twins there in Boise, while just the two of them slipped away for a short vacation at the ski lodge where they'd spent their honeymoon nearly three years earlier.

Chris shook her head. She understood completely.

A chuckle vibrated in his chest a second later. "You know what everyone's going to say when we tell them we're pregnant again, don't you?"

Her eyes glowed up at him. "That we obviously didn't do any skiing!"

She didn't know that happened to be the very subject under discussion in the room down the hall. Paul was shaking his head as he climbed into bed beside his wife. "It's hard to believe Chris and Logan have been married as long as they have. Sometimes they act like they're still on their honeymoon!"

Elaine smiled mysteriously. "You know what happened the last time they went skiing in Washington, don't you?"

"Heidi and Julie appeared on the scene nine months later." Even the darkness couldn't hide the gleam in his eyes. "You know, our daughter and her husband have two little girls already. One more and they'll be well on their way to having a basketball team of their own."

That proved to be quite an accurate prediction.

Harlequin
Superromance

COMING NEXT MONTH

#310 THE MOON GATE • Rosalind Carson
Videographer Allison Bentley is in Bermuda to trace an ancestor, but that's not the only mystery she has to solve. The history of the islands is an open book to Colin Endicott, yet he is strangely reluctant to help Allison by digging into his past....

#311 THE SECOND TIME AROUND • Ruth Alana Smith
Playwright Noah Kincaid is shocked to learn that his dear Aunt Maisie's will requires him to move back to Broken Bow, Colorado. Even more incredible is the still-electric spark between him and the beautiful Devon Parnell. Suddenly, living in Broken Bow no longer seems such punishment....

#312 THE RIGHT COMBINATION • Aimee Thurlo
Inventor Sara Cahill has an iron-clad lease, but Ben Lowell wants her out of his building. Sara's off-the-wall approach to negotiation has Ben stymied until his young son comes up with a plan—hire Sara to develop new products for Ben's own company. Sara considers the contract a real coup until the unexpected happens. Suddenly she's no longer in control of her experiments or her emotions!

#313 TILL THERE WAS YOU • Eleni Carr
Lawyer Meghan O'Brien is unable to believe that a sexy, witty man like Justin Forbes is the director of a women's shelter. But then, since meeting Justin, Meghan has found *all* of her previous conceptions turned upside down. Meghan used to believe that falling in love was for other people. Now she's beginning to think she just might change her mind....

HARLEQUIN SIGNATURE EDITION

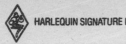

JUST ONE NIGHT

Hawk Sinclair—Texas millionaire and owner of the exclusive
Sinclair hotels, determined to protect his son's inheritance.
Leonie Spencer—desperate to protect her sister's happiness.

They were together for just one night.
The night their daughter was conceived.

Blackmail, kidnapping and attempted murder add suspense
to passion in this exciting bestseller.

The success story of Carole Mortimer continues with *Just
One Night*, a captivating romance from the author of the
bestselling novels, *Gypsy* and *Merlyn's Magic*.

★

**Available in March
wherever paperbacks are sold.**

WTCH-1

ATTRACTIVE, SPACE SAVING BOOK RACK

Display your most prized novels on this handsome and sturdy book rack. The hand-rubbed walnut finish will blend into your library decor with quiet elegance, providing a practical organizer for your favorite hard-or soft-covered books.

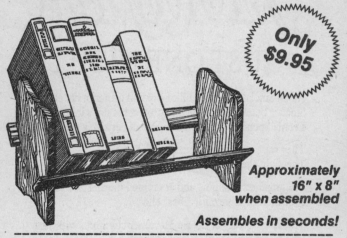

Only $9.95

Approximately 16" x 8" when assembled

Assembles in seconds!

To order, rush your name, address and zip code, along with a check or money order for $10.70* ($9.95 plus 75¢ postage and handling) payable to *Harlequin Reader Service*:

Harlequin Reader Service
Book Rack Offer
901 Fuhrmann Blvd.
P.O. Box 1396
Buffalo, NY 14269-1396

Offer not available in Canada.

BKR-1A

*New York and Iowa residents add appropriate sales tax.

HARLEQUIN SUPERROMANCE BRINGS YOU...

Lynda Ward

Superromance readers already know that Lynda Ward possesses a unique ability to weave words into heartfelt emotions and exciting drama.

Now, Superromance is proud to bring you Lynda's tour de force: an ambitious saga of three sisters whose lives are torn apart by the conflicts and power struggles that come with being born into a dynasty.

In *Race the Sun, Leap the Moon* and *Touch the Stars*, readers will laugh and cry with the Welles sisters as they learn to live and love on their own terms, all the while struggling for the acceptance of Burton Welles, the stern patriarch of the clan.

Race the Sun, Leap the Moon and *Touch the Stars* . . . a dramatic trilogy you won't want to miss. Coming to you in July, August and September.

The Welles Family Trilogy

LYNDA-1A

PAMELA BROWNING

...is fireworks on the green at the Fourth of July and prayers said around the Thanksgiving table. It is the dream of freedom realized in thousands of small towns across this great nation.

But mostly, the Heartland is its people. People who care about and help one another. People who cherish traditional values and give to their children the greatest gift, the gift of love.

American Romance presents HEARTLAND, an emotional trilogy about people whose memories, hopes and dreams are bound up in the acres they farm.

HEARTLAND...the story of America.

Don't miss these heartfelt stories: American Romance #237 SIMPLE GIFTS (March), #241 FLY AWAY (April), and #245 HARVEST HOME (May).

HRT-1